The Havenfall Accord

A Torlan Tarsen Adventure

The Havenfall Accord

Russell V McFall

Ordained Path Books

Published by **Ordained Path Books**
For permissions or inquiries, contact:
ordainedpathbooks@gmail.com

Cover illustration and interior artwork generated by AI under direction of the author.

First Edition.

ISBN (Paperback): 978-1-972724-02-6
ISBN (Hardcover):

Printed in the United States of America.

Version 1.00 -- March 2026

Dedication

To my family, whose curiosity and imagination first turned simple bedtime stories into journeys among the stars.

Contents

Chapter 1 — Two Years Later

The Mentored Six

Two years had passed since Torlan Tarsen returned to Earth.

Torlan had never believed the universe needed more conquerors.

It needed observers—people patient enough to understand a problem before trying to solve it.

That had been the first lesson he learned on Cyrion – and the one he trusted most.

Dr. Ziv had often reminded his students: *"The quiet mind sees farther."*

The office tower of Arden Global rose above the city skyline, its glass walls reflecting the pale light of early morning. From the top floor the world below looked quiet and distant. The streets were just beginning to wake as the first traffic of the day started to move.

Six people sat around the long conference table, waiting.

Each of them had been invited personally by Torlan Tarsen.

At the far end of the table, **Samir Patel** studied the city skyline through the tall glass wall, his attention drifting between the distant horizon and the silent door.

Across from him, **Mateo Alvarez** tapped a pen lightly against the table, the steady rhythm suggesting patience had never been one of his strongest qualities.

Beside him, **Dr. Lila Chen** reviewed several lines of data on a tablet, her calm expression showing the quiet concentration of someone used to solving complicated problems.

Next to her, **Owen Tark** turned a small mechanical part slowly between his fingers, examining it from every angle as though the meeting had already given him something to repair.

Two others sat farther down the table, each waiting in thoughtful silence, unsure exactly why they had been called to this meeting.

The room grew still.

The door opened quietly.

Torlan Tarsen stepped into the room and paused just inside the doorway.

His eyes moved slowly around the table, studying each of the six people as though measuring something far more important than their names or resumes.

For a moment he said nothing.

Then he closed the door behind him and walked to the head of the table.

"Thank you for coming."

Inside the conference room, however, the atmosphere was anything but quiet.

Everyone at the table understood that this meeting mattered.

Each of them now ran one of the Arden companies.

Two years earlier they had been senior managers, engineers, analysts, and project leaders. Now they were chief executives.

Torlan had chosen them carefully.

Torlan had trained them himself.

At six feet five inches tall he naturally stood above most people in the room, yet nothing in his manner suggested authority or command. He moved calmly to the head of the table and greeted them with a simple nod.

"Good morning."

"Morning, Torlan," several replied.

He took his seat and opened the tablet in front of him.

"Let's begin with your reports."

The first executive spoke.

Daniel Mercer, the financial director of Arden Infrastructure, was known for caution and meticulous planning. His company managed orbital construction and large-scale planetary engineering projects.

"Quarterly results are stable," Mercer said. "We've increased output by eleven percent while reducing operating costs."

Torlan listened quietly.

He had already read the report.

Four hundred pages of data, projections, and analysis.

It had taken him less than a minute to absorb it.

Years on Cyrion had trained his mind to absorb information quickly, but he rarely mentioned it. Instead, he asked a simple question.

"What caused the efficiency gain?"

Mercer glanced down at his notes.

"Improved logistics scheduling."

Torlan nodded slightly.

"That explains most of it," he said. "But not all."

The room became quiet.

Mercer looked at him curiously.

Torlan turned the tablet toward him.

"You reduced transport delays by reorganizing the launch windows," Torlan said. "But the larger gain came from the automated scheduling system your engineers introduced in February."

Mercer blinked.

"Yes… that's correct."

Torlan closed the tablet.

"Good work."

The meeting continued around the table.

Each of the six executives presented their reports.

A technology entrepreneur described a new research initiative.
A manufacturing director outlined improvements to production systems.
A logistics coordinator explained expanded trade routes.

Torlan listened carefully to each one.

Occasionally he asked a quiet question.

Sometimes he made a suggestion.

But he never took control of their decisions.

At the far end of the room sat two members of the Arden corporate board.

They had watched this pattern for two years.

Finally one of them spoke.

"Torlan," the man said carefully, "you realize that most founders would maintain tighter control over companies of this size."

The room grew still.

Torlan considered the question before answering.

Then he spoke calmly.

"If leaders never learn to lead," he said, "they will always wait for someone else to decide."

The board member frowned slightly.

"But these companies are worth billions."

Torlan nodded.

"Yes."

He paused for a moment before continuing.

"That is why they must be led by people who understand them."

He gestured toward the six executives.

"They built these systems. They know the work better than anyone."

Silence settled over the room.

One of the CEOs finally smiled.

"I think he's saying we're responsible now."

Torlan returned the smile.

"You always were."

The meeting ended shortly afterward.

The six CEOs gathered their materials and left the conference room, discussing plans for their next projects.

As the door closed behind them, the board members remained seated.

One of them shook his head slightly.

"You've effectively handed control of six corporations to other people."

Torlan stood and walked toward the window.

Outside, the city stretched to the horizon.

"Yes," he said.

"And that doesn't concern you?"

Torlan looked out across the skyline for a moment before answering.

"No."

He turned back toward them.

"Leadership is not about holding control," he said quietly.

"It's about preparing others to carry it."

The Factory Floor Lesson

Two days after the executive meeting, Torlan arrived at one of the Arden manufacturing facilities on the edge of the city.

The building stretched across several acres, its long metal roof reflecting the afternoon sun. Inside, the steady rhythm of machinery filled the air.

This plant produced specialized components used in orbital construction projects. Thousands of parts moved through the production lines each day.

A plant manager waited for him near the entrance.

"Welcome, Mr. Arden," the man said. "We've prepared a full tour of the facility."

Torlan shook his hand politely.

"Thank you," he said. "But I'd like to start on the production line."

The manager hesitated.

"I'm sorry… the production line?"

"Yes."

Torlan gestured toward the interior of the building where rows of workers operated assembly stations.

"I'd like to work there for a while."

The manager looked uncertain.

"Sir… you're the owner."

Torlan nodded.

"Today I'm learning."

The manager studied him for a moment, then smiled slightly.

"Well," he said, "I suppose we can arrange that."

A few minutes later Torlan stood beside a workbench wearing protective gloves and safety glasses.

A veteran technician named Maria Alvarez showed him how the assembly station worked.

"This part slides into the frame here," she explained, demonstrating the process. "Then you lock the coupling ring before passing it to the next station."

Torlan watched closely.

Then he tried the process himself.

The first attempt was slow.

The second was smoother.

By the fourth unit he was keeping pace with the line.

Maria raised an eyebrow.

"You've done this before?"

Torlan shook his head.

"No."

"Well," she said, "you're picking it up quickly."

The line supervisor walked by and paused when he noticed who was working the station.

"Is that…?"

Maria nodded casually.

"Yep."

The supervisor folded his arms and watched for a moment.

Torlan continued assembling components without comment.

Finally one of the workers farther down the line called out.

"Careful, boss!"

Several workers looked over.

"If you're too good at this," the man said with a grin, "they'll make you stay."

Laughter spread along the line.

Torlan looked up briefly.

"Then I'll need better gloves," he said.

The laughter grew louder.

For the next hour Torlan worked alongside the line workers.

He asked questions occasionally.

Why this step?

Why that tool?

Maria explained patiently.

Eventually Torlan noticed something.

The line slowed briefly every few minutes.

He watched several cycles carefully.

Then he spoke quietly.

"The delay happens when the coupling rings arrive," he said.

Maria glanced toward the supply cart.

"You're right," she said. "We've had trouble with that delivery timing."

Torlan studied the station layout for a moment.

"What if the rings were staged here instead?" he suggested, pointing to an empty rack beside the bench.

Maria considered it.

"That might work."

The supervisor overheard and nodded.

"Let's try it."

Within minutes the adjustment was made.

The line resumed moving.

This time it flowed smoothly.

Maria watched the process for several cycles.

"Well," she said, "that solved it."

Torlan removed his gloves and set them on the bench.

"You already understood the problem," he said.

"You just needed a moment to see it differently."

Maria smiled.

"Still," she said, "not bad for someone on their first day."

Torlan returned the smile.

"Thank you for teaching me."

When he left the facility later that afternoon, the plant manager walked him back toward the entrance.

"I have to admit," the manager said, "I've never seen a company owner work an assembly station before."

Torlan looked back toward the busy production floor.

"The people here understand the work," he said.

"If I want to improve it, I should understand it too."

The Support Assistance Resource Groups

Later that week Torlan met with the directors of the Support Assistance Resource organizations.

The meeting took place in a smaller conference room on a lower floor of the Arden tower. Unlike the executive boardroom upstairs, this room felt more practical than ceremonial. Maps and project displays covered the walls.

Three groups had gathered around the table.

Each group represented one of the Support Assistance Resource initiatives.

Medical relief.

Agricultural development.

Infrastructure support.

These organizations operated quietly in places where traditional investment rarely reached—remote settlements, recovering regions, and struggling communities that needed practical help.

Torlan entered the room and greeted the group.

"Good afternoon."

A woman near the center of the table stood.

Dr. Elena Markovic directed the medical relief division. Her teams coordinated mobile clinics and emergency medical shipments across several frontier regions.

"Good afternoon, Torlan," she said. "We've prepared the quarterly reports."

Torlan nodded.

"Let's begin."

The medical team spoke first.

Dr. Markovic projected a map onto the wall showing dozens of small outposts scattered across distant systems.

"Our teams delivered supplies to fourteen settlements this quarter," she explained. "Vaccination programs are now operating in three additional colonies."

Torlan studied the map carefully.

"Excellent," he said.

The agricultural director spoke next.

His group focused on helping colonies develop sustainable food systems.

"We've been assisting two frontier worlds with soil stabilization," he explained. "The results look promising."

Finally the infrastructure team described their work.

They specialized in wells, water purification systems, and basic construction support.

"In many of these communities," the director said, "one functioning water system can change everything."

Torlan listened quietly as each group spoke.

This work interested him far more than corporate earnings reports.

Near the end of the meeting one of the financial advisors cleared his throat.

"There is one concern we should address."

Torlan looked toward him.

"Yes?"

The advisor folded his hands carefully.

"These programs require significant funding. Some members of the corporate board believe the resources might be better invested directly into expanding the companies."

The room grew quiet.

Several of the SAR directors watched Torlan carefully.

He considered the question for a moment before answering.

Then he spoke calmly.

"The companies exist to create opportunity."

He gestured toward the maps on the wall.

"Opportunity should help people."

The advisor hesitated.

"But shareholders—"

Torlan interrupted gently.

"Prosperity that benefits only a few people is fragile," he said.

He pointed again toward the map of settlements.

"Communities that grow stronger create stability for everyone."

The advisor slowly nodded.

"That is… a different way of measuring success."

Torlan smiled slightly.

"Yes."

Dr. Markovic looked back toward the map.

"Many of these communities struggle simply because no one notices them," she said.

Torlan nodded.

"Then we should notice them."

As the meeting ended, the directors gathered their materials and prepared to leave.

Torlan remained seated for a moment studying the map.

Hundreds of small lights marked distant settlements.

Each one represented people trying to build a life somewhere far from the centers of power.

Helping them felt like meaningful work.

Much more meaningful than managing corporations.

Reflection on Cyrion

Late that evening the Arden tower had grown quiet.

Most of the offices had emptied as employees finished their work for the day. Only a few lights remained on in the upper floors of the building.

Torlan stood alone in his office.

The large window behind his desk looked out across the city. Thousands of lights stretched toward the horizon, forming a quiet sea of movement and activity.

Two years earlier he had returned to Earth.

In that time he had stabilized the Arden companies, trained new leaders, and established the Support Assistance Resource groups.

The work had been necessary.

But tonight he felt something shifting inside him.

The companies were running well now.

They no longer required his constant attention.

He rested his hands lightly on the window frame and looked down at the city streets far below.

Earth was impressive in its own way—vast, energetic, constantly changing.

Yet in moments like this his thoughts often returned to another place.

Cyrion.

He remembered the quiet valley of Valaryn.

The stone forests that rose from the plains.

The long walks through Lyara's garden where Dr. Arel Ziv had patiently explained the deeper rhythms of life.

Ziv rarely lectured.

He simply spoke truths and allowed time to reveal their meaning.

Torlan could still hear the old teacher's calm voice.

"Strength grows slowly."

At the time Torlan had thought Ziv was speaking about the heavy gravity of Cyrion and the endurance required to live there.

Now he understood the words differently.

Strength did grow slowly.

Leadership grew slowly.

Wisdom grew slowly.

He had spent two years preparing others to lead the companies.

Perhaps that had been part of the long path Ziv had spoken about.

Torlan looked again at the lights of the city.

Running the companies had been important.

But it had never been the destination.

It was only the beginning.

The Assistant Problem

The following morning Torlan arrived early at the Arden tower.

The office floor was still quiet when he entered. Only a few lights were on in the administrative wing.

As he walked toward his office, his current assistant was already waiting outside the door.

She looked slightly uncomfortable.

"Good morning, Mr. Arden."

Torlan nodded politely.

"Good morning."

She hesitated for a moment before speaking.

"I wanted to let you know that today will be my last day."

Torlan studied her expression calmly.

"I see."

She shifted her folder from one hand to the other.

"You've been very fair to work with," she said quickly. "But the schedule is… demanding."

Torlan nodded again.

"That is understandable."

She seemed relieved that he had not argued.

"I've prepared transition notes for the next assistant," she said. "All the schedules and contact lists are organized."

"Thank you," Torlan replied.

After a brief exchange she gathered her things and left the office floor.

Torlan entered his office and set his tablet on the desk.

A few minutes later the administrative director appeared in the doorway.

"I heard the news," the man said.

Torlan looked up.

"Yes."

The director rubbed the back of his neck.

"That makes four assistants in a year."

Torlan considered the number for a moment.

"Yes."

The director sighed.

"Most people can't keep up with your schedule."

Torlan leaned back slightly in his chair.

"Then we should continue searching for someone who can."

The director gave a small, uncertain laugh.

"That may take some time."

Torlan opened the tablet on his desk.

"Begin the search again."

Later that afternoon the human resources department delivered the first group of new applicants.

Torlan reviewed the list quietly.

Most of the candidates had strong resumes.

Some had experience in corporate administration.

Others had backgrounds in logistics or government work.

He moved through the list quickly.

Then one name caused him to pause.

Alexandra Hale.

Torlan looked at the name again.

There was nothing unusual about the application at first glance.

Strong academic background.

Leadership experience.

Military family.

Several recommendations describing her as disciplined and dependable.

Torlan studied the file for another moment.

Something about the name caught his attention.

He closed the tablet and set it on the desk.

"Schedule an interview," he said quietly.

Chapter 2 — Alexandra Hale

Alex at Home

Alexandra Hale's family home sat on a quiet street just outside the city.

The house had been in the Hale family for nearly thirty years. It was solid, practical, and well cared for—much like the people who lived there.

Inside the kitchen, Alex sat at the table with her father and two older brothers.

The dinner plates had been pushed aside, but the conversation was still going strong.

"So let me understand this," her brother Daniel said, leaning back in his chair. "You're planning to move into the city."

Alex nodded.

"Yes."

"And you're applying to work for William Arden."

"Yes."

Daniel exchanged a glance with their other brother, Marcus.

"The same William Arden who runs half the companies in the northern hemisphere?"

"The same one."

Marcus folded his arms.

"I heard he's burned through four assistants in one year."

Alex took a sip of water and set the glass down calmly.

"Then the position is clearly available."

Daniel laughed.

"That's one way to look at it."

Their father, Colonel Nathan Hale, sat quietly at the head of the table listening to the exchange.

He had spent most of his life in military service. Even in retirement his posture remained straight, and his voice carried the calm authority of someone accustomed to responsibility.

"You've researched the position carefully?" he asked.

Alex nodded.

"Yes."

"And you understand the workload will be demanding."

"I do."

Colonel Hale studied her expression for a moment.

"You know," Marcus said, "most people would apply for something easier."

Alex shrugged slightly.

"I'm not most people."

Daniel grinned.

"That part is definitely true."

Alex had grown up in a house where service was expected.

Her father had served more than twenty-five years in the military.

Both of her brothers had followed the same path.

The family valued discipline, honesty, and responsibility.

Yet Alex had always known her own path would be different.

She admired the military, but her strengths lay elsewhere.

Planning.

Organization.

Leadership.

She enjoyed solving complicated problems and helping groups work together effectively.

That was why the assistant position interested her.

Not because of the title.

Because of the opportunity to make a difference.

Colonel Hale leaned forward slightly.

"Tell me why this position matters to you."

Alex met his gaze.

"I've been studying the work Arden's companies are doing," she said.

"The infrastructure projects. The agricultural support programs. The medical relief shipments."

Her father nodded slowly.

"And?"

"I want to be part of something like that," she said.

"Helping people."

"Just in a different way."

Colonel Hale's expression softened slightly.

"Service takes many forms," he said.

Alex smiled.

"That's what I was hoping you'd say."

Marcus stood and carried the plates toward the sink.

"So when is the interview?"

"Next week," Alex said.

Daniel shook his head.

"Well," he said, "if you survive the interview, I suppose we'll start calling you 'executive assistant.'"

Alex leaned back in her chair.

"I'd settle for 'employed.'"

The room filled with quiet laughter.

Hearing About Bill

Two days later Alex sat at a small café near the transit station, reviewing the information she had gathered about Arden Global.

Her tablet lay open on the table in front of her. The screen displayed company reports, organizational charts, and a collection of articles about William Arden.

Or Torlan Tarsen, as some publications had begun calling him.

Most of the articles focused on the scale of his businesses.

Six major companies.

Infrastructure construction.

Agricultural technology.

Medical logistics.

Yet the more Alex read, the more she noticed something unusual.

Several of the companies quietly funded humanitarian projects in remote settlements.

Mobile medical clinics.

Agricultural support programs.

Water infrastructure systems.

That caught her attention.

Across the table her friend Rachel leaned forward.

"So," Rachel said, "this is the famous job interview?"

Alex nodded.

"Yes."

Rachel glanced at the tablet.

"Isn't that the guy who made four assistants quit?"

"That seems to be the rumor."

Rachel raised an eyebrow.

"And you still want the job?"

Alex closed the tablet for a moment.

"Yes."

Rachel shook her head slowly.

"I heard he works constantly," she said. "Long hours. No breaks. Impossible schedule."

Alex considered that.

"That doesn't bother me."

"Most people would call that a warning sign."

Alex smiled slightly.

"Most people probably aren't applying for the job."

Rachel laughed.

"You're serious."

Alex nodded.

"Yes."

She opened the tablet again and looked at one of the reports describing the Support Assistance Resource programs.

The article mentioned water systems installed in several frontier colonies.

Another report described medical shipments sent to struggling settlements.

That kind of work mattered.

If the rumors were true, working for William Arden would require energy, discipline, and patience.

But it might also allow her to help people.

And that was the part that interested her most.

Rachel watched her for a moment.

"You know," she said, "there are much easier jobs you could apply for."

Alex nodded.

"I know."

"Better hours too."

"I know."

Rachel leaned back in her chair.

"So why this one?"

Alex closed the tablet and looked out the café window for a moment before answering.

"Because this one might matter."

The Journey to the City

The morning Alex left home arrived earlier than expected.

Sunlight filtered through the kitchen window as she carried her travel bag toward the door. The house was quiet except for the soft sound of coffee brewing.

Her mother stood near the counter watching her.

"You packed everything?" she asked.

"I think so," Alex replied.

"You *think* so?"

Alex smiled slightly.

"Yes."

Her mother shook her head with a small laugh.

"You've always been confident."

Alex set her bag beside the door and walked back into the kitchen.

"I'll visit often," she said.

"I know you will."

Her mother studied her for a moment.

"You've worked hard for this opportunity."

Alex nodded.

"I just hope I can do the job well."

Her mother stepped forward and adjusted the collar of Alex's jacket.

"You've been preparing for this your whole life," she said gently.

Then she added quietly,

"Just remember who you are."

Alex nodded.

"I will."

Her father entered the kitchen a moment later.

Colonel Nathan Hale rarely made dramatic speeches. Most of his advice came in short, direct statements.

He looked at the travel bag near the door.

"So," he said, "today's the day."

"Yes."

He studied her posture carefully.

"Feeling nervous?"

"A little."

"That's normal."

He walked over and placed a hand on her shoulder.

"You know what to do."

Alex waited.

Her father rarely used many words when something important needed to be said.

Finally he spoke.

"Stand steady."

Alex nodded again.

"I will."

Outside the house, the morning air was cool and clear.

Alex loaded her bag into the car and paused for a moment before closing the door.

Her brothers had already left for work earlier that morning, but she knew they were proud of her decision even if they enjoyed teasing her about the interview.

The road toward the city stretched ahead.

Somewhere beyond the skyline stood the Arden tower.

And inside that tower was the man whose reputation had made four assistants quit in one year.

Alex smiled slightly.

"Well," she said to herself, starting the car.

"Let's see what the job is really like."

Chapter 3 — The Fifth Assistant

"Observe first. Act second."
Understanding a problem is often more powerful than reacting quickly.
— Wisdom of Cyrion

Arrival

Alex stepped out of the elevator onto the executive floor of the Arden tower.

The hallway was quieter than the rest of the building, yet the pace of activity was unmistakable.

People moved quickly from office to office carrying tablets, reports, and folders. Conversations were brief and efficient.

No one appeared idle.

Alex paused for a moment to take it all in.

The rumors about William Arden suddenly felt more believable.

This place operated with the quiet intensity of a command center.

A receptionist sat behind a polished desk near the center of the hallway.

Alex approached and introduced herself.

"Alexandra Hale. I'm here for the assistant interview."

The receptionist checked her tablet.

"Yes, Ms. Hale. Please have a seat. Mr. Arden will see candidates shortly."

Alex nodded and took a seat along the wall.

Several other applicants were already waiting.

Some reviewed notes nervously.

Others stared at the floor.

One candidate tapped his foot repeatedly.

Alex noticed something else.

The assistants already working in the office moved with remarkable speed.

Phones rang.

Messages arrived.

Doors opened and closed.

The entire floor seemed to run on an invisible schedule that never slowed down.

After watching for a few minutes, Alex turned back toward the receptionist.

"Busy morning?" she asked.

The receptionist smiled politely.

"It's always a busy morning here."

Alex glanced toward the hallway where several assistants hurried past.

"I can see that."

The receptionist leaned slightly closer and lowered her voice.

"Good luck."

Alex raised an eyebrow.

"Is that encouragement or a warning?"

The receptionist smiled again.

"Both."

Alex leaned back in her chair and waited calmly.

The Waiting Room

More applicants arrived during the next few minutes.

Soon nearly a dozen candidates sat along the wall outside the executive offices.

The atmosphere felt strangely quiet for such a large group of people.

Everyone seemed to understand that this interview was different from a normal job meeting.

Alex watched the room calmly.

The man sitting beside her tapped his foot rapidly against the floor.

He held a tablet in one hand and kept scrolling through notes.

"First time applying here?" he asked suddenly.

"Yes," Alex said.

He nodded quickly.

"Same."

He leaned closer and lowered his voice.

"I heard the last assistant lasted three months."

Alex raised an eyebrow.

"That long?"

The man gave a nervous laugh.

"Apparently that was considered impressive."

Across the room another candidate sat with remarkable confidence.

He leaned back in his chair, arms folded, looking completely relaxed.

When he noticed Alex watching, he smiled.

"I've managed executive schedules before," he said.

"Shouldn't be too difficult."

Alex nodded politely.

"That's encouraging."

He seemed pleased with the response.

A few minutes later the office door opened.

One of the assistants stepped out and called a name.

The confident candidate stood immediately.

"That's me."

He straightened his jacket and walked into the office.

The door closed behind him.

The waiting room grew quiet again.

Several minutes passed.

Then the door opened once more.

The same man walked out.

His confident expression had disappeared.

He avoided eye contact with the other candidates and walked quickly toward the elevator.

As he passed the receptionist she asked politely,

"Would you like to schedule a follow-up meeting?"

The man shook his head.

"No."

Then he continued down the hallway.

The door to the executive office closed again.

The room remained silent for several seconds.

Finally the nervous candidate beside Alex whispered,

"That seems… concerning."

Alex smiled slightly.

"Yes."

"It does."

The Entrance

After several more interviews the receptionist looked toward Alex.

"Ms. Hale?"

Alex stood.

"Yes."

"You may go in now."

She walked toward the door at the end of the hallway. The assistant waiting there opened it and gestured her inside.

"Right through there."

Alex nodded and stepped into the office.

The room was larger than she expected but surprisingly simple. A wide window stretched across the far wall, overlooking the city far below.

Near the window stood William Arden.

He was reviewing a report on a tablet, his attention completely focused on the screen.

For a moment Alex simply waited.

The office surprised her.

There were no trophies, no awards, no displays of success—only a desk, a meeting table, and the wide window overlooking the city.

Someone who ran corporations worth billions could easily have filled the room with symbols of power.

William Arden had chosen not to. That told her something important about the man she was about to work for.

She wondered if he had done that intentionally.

Then he finished reading, lowered the tablet, and turned.

This was the first time they stood face to face.

Alex noticed several things immediately.

He was tall—easily six feet five.

But what struck her more was the calm steadiness in the way he stood. Nothing about him suggested hurry or pressure, even though the entire office outside seemed to move at a constant rush.

His eyes met hers directly.

Observant.

Clear.

Alex returned the look without hesitation.

Torlan studied her just as carefully.

He had expected another nervous applicant.

Instead he saw something different.

Alexandra Hale stood nearly six feet tall herself, with a posture that suggested confidence rather than uncertainty.

She met his eyes without trying to impress him and without looking away.

Steady.

That interested him.

He gestured toward a chair near the table.

"Please come in."

Alex stepped forward.

"Thank you."

Torlan set the tablet on the table.

"Alexandra Hale."

"Yes."

He nodded once.

"Please sit."

Alex sat calmly.

For a brief moment the room was quiet.

Torlan studied her for another second.

Most applicants filled the silence with explanations or nervous conversation.

Alexandra Hale simply waited.

That interested him.

He nodded once.

"Let's begin."

The Interview

Torlan sat across the table from Alex and opened her file on the tablet.

He read silently for several seconds.

Alex waited.

She had already noticed something unusual.

He read extremely fast.

Faster than anyone she had ever seen.

Within moments he finished reviewing the file and placed the tablet on the table.

"Why do you want this position?" he asked.

The question was direct.

Alex answered just as directly.

"Because the work matters."

Torlan studied her expression.

"You're referring to the companies?"

"Partly."

"And the rest?"

"The humanitarian programs."

Torlan leaned back slightly.

"You've researched them."

"Yes."

"Why?"

Alex considered the question briefly.

"Because they solve real problems."

Torlan nodded once.

"That is their purpose."

He glanced down at the tablet again.

"You know four assistants resigned this year."

"Yes."

"That does not concern you?"

Alex shook her head.

"Not particularly."

Torlan raised an eyebrow.

"Why not?"

Alex folded her hands calmly on the table.

"Because the expectations are clear."

Torlan watched her carefully.

"And you believe you can meet them?"

"I believe I can try."

For a moment the room was quiet again.

Then Torlan asked another question.

"If a problem appears impossible to solve," he said, "what do you do?"

Alex thought for a moment before answering.

"Understand it better."

Torlan tilted his head slightly.

"Explain."

"Most problems look impossible at first," she said. "But once you understand the situation completely, a solution usually becomes visible."

Torlan studied her for several seconds.

Then he nodded.

"That is often true."

Alex hesitated for a moment before speaking again.

"May I ask a question?"

Torlan looked slightly surprised.

"Yes."

"You've gone through four assistants," she said.

"Why?"

Torlan answered honestly.

"The work requires patience."

"And?"

"Endurance."

Alex nodded slowly.

"That sounds manageable."

Torlan allowed himself the faintest smile.

"We will see".

The Test

Torlan remained seated for a moment after their last exchange.

Then he reached to the side of the table and picked up three thick folders.

He slid them across the table toward Alex.

"These arrived this morning," he said.

Alex looked down at them.

Each folder was filled with reports, diagrams, and technical summaries.

Torlan folded his hands calmly.

"Summarize them."

Alex opened the first folder.

The documents were dense—logistics reports, engineering projections, and supply schedules from several departments.

A less experienced assistant might have rushed immediately.

Alex did not.

Instead she took a breath and began organizing the information.

First she scanned the titles and headings.

Then she marked key sections.

She placed the folders side by side, comparing the data.

Torlan watched quietly.

She wasn't rushing.

She wasn't overwhelmed.

She was thinking.

Several minutes passed.

Alex closed the first folder and spoke.

"These reports describe the same problem from three different departments."

Torlan said nothing.

She continued.

"The logistics team is concerned about delivery delays."

She tapped the second folder.

"The engineering team believes the delays are caused by equipment failures."

Then she pointed to the third folder.

"But the supply report suggests the real issue is scheduling conflicts between transport routes."

Torlan nodded slightly.

"Continue."

Alex organized the papers into a small stack.

"The actual problem isn't mechanical failure," she said.

"It's coordination."

She looked up.

"The departments are solving the same problem separately."

Torlan leaned back slightly.

"And your summary?"

Alex answered calmly.

"Centralize the scheduling system."

Torlan watched her for a moment longer.

Then he reached forward and closed the folders.

"That is correct."

Alex sat back.

"Was that the test?"

Torlan allowed himself the smallest hint of a smile.

"Yes."

Quiet Respect

The folders now sat neatly stacked in the center of the table.

Torlan rested his hands lightly on the tabletop and studied Alex for a moment.

The test had confirmed something he had suspected during the interview.

She remained calm under pressure.

That alone was rare.

But he had one more question.

"What do you do," he asked, "when a task seems impossible?"

Alex did not answer immediately.

She thought about the question for a moment.

Then she said simply,

"Break it into smaller tasks."

Torlan waited.

"And start with the first one," she finished.

The room became quiet.

Torlan watched her carefully.

There was no hesitation in her voice.

No attempt to impress him.

Just a clear answer.

Her words stirred a memory.

Years earlier, in the valley of Valaryn on Cyrion, Dr. Arel Ziv had once pointed toward the mountains that rose along the horizon.

Torlan had been younger then, struggling with the heavy gravity of the world.

Climbing even a small ridge had felt exhausting.

Ziv had smiled gently and said,

"Even the highest mountain is climbed one step at a time."

At the time Torlan had thought the lesson was about endurance.

Later he understood it was about patience.

And understanding.

Torlan returned his attention to Alex.

She sat quietly across the table, waiting for his response.

He nodded once.

"That is a useful approach."

Alex gave a small shrug.

"It usually works."

Torlan allowed himself a faint smile.

"Yes," he said quietly.

"It usually does."

The Offer

Torlan sat quietly for a moment after their last exchange.

Then he leaned back slightly in his chair.

"You should understand something about this position," he said.

Alex nodded.

"I assumed there might be something."

Torlan allowed a faint smile.

"There are several things."

He spoke plainly.

"The hours are long."

Alex nodded again.

"The work rarely slows down."

She remained silent, listening.

"There will be constant pressure," he continued.

"Unexpected problems."

"Sudden travel."

"Complicated decisions."

He paused.

"And absolute honesty is required."

Alex tilted her head slightly.

"In what sense?"

Torlan answered calmly.

"If something goes wrong, I need to know immediately."

"No delays."

"No softened explanations."

"No convenient omissions."

Alex considered that for a moment.

Then she said simply,

"That seems reasonable."

Torlan studied her expression.

"You understand that four assistants resigned this year."

"Yes."

"And this description does not concern you?"

Alex leaned back slightly in her chair.

Then she said something that surprised him.

"Actually," she said, "it helps."

Torlan raised an eyebrow.

"Explain."

"If the expectations are clear," she said, "then the work is clear."

She met his eyes calmly.

"Then we understand each other."

For a moment Torlan said nothing.

Then he nodded once.

"Yes," he said quietly.

"I believe we do."

He stood.

Alex stood as well.

Torlan extended his hand.

"If you are willing to accept the position," he said,

"I would like you to begin next week."

Alex shook his hand.

"I'm here now," she said.

"If there's work to begin, I'd like to start."

Torlan studied her for a moment—then, just slightly, nodded.

Immediate Work

Alex stepped out of Torlan's office and followed the receptionist to a nearby desk.

"This will be your workspace," the receptionist said.

Alex set down her bag and looked around.

The desk was covered with neatly stacked reports, incoming messages, and a digital schedule screen that was already filled with appointments.

She turned the screen toward herself and began reviewing the schedule.

Torlan returned to his office, leaving the door partially open.

Alex studied the calendar carefully.

Her eyebrows lifted slightly.

Then she stood and stepped into the office doorway.

"Mr. Arden?"

Torlan looked up from his tablet.

"Yes?"

Alex turned the schedule display so he could see it.

"You have meetings scheduled for the next sixteen hours."

Torlan glanced at the screen.

"Yes."

Alex hesitated.

"Do you eat during those meetings?"

Torlan thought for a moment.

"Sometimes."

Alex nodded slowly.

"That will need improvement."

For the first time during the entire interview process—

Torlan smiled.

Alex returned to the desk and continued reviewing the incoming messages.

Most were routine:

• corporate reports

• meeting confirmations

• logistics updates

Then one message caught her attention.

It was different.

Short.

Direct.

And marked with a priority tag from one of Torlan's humanitarian organizations.

Alex opened the message and read it carefully.

Her expression grew more serious.

She stood again and walked back into the office.

"Mr. Arden?"

Torlan looked up.

"Yes?"

She handed him the tablet.

"You may want to see this."

Torlan read the message slowly.

A distant colony.

A neutral settlement caught between two war zones.

Cargo ships damaged.

Medical supplies nearly gone.

Agricultural systems failing.

They were asking for help.

Torlan read the message a second time.

Then he set the tablet down quietly.

"Schedule them for tomorrow," he said.

Alex nodded.

"I will."

As she returned to her desk, Torlan looked out the window toward the distant horizon.

Somewhere far beyond Earth—

people needed help.

Chapter 4 — The Visitors

(The Inciting Incident)

Alex Organizes the Meeting

The following morning began earlier than usual.

Alex arrived before sunrise and found that Torlan was already in his office reviewing reports.

That did not surprise her.

What surprised her was the message waiting in her system.

The delegation requesting the meeting had already arrived.

Two hours early.

Alex checked the building entrance log.

Three visitors.

All registered through Torlan's Support Assistance Resource network.

Their request for help had been marked urgent.

Alex stood and walked toward the reception area.

The three visitors were waiting quietly.

Their clothing suggested long-distance travel—practical garments, slightly worn from use.

They looked tired.

More than tired.

Concerned.

The oldest of the three stood when Alex approached.

"Good morning," he said politely.

"We apologize for arriving early."

Alex gave a small reassuring nod.

"That's quite alright."

She studied them briefly.

Their posture told her something immediately.

These were not people used to asking for help.

Yet here they were.

"Mr. Arden will see you shortly," she said.

"Please follow me."

Alex led them to a conference room overlooking the eastern side of the city.

Morning sunlight had just begun to reach the glass walls.

She arranged several chairs and activated the display table.

"Can I bring you anything?" she asked.

"Water would be appreciated," the older man said.

Alex nodded and left briefly.

As she walked back toward Torlan's office, she reviewed the message again.

Neutral settlement.

War zone nearby.

Medical shortages.

Agricultural system failures.

That combination rarely ended well.

She knocked lightly on Torlan's door.

"Yes," he said.

Alex stepped inside.

"The visitors have arrived."

Torlan looked up from his report.

"Already?"

"Yes."

He closed the tablet and stood.

"What do you think?" he asked.

Alex answered honestly.

"They appear worried."

Torlan nodded once.

"Then we should listen."

The Delegation Arrives

Torlan entered the conference room quietly.

The three visitors stood as he approached.

For a moment no one spoke.

Torlan noticed several details immediately.

Their clothing was practical—durable travel garments designed for long voyages rather than comfort. Dust from several different environments still clung to the seams.

Their boots were worn.

Their shoulders carried the stiffness of people who had spent too many hours in cramped transport seats.

They had come a long way.

But it was their faces that told the real story.

Tired.

Concerned.

And carrying the quiet tension of people who had been dealing with the same problem for far too long.

Torlan had seen that expression before.

Usually it meant someone had run out of options.

The oldest of the three stepped forward.

His hair had begun to gray at the temples, and the lines around his eyes suggested years spent outdoors rather than behind a desk.

"Mr. Arden," he said.

"Thank you for agreeing to see us."

Torlan shook his hand.

"You traveled a long distance."

"Yes," the man replied.

"But the matter is important."

Torlan gestured toward the chairs around the table.

"Please sit."

The visitors took their seats.

Alex entered quietly behind Torlan and placed several glasses of water on the table.

"Thank you," the older man said.

Alex nodded politely and took a seat near the display console.

Torlan noticed something else.

The three settlers kept exchanging brief glances with each other.

They were deciding who should speak.

Finally the older man took a breath.

"My name is Daniel Marris," he said.

"I represent the Havenfall settlement."

Torlan nodded once.

"I'm listening."

The Problem Explained

Daniel Marris rested his hands on the table and looked toward Torlan.

"Our settlement is located in the Havenfall system," he began.

Torlan nodded slightly.

"I'm familiar with the region."

Marris looked faintly relieved.

"That will make this easier to explain."

He activated the display table.

A star map appeared above the surface, projecting the surrounding systems in soft blue light.

Alex leaned forward slightly, studying the map.

Marris pointed to a small world orbiting a yellow star.

"This is Havenfall."

The projection shifted to show two neighboring systems.

"These," Marris continued, "are the planets currently at war."

Torlan recognized the names immediately.

The conflict had been reported for months.

"What is your connection to them?" he asked.

"None," Marris said.

"We are an agricultural settlement."

He zoomed the display further.

"Our world produces food, plant cultures, and soil regeneration compounds."

Torlan nodded.

"Useful exports."

"Yes."

"Until recently we shipped regularly through the regional trade routes."

Marris tapped a series of blinking markers that appeared along the map.

"These routes now pass through active military patrol zones."

Alex studied the data.

"How many ships have been affected?" she asked.

Marris hesitated.

"Seven."

Torlan's expression remained calm.

"Destroyed?"

"Two destroyed," Marris said quietly.

"Five damaged."

He paused before continuing.

"Fortunately the crews survived."

Alex's voice was steady.

"But the cargo was lost."

"Yes."

Another settler spoke for the first time.

She was younger, with dark hair tied back tightly.

"Our medical equipment is nearly gone," she said.

"We expected resupply shipments months ago."

Marris nodded toward her.

"Doctor Elina Voss," he said.

"Our settlement physician."

Torlan inclined his head slightly.

"How serious is the shortage?"

Dr. Voss answered honestly.

"We are managing."

Torlan understood the tone.

That meant they were **barely managing**.

Marris gestured again toward the map.

"There's another problem."

The display shifted to show Havenfall's agricultural regions.

"Several of our irrigation systems depend on imported replacement parts."

Alex asked quietly,

"And those parts are now stuck in the trade routes."

"Yes."

Torlan considered the situation.

"So your food production is declining."

"Slowly," Marris said.

"But steadily."

For a moment the room was quiet.

Then Marris added something with a faint trace of humor.

"We tried very hard to stay out of the war."

Torlan looked at him calmly.

"How successful has that been?"

Marris gave a dry smile.

"Not very."

Even Alex allowed herself a small smile at that.

Marris leaned forward again.

"We have tried every neutral shipping service we could find."

"No one will enter the region anymore."

"Not with two fleets fighting nearby."

He looked directly at Torlan.

"So we came here."

The War Description

Daniel Marris adjusted the star map again.

Two larger worlds appeared on opposite sides of Havenfall.

"These are the two planets currently at war," he said.

He pointed to the first.

"Helior."

The projection shifted to highlight a bright desert world orbiting a slightly hotter star.

"Helior's government controls most of the industrial mining operations in this sector."

Torlan nodded slightly.

"And the other?"

Marris touched the second marker.

"Virella."

The display changed to show a blue-green world with wide oceans and scattered continents.

"Virella controls the trade routes through this region of space."

Alex studied the map carefully.

"So Havenfall lies between them."

"Yes," Marris said quietly.

"Unfortunately."

Dr. Voss added,

"The conflict began several years ago."

"At first it was mostly economic pressure and border disputes."

"But eventually both sides deployed fleets."

Torlan watched the map.

"How many years?"

Marris answered.

"Seven."

Torlan nodded once.

"And neither side is winning."

Marris looked surprised.

"No."

"How did you know?"

Torlan answered simply.

"If either side had won, the patrols would not still be active."

Alex glanced at him briefly.

That was a very fast conclusion.

Marris zoomed the map closer.

"Our supply routes pass through this region."

Several blinking markers appeared between the two worlds.

"This area has become the primary patrol zone."

Torlan asked his next question.

"How often are ships intercepted?"

Marris hesitated.

"Frequently."

Torlan's eyes remained on the display.

"By both sides?"

"Yes."

"And the inspections?"

"Thorough."

Torlan nodded slowly.

"So neither side trusts outsiders."

"That's correct."

Dr. Voss leaned forward slightly.

"The problem is that neither side intends to attack Havenfall."

"But their fleets are operating so close to our trade routes that civilian traffic is constantly at risk."

Torlan asked one final question.

"Have either governments declared Havenfall neutral?"

Marris shook his head.

"No."

"And have you requested such a declaration?"

"Yes."

"And the response?"

Marris gave a tired smile.

"They were both… considering it."

Alex translated that silently.

Which meant:

Neither side trusted the other enough to agree.

Torlan studied the map one last time.

Then he looked back toward the settlers.

"I understand."

The Request

The star map slowly faded from the display table.

For a moment no one spoke.

Torlan rested his hands lightly on the table and waited.

He had learned long ago that people eventually say what matters most if they are given the time to do so.

Daniel Marris finally broke the silence.

"Mr. Arden," he said quietly, "we did not come here simply to explain our situation."

Torlan nodded.

"I assumed that."

Marris folded his hands together.

"Our settlement is reaching a point where we cannot solve these problems alone."

He glanced briefly toward Dr. Voss before continuing.

"Our medical supplies are running dangerously low."

Dr. Voss spoke next.

"We expected replacement equipment months ago."

"Without it we can treat only the most basic conditions."

Torlan listened carefully.

Marris continued.

"Our agricultural systems are also beginning to fail."

He brought up another image on the display.

Large irrigation grids spread across the surface of Havenfall.

"Several of our well pumps require specialized replacement parts."

He looked directly at Torlan.

"Those parts are currently sitting in cargo depots we can no longer reach."

Alex studied the image quietly.

"If the irrigation fails," she said, "your food production will collapse."

Marris nodded.

"Yes."

The third settler, a younger man who had remained silent until now, finally spoke.

"Our cargo routes are gone."

"No captain is willing to fly through the patrol zones."

Torlan asked calmly,

"And you cannot build the equipment locally?"

"We can repair some systems," the man replied.

"But the specialized components must be imported."

Marris took a breath.

"Mr. Arden… we have heard about your Support Assistance Resource organizations."

Torlan said nothing.

"We know your groups have helped communities in difficult situations before."

He paused for a moment.

"We hoped you might be willing to help Havenfall."

The room grew quiet again.

Torlan looked briefly toward Alex.

She understood the question immediately.

They were not asking for advice.

They were asking for **action**.

Marris spoke again.

"We need several things."

He counted them carefully.

"Medical supplies."

"Agricultural equipment."

"Replacement parts for our wells."

He paused briefly.

"Nearly everything is already paid for," he added, his tone steady.

"What we lack is a safe way to bring it in."

"And most importantly…"

He met Torlan's eyes.

"A way to move cargo safely through the region."

Torlan listened without interrupting.

Marris finished simply.

"That is why we came."

Torlan's Response

After Marris finished speaking, the room became quiet again.

Torlan remained seated for several seconds, his hands resting lightly on the table.

He had listened carefully to everything the settlers had said.

Medical shortages.

Agricultural failures.

Trade routes cut off by war.

The problem was serious.

But serious problems were rarely solved by moving too quickly.

Torlan finally looked up.

"I understand your situation," he said.

Marris nodded.

"We hoped you might."

Torlan leaned back slightly in his chair.

"But before I give you an answer," he continued, "I will need to understand the war."

The settlers exchanged brief glances.

Torlan continued calmly.

"If supplies are to reach Havenfall, they must pass through the region controlled by both sides."

"That means I must understand the motives of both governments."

Alex watched him carefully.

She was already beginning to see how his mind worked.

He was not thinking about sympathy.

He was thinking about **solutions**.

Torlan stood and walked slowly toward the window.

The city stretched out far below.

Ships moved through the sky lanes in steady patterns.

Behind him the conference room remained silent.

He remembered something Dr. Arel Ziv had told him many years earlier in the Valley of Valaryn.

When Torlan had once rushed into a difficult problem, Ziv had smiled patiently and said,

"Observe first. Act second."

At the time Torlan had thought the advice was simple.

Later he learned how powerful it was.

Most mistakes happened because people acted too quickly.

Torlan turned back toward the table.

"I will review everything you have provided," he said.

"I will also gather additional information about the conflict."

Marris leaned forward slightly.

"And then?"

Torlan answered simply.

"Then we will see what can be done."

The Investigation Begins

The meeting concluded quietly.

Torlan walked with the settlers toward the reception area.

Daniel Marris shook his hand firmly.

"Thank you for hearing us," he said.

"You traveled a long distance," Torlan replied.

"It was the least I could do."

Dr. Voss gave a grateful nod.

"Whatever your decision, we appreciate the time."

Torlan inclined his head slightly.

"Safe travels."

The three settlers left the building a few minutes later, returning to their transport to await his answer.

Havenfall could not wait much longer.

For a moment the office became unusually quiet.

Torlan returned to the conference room.

Alex was already standing beside the display table reviewing the star map again.

He studied the projection for a moment.

Then he turned toward her.

"Alex."

"Yes."

"Gather everything we can learn about this conflict."

Alex nodded and opened a new data file.

"What specifically?"

Torlan answered without hesitation.

"Historical records."

"Economic trade routes."

"Political leadership on both planets."

"Military movements during the past seven years."

He paused briefly.

"And shipping traffic through the region."

Alex typed quickly.

"Understood."

Torlan added one final instruction.

"Nothing is too small."

Alex glanced up.

"I suspected that."

The star map slowly rotated above the display table.

Two worlds.

One neutral settlement caught between them.

Alex finished entering the request parameters.

Then she looked toward Torlan.

"Do you think we can help them?"

Torlan considered the question for a moment.

"I don't know yet," he said.

Alex waited.

Torlan studied the map again.

Then he said quietly,

"But we will find out."

Chapter 5 — The Quiet Investigation

The Data Request

Location: Torlan's Office

The following morning began quietly.

Alex arrived carrying a tablet filled with preliminary reports.

Torlan was already seated near the window reviewing a series of historical star charts.

He glanced up as she entered.

"How much information exists about the conflict?" he asked.

"More than I expected," Alex replied.

"Good," Torlan said.

He stood and walked toward the display table in the center of the room.

The table activated automatically as Alex placed the tablet on its surface.

Several layers of information appeared:

- star system maps
- shipping routes
- diplomatic communications
- military patrol records

Torlan studied the data silently for a moment.

Then he began giving instructions.

"I want everything we can find about the origin of the conflict."

Alex began typing.

"Historical archives," Torlan continued.

"Diplomatic records between Helior and Virella."

"Economic trade routes through the region."

"Military deployments during the past seven years."

Alex added the categories quickly.

Torlan continued.

"Leadership changes on both planets."

Alex paused briefly.

"That could be a large amount of information."

Torlan nodded.

"Yes."

She looked up.

"You want all of it?"

"Yes."

Alex continued entering the request parameters.

Torlan watched the rotating star map above the table.

Then he added one final instruction.

"As I said before—nothing is too small."

Alex looked at him curiously.

Torlan spoke quietly.

"Sometimes the smallest detail explains the largest conflict."

Alex nodded slowly.

"I'll begin filtering the data."

Torlan returned his attention to the map.

Two planets at war.

One settlement caught between them.

Somewhere in the history of the conflict, he suspected there was a detail everyone else had overlooked.

And that detail might be the key to helping Havenfall.

Alex Builds the File System

Location: Operations Office

The operations office was quieter than the executive floor.

Here the walls were lined with large display panels used for planning logistics and research projects.

Alex activated the central display table.

A wide projection appeared above the surface.

Torlan entered a few minutes later and stopped beside the table.

Alex had already begun constructing the research framework.

Layers of information floated in the air above the display.

Star systems.

Trade routes.

Military patrol regions.

Torlan watched silently.

Alex began explaining her system.

"I've started organizing the information into four primary layers," she said.

She expanded the first layer.

A map of the sector appeared.

Two large systems glowed in red.

"Helior."

"Virella."

Between them a smaller system appeared in soft green.

"Havenfall."

Torlan nodded.

"Continue."

Alex activated the second layer.

Thin blue lines appeared across the map.

"These are the historical trade routes."

Several of the lines passed directly between the two war systems.

Torlan studied them carefully.

"That explains why Havenfall depended on those routes."

"Yes," Alex said.

"They were the most efficient paths for cargo traffic."

She expanded the third layer.

Red markers appeared across the region.

"These are the known military patrol zones."

Several of the patrol areas overlapped the old trade routes.

Torlan understood the implication immediately.

"No captain wants to fly through that."

"Correct," Alex said.

Finally she activated the fourth layer.

A timeline appeared along the bottom of the display.

"This tracks major events during the past seven years."

Diplomatic messages.

Fleet movements.

Trade disruptions.

Leadership changes.

Torlan looked at the growing network of information.

"You built this quickly."

Alex shrugged slightly.

"It's easier to understand a problem once everything is visible."

Torlan nodded.

"That is true."

The map rotated slowly above the display table.

For the first time the entire situation became clear.

Two war worlds.

One neutral settlement between them.

And every supply route passing directly through the conflict.

Torlan studied the projection carefully.

Somewhere in that web of information was the answer.

He was certain of it.

Late Night Research

The building had grown quiet.

Most of the offices on the executive floor were dark.

Only a few lights remained on in the operations room.

Torlan sat alone at the display table.

The star map hovered in front of him, slowly rotating.

Helior.

Virella.

Havenfall.

Dozens of shipping routes and patrol zones crossed the region like threads in a complicated web.

Torlan studied the pattern carefully.

He had spent several hours reviewing the records Alex had gathered.

Trade agreements.

Military deployments.

Diplomatic messages.

Convoy logs.

Most of it was routine information.

But somewhere in that data, something had started a war.

Torlan expanded the timeline display.

The past seven years appeared along the bottom of the map.

Key events were marked with small glowing symbols.

Fleet movements.

Economic sanctions.

Border patrols.

He studied the earliest entries again.

The beginning.

Wars rarely started without a cause.

Yet the first reports were surprisingly unclear.

Two cargo convoys had been destroyed.

Each side accused the other.

Neither explanation seemed complete.

Torlan leaned back slightly in his chair.

For a moment he closed his eyes.

Years earlier, on the world of Cyrion, Dr. Arel Ziv had often taken his students outside the learning halls at night.

They would sit quietly in Lyara's garden and watch the stars move slowly across the sky.

One evening Torlan had asked why Ziv preferred teaching astronomy in silence.

Ziv had smiled and said,

"The quiet mind sees the farthest."

At the time Torlan had not fully understood.

Later he realized that silence helped the mind notice things that noise often hid.

Torlan opened his eyes again.

He studied the data once more.

This time he looked not at the reports themselves—

but at the patterns surrounding them.

Convoy routes.

Patrol schedules.

Economic shipments.

And something began to stand out.

A small detail.

One that most analysts would probably overlook.

But small details had a habit of explaining large problems.

Torlan leaned forward slightly.

The investigation had only just begun.

The First Strange Detail

Torlan continued reviewing the early records of the conflict.

The display table shifted to show the first major event recorded in the timeline.

Year Seven — Month Three

Two cargo convoys destroyed.

The marker pulsed faintly on the star map.

Torlan expanded the report.

The incident had occurred in open space between Helior and Virella.

Exactly along one of the major trade routes.

Alex entered the operations room a few minutes later carrying another data tablet.

"You're still working," she said.

Torlan nodded slightly.

"Yes."

Alex stepped beside the display.

"What have you found?"

Torlan pointed toward the incident marker.

"The war began here."

Alex studied the report.

"The convoy destruction."

"Yes."

She expanded the historical file.

Two civilian cargo fleets had been traveling through the corridor.

One convoy from Helior.

One convoy from Virella.

Both carrying industrial materials.

Both destroyed within minutes of each other.

Alex frowned.

"That seems unlikely."

Torlan nodded.

"Very."

Alex scrolled through the investigation reports.

"Helior claims Virella attacked first."

"And Virella claims Helior opened fire."

Torlan studied the data again.

"Both reports say the same thing."

Alex looked up.

"That the other side started the battle."

"Yes."

Alex leaned back slightly.

"So each side believes it was defending itself."

Torlan nodded slowly.

"Exactly."

Alex continued reading.

"The convoys were traveling near Havenfall's outer corridor."

Torlan's eyes returned to the map.

"Yes."

Alex studied the flight logs carefully.

"Something about this report feels incomplete."

Torlan nodded.

"That is because it is."

Alex looked at him.

"What do you mean?"

Torlan expanded the navigation data.

Several flight paths appeared around the convoy location.

"According to these records," he said quietly,

"both convoys arrived in the corridor at almost exactly the same moment."

Alex frowned.

"That's a very unusual coincidence."

Torlan nodded again.

"Yes."

He looked at the star map thoughtfully.

"Wars rarely begin because of coincidence."

The map rotated slowly above the table.

Helior.

Virella.

Havenfall.

Three systems tied together by trade routes.

Torlan studied the pattern again.

"The official explanation is simple," he said.

"But the situation is not."

Alex asked the obvious question.

"What do you think really happened?"

Torlan answered calmly.

"I don't know yet."

He zoomed the map closer to the convoy location.

"But something important happened here."

"And someone misunderstood it."

Discussion with Alex

Alex returned to the operations room carrying a stack of additional records.

Torlan was still standing beside the display table.

The star map hovered above the surface, now filled with layers of information.

Convoy routes.

Patrol zones.

Diplomatic reports.

The timeline stretched across the bottom of the projection like a long thread of events.

Alex placed the new files on the table.

"I found additional shipping logs from the first year of the conflict."

Torlan nodded.

"Add them to the timeline."

Alex worked quickly, inserting the records into the display.

New markers appeared across the early months of the war.

For several minutes they studied the data in silence.

Alex noticed something first.

"These dates don't align."

Torlan looked at the section she indicated.

Two diplomatic messages appeared several days after the convoy incident.

Yet according to the military records, patrol fleets had already begun mobilizing before those messages were sent.

"That is unusual," Alex said.

Torlan nodded slowly.

"Yes."

Alex continued reviewing the files.

"There are also gaps in the witness reports."

She highlighted several missing entries.

"The first convoy captains recorded distress transmissions."

"But the final investigation reports contain no surviving testimony."

Torlan leaned closer to the display.

"Vanished?"

Alex nodded.

"The ships were destroyed."

"And most of the crews were rescued."

She paused.

"But the original witnesses never appear in the official hearings."

Torlan studied the timeline again.

Something about the sequence of events was wrong.

Alex expanded another report.

"There's more."

She highlighted a section of the diplomatic archive.

"Both governments issued accusations within hours of the incident."

Torlan nodded.

"Too quickly."

Alex looked at him.

"You think the reports were incomplete."

Torlan considered the data carefully.

"Possibly."

He stepped back from the display table.

Orbits and patrol routes glowed softly in the dim room.

For several seconds he said nothing.

Finally Torlan spoke quietly.

"This war did not begin the way they believe."

Alex looked up from the display.

"What do you mean?"

Torlan pointed to the convoy incident marker.

"Both sides believe they were attacked."

"Yes."

Torlan studied the surrounding records again.

"But the evidence suggests something else happened first."

Alex waited.

Torlan finished the thought slowly.

"Someone misunderstood something important."

Alex looked back at the timeline.

Then she asked the question that followed naturally.

"Or someone wanted them to misunderstand?"

Torlan did not answer immediately.

He studied the map again.

Helior.

Virella.

Havenfall.

Three systems connected by trade routes and suspicion.

"Perhaps," he said quietly.

Chapter 6 — War Files

The Archive Files

Location: Torlan's Office

Alex entered the office carrying a large data slate.

"I've compiled the first complete archive set," she said.

Torlan looked up from the star charts spread across his desk.

"That was fast."

Alex set the slate on the display table.

"Most of the records were public diplomatic archives. The military files were harder to locate."

The table activated automatically.

Layers of information appeared in the air above the surface.

Diplomatic messages.

Trade records.

Fleet movement reports.

Navigation logs.

Torlan stood and walked around the table slowly, studying the information.

Alex organized the files into categories.

"I grouped the data into four primary sections," she explained.

"Diplomatic archives between the two systems."

"Military activity reports."

"Economic trade records."

"And civilian navigation logs."

Torlan nodded.

"Good."

Alex opened the diplomatic archive first.

Hundreds of communications appeared on the display.

"The early exchanges are surprisingly calm," she said.

Torlan read one of the messages.

Valyra had issued a complaint regarding mining access.

Dravakar responded with a request for negotiation.

Neither side sounded hostile.

"At first this appears to be a standard economic dispute," Alex said.

Torlan nodded.

"Many wars begin that way."

She switched to the economic records.

Trade routes appeared across the sector map.

Cargo shipments flowed steadily between the systems.

Industrial metals.

Food supplies.

Energy crystals.

Torlan studied the routes carefully.

"The systems depended on each other," he observed.

"Yes," Alex said.

"Which makes the war economically destructive for both sides."

Torlan nodded slowly.

"That is rarely a good sign."

Alex expanded the military reports.

Fleet patrol zones appeared in red across the map.

Over time the patrol areas grew larger.

More ships.

More interceptions.

More accusations.

Torlan watched the pattern unfold.

"This war escalated gradually," he said.

"Yes."

Alex pointed to the early months of the conflict.

"The convoy incident changed everything."

Torlan studied the records again.

"Yes."

Finally Alex opened the navigation logs.

Flight paths from dozens of ships appeared in thin white lines across the map.

Cargo vessels.

Diplomatic transports.

Mining ships.

Torlan watched the lines intersect near Havenfall.

The same region where the first convoy incident had occurred.

He leaned closer to the display.

"Interesting."

Alex looked at him.

"What did you notice?"

Torlan did not answer immediately.

He simply studied the map a little longer.

The war had begun here.

But the records suggested something more complicated than a simple attack.

And somewhere in these archives—

the truth was still waiting.

Valyra

The star map shifted as Alex activated the next data layer.

The system of **Valyra** appeared in the center of the display.

A large amber world rotated slowly above the table.

Several smaller moons orbited it like silent sentinels.

Torlan studied the planet carefully.

"Valyra," he said quietly.

Alex nodded.

"I've compiled the primary cultural and political data."

She expanded the file.

Several summary notes appeared beside the rotating world.

"Valyra is governed by a **constitutional monarchy**," Alex explained.

"The royal house remains the symbolic center of authority, but legislative councils manage most civil policy."

Torlan nodded slightly.

"Stable leadership structure."

"Yes," Alex said.

"Very stable."

Alex activated another layer.

Military formations appeared around the system.

A network of patrol routes and fleet bases circled the planet.

"Valyra maintains a **disciplined naval fleet**," she continued.

"Highly structured command hierarchy."

"Fleet officers are trained from an early age."

Torlan studied the formation patterns.

"Their patrol routes are precise."

Alex nodded.

"They place a high value on order and discipline."

She opened another section of the file.

Cultural records appeared.

Ceremonial events.

Military academies.

Historical celebrations.

"Valyra's society is heavily influenced by **honor traditions**," Alex said.

"Reputation and loyalty are extremely important."

Torlan looked at the records thoughtfully.

"That would explain their reaction."

Alex glanced at him.

"To the convoy incident?"

"Yes."

Alex expanded the historical report connected to the beginning of the war.

A convoy marker appeared on the map.

"According to Valyra's official account," she said,

"a **royal diplomatic convoy** was traveling through the corridor near Havenfall."

The marker pulsed softly on the display.

"They report that Dravakar ships intercepted the convoy and opened fire."

Torlan studied the report carefully.

"And the diplomatic passengers?"

"Several were killed," Alex said quietly.

Torlan nodded slowly.

"For a society built on honor, that would be unforgivable."

Alex agreed.

"Yes."

The planet continued rotating above the table.

Valyra's fleets guarded the system like an armored shield.

Torlan studied the cultural reports one more time.

"They believe they were attacked without provocation."

"That is their official position," Alex said.

Torlan nodded.

"And if their honor culture believes that narrative…"

Alex finished the thought.

"Then they would see the war as justified."

Torlan looked back toward the convoy marker.

"Yes."

Dravakar

Alex shifted the star map again.

The image of Valyra faded slightly as another system brightened on the opposite side of Havenfall.

"This is **Dravakar**," she said.

A deep blue world appeared above the display table.

Several orbital stations circled the planet like busy crossroads.

Trade lanes radiated outward from the system in every direction.

Torlan studied the projection carefully.

"Very different from Valyra," he said.

Alex nodded.

"Yes."

She opened the political file.

"Dravakar operates under a **commercial council government**."

Several council emblems appeared beside the planet.

"The system is governed by a coalition of merchant guilds, shipping alliances, and trade consortiums."

Torlan raised an eyebrow slightly.

"Economics as government."

"Essentially," Alex said.

"Major policy decisions are made by representatives of the largest trading organizations."

Torlan studied the council structure.

"That would create a strong focus on trade routes."

"Yes."

"Trade is the foundation of their economy."

Alex activated the military layer.

Dozens of small fleet formations appeared along the system's outer routes.

"These are Dravakar's naval forces."

Torlan noticed something immediately.

"Their ships are smaller."

"Yes," Alex said.

"But faster."

She expanded the tactical report.

"Dravakar fleets operate using **raider-style formations**."

"Light vessels."

"Rapid interception capability."

"Designed to move quickly between trade corridors."

Torlan nodded slowly.

"They protect their shipping lanes."

"Exactly."

Alex expanded the historical report connected to the convoy incident.

A second convoy marker appeared on the map.

"Dravakar's official record states that one of their cargo convoys was traveling through the corridor near Havenfall."

Torlan watched the data carefully.

"What were they carrying?"

"Industrial metals and navigation components," Alex replied. "Standard trade cargo."

Torlan nodded.

"And the incident?"

Alex opened the report.

"Dravakar claims that Valyra's fleet suddenly intercepted the convoy and opened fire without warning."

Torlan studied the record.

"Ambush."

"That is how Dravakar describes it."

The star map slowly rotated.

Valyra's disciplined fleet formations appeared on one side.

Dravakar's fast trade patrols appeared on the other.

Between them sat Havenfall.

A small green world surrounded by the traffic lanes both civilizations depended on.

Torlan looked at the reports again.

"So Dravakar believes Valyra attacked their cargo ships first."

"Yes."

"And they see the war as defending their trade routes."

Alex nodded.

"That is their official position."

Torlan folded his arms thoughtfully.

"For a trade civilization," he said, "control of shipping lanes would be essential."

"Yes."

"And losing them would threaten their entire economy."

Alex nodded again.

"Which makes the war… necessary from their perspective."

Torlan looked back at the map.

Two civilizations.

Two completely different ways of thinking.

Both convinced the other side had started the conflict.

And somewhere between their stories—

the truth had been lost.

Timeline Mapping

Alex expanded the display across the entire operations wall.

The star map faded into the background as a long visual timeline appeared from left to right, stretching nearly the full length of the room.

Dates, fleet movements, diplomatic messages, and trade disruptions arranged themselves into clear sequence.

Torlan stood with his hands loosely folded behind his back, studying the progression in silence.

Alex moved to the first major marker and activated it.

A convoy symbol appeared in red.

"The opening incident," she said.

"The convoy collision near Havenfall's outer corridor."

Two smaller route lines unfolded beneath it—one from Valyra, one from Dravakar.

Torlan nodded once.

"And after that?"

Alex advanced the timeline.

New markers appeared.

"Military mobilization."

Patrol routes expanded outward from both systems.

Fleet readiness notices.

Emergency command authorizations.

Early deployment orders.

Torlan watched the sequence carefully.

"They mobilized quickly," he said.

Alex nodded.

"Within hours, according to the official records."

She advanced the timeline again.

Two more events appeared almost immediately after the mobilization.

"Trade embargoes."

Economic restrictions spread across the route networks between the systems.

Ports were closed.

Civilian cargo traffic collapsed.

Insurance carriers withdrew coverage.

Torlan studied the dates.

"Too fast," he said quietly.

Alex glanced at him.

"You think the embargoes were prepared in advance?"

"Possibly."

He did not look away from the display.

"Or both governments were already expecting the conflict to worsen."

Alex activated the next layer.

The earliest battles appeared as bright markers along the corridor routes.

Small engagements at first.

Patrol interceptions.

Cargo seizures.

Warning shots.

Then larger fleet actions.

The entire region near Havenfall became crowded with overlapping military movements.

Torlan studied the pattern.

The war had not exploded in a single moment.

It had tightened around the corridor like a net.

Convoy collision.

Military mobilization.

Trade embargoes.

Early battles.

Every step followed the previous one with almost unnatural speed.

Alex stood beside the display, watching Torlan's expression.

"What are you seeing?"

Torlan did not answer immediately.

He stepped closer to the wall and studied the dates again.

Then he pointed to the earliest section.

"The collision happened here."

"Yes."

"Valyra issued a military alert here."

Alex nodded.

"And Dravakar responded here."

Torlan moved his hand down the line.

"But the trade embargoes were implemented almost immediately."

Alex looked at the same data.

"That would take preparation."

"Yes."

He stepped back.

"And the first battle patrols were already in position before some of the diplomatic messages were even delivered."

Alex frowned.

"That shouldn't be possible."

Torlan nodded slowly.

"No."

The room grew quiet again.

Alex looked back at the timeline.

"So what does that mean?"

Torlan kept his eyes on the display.

"It means the war did not unfold naturally."

Alex folded her arms.

"You think someone accelerated it."

Torlan looked at the convoy marker one more time.

"Or they were already moving toward war before the convoy incident gave them a reason."

The Strange Gap

The timeline still filled the operations wall.

Convoy collision.

Fleet mobilization.

Trade embargoes.

Early battles.

The sequence of events looked logical at first glance.

But Torlan continued studying the earliest section of the timeline.

Something about it still felt incomplete.

Alex began opening the original convoy reports again.

"These are the first investigation files released by both governments," she said.

Torlan stepped closer.

"Show me the navigation logs."

Alex expanded the file.

Two flight paths appeared near Havenfall's outer corridor.

One convoy from Valyra.

One convoy from Dravakar.

The two routes crossed almost exactly at the same point.

Torlan studied the data carefully.

"Where are the full sensor reports?"

Alex searched through the file system.

A moment later she frowned.

"That's strange."

Torlan waited.

"The long-range sensor records stop several minutes before the incident."

Torlan looked back at the timeline.

"Both sides?"

"Yes."

She checked the second archive.

"Both."

Alex opened another file.

"These should be the bridge communications."

Several short transcripts appeared.

Emergency alerts.

Distress calls.

Fragments of conversations.

But the messages were incomplete.

Some sections ended abruptly.

Others referenced signals that were not included in the records.

Alex leaned back slightly.

"These reports were heavily edited."

Torlan nodded slowly.

"Yes."

Alex continued searching the archive.

"What about witness reports?" she asked.

She opened the investigation summaries.

Several crew members had survived the convoy destruction.

But the official records contained only brief statements.

Many names listed in the rescue logs never appeared in the final investigation reports.

Alex looked at the screen again.

"That's not normal."

Torlan agreed.

"No."

He studied the incomplete files quietly for a moment.

"Navigation logs missing."

"Sensor reports inconsistent."

"Witness accounts absent."

Alex folded her arms thoughtfully.

"That's a lot of missing information."

Torlan nodded.

"Yes."

He looked again at the convoy marker on the timeline.

Then he said quietly,

"This war began with incomplete information."

The room fell silent again.

Alex stared at the timeline.

"You think both sides reacted before they knew what actually happened."

Torlan nodded slowly.

"Yes."

He stepped away from the display and walked toward the window.

Beyond the glass, cargo ships crossed the morning sky above the city.

Years earlier, in the Valley of Valaryn, Dr. Arel Ziv had once spoken a lesson that seemed simple at the time.

"Hear the wind before it rises."

Torlan had later understood what Ziv meant.

Small signs often appear long before larger events.

But most people do not notice them until the storm has already begun.

Torlan returned to the display table.

"The warning signs were there," he said quietly.

"But no one listened."

Alex's Insight

The operations room remained quiet except for the soft hum of the display wall.

Alex continued reviewing the timeline she had assembled.

Convoy collision.

Fleet mobilization.

Trade embargoes.

Early battles.

Torlan stood near the display studying the earliest section again.

Something about the sequence still bothered him.

Alex leaned closer to the timeline markers.

"Something else stands out," she said.

Torlan looked toward her.

"What is it?"

Alex highlighted several military alerts issued by both planets.

"These mobilization orders."

Torlan studied the dates.

They appeared only hours after the convoy incident.

"Yes."

Alex zoomed in further.

"But the fleets began deploying even before the official investigation reports were transmitted."

Torlan nodded slowly.

"That would require preparation."

Alex folded her arms thoughtfully.

"Almost as if both sides were expecting hostility."

Torlan looked again at the timeline.

"That suggests the tension already existed."

Alex nodded.

"Yes."

"The convoy incident may not have started the war."

"It may have simply triggered it."

Torlan turned back toward the star map.

Helior's patrol routes.

Dravakar's trade lanes.

Havenfall resting quietly between them.

He activated the navigation logs again.

Two thin white lines appeared.

The flight paths of the two convoys.

Torlan studied the routes carefully.

Then he leaned slightly closer to the display.

Alex noticed the change in his expression.

"What is it?"

Torlan did not answer immediately.

Instead he expanded the navigation grid and overlaid the standard shipping lanes used before the war.

Several additional lines appeared across the map.

Torlan compared the routes carefully.

Then he spoke quietly.

"The two convoys should never have crossed paths."

Alex stepped closer.

"What do you mean?"

Torlan pointed to the routes.

"These ships were following secondary corridors."

Alex studied the map.

"You mean they were rerouted?"

Torlan kept his eyes on the display.

"Or misdirected."

The room became silent again.

Two convoys.

Two civilizations.

One corridor where they were never supposed to meet.

Torlan looked again at the convoy marker glowing near Havenfall.

Somewhere in that moment—

something had gone very wrong.

Chapter 7 — The Hidden Beginning

"The patient traveler arrives safely."
Haste often leads people into dangers they could have avoided.
— *Wisdom of Cyrion*

The Navigation Logs

Location: Torlan's Office

The next morning Alex entered Torlan's office carrying a thick data slate.

"I found additional navigation archives," she said.

Torlan looked up from the star charts covering his desk.

"That was quicker than I expected."

Alex placed the slate on the display table.

"It took some effort," she admitted.

"Several of the records were buried in older maintenance systems."

Torlan stood and walked toward the table.

The display activated automatically.

Several layers of data appeared:

• historical navigation logs

• long-range sensor records

• beacon maintenance reports

• archived flight plans

Torlan studied the information quietly.

"These are from the week of the convoy incident?" he asked.

"Yes," Alex said.

"Some of the archives were incomplete, but I managed to reconstruct most of the flight paths."

Torlan nodded.

"Show me the convoy routes."

Alex expanded the navigation records.

Two thin lines appeared across the star map.

One line represented the **Valyra convoy**.

The other represented the **Dravakar cargo fleet**.

The two routes curved slowly through the outer corridor near Havenfall.

Torlan studied the paths carefully.

"They intersect here."

A small marker appeared where the lines crossed.

"Yes," Alex said.

"That's the reported collision zone."

Torlan looked closer.

"These routes still don't make sense."

Alex expanded the surrounding navigation grid.

"These were the standard shipping corridors before the war."

Several larger routes appeared across the sector.

Torlan compared the old corridors with the convoy paths.

The difference was obvious.

"These convoys were not using the main trade routes," he said.

"No," Alex replied.

"They were traveling along secondary corridors."

Torlan folded his arms thoughtfully.

"Which means something redirected them."

Alex nodded slowly.

"That's what it looks like."

Torlan activated another data layer.

Beacon maintenance reports appeared across the map.

Navigation beacons marked the safe routes between systems.

Torlan studied their operational records carefully.

One beacon near Havenfall caught his attention.

"This beacon malfunctioned two days before the incident," he said.

Alex leaned closer.

"That would affect navigation guidance in the corridor."

"Yes."

Torlan looked again at the convoy routes.

"If the beacon transmitted incorrect coordinates…"

Alex finished the thought.

"The convoys could have been directed into the same corridor."

Torlan stepped back from the display.

Two fleets.

Both believing they were following safe navigation routes.

Both arriving in the same narrow corridor.

Alex looked at the map quietly.

"That would explain the collision."

Torlan nodded slowly.

"Yes."

But he was not satisfied yet.

Something still felt incomplete.

The Beacon Report

The star map still hovered above the operations table.

Two thin navigation lines crossed the outer corridor near Havenfall.

The location of the convoy collision.

Torlan studied the surrounding sector carefully.

“Expand the navigation infrastructure,” he said.

Alex nodded and added another data layer to the display.

Small markers appeared across the map.

Navigation beacons.

Each beacon acted as a reference point for ships traveling through deep space corridors.

Without them, accurate navigation across the sector would be difficult.

Torlan moved closer to the display.

“Show the beacon maintenance records.”

Alex opened another archive.

Several diagnostic logs appeared beside the star map.

Routine calibration checks.

Signal verification reports.

System maintenance requests.

Most of the records were ordinary.

Until Torlan noticed one entry.

“This one,” he said.

Alex enlarged the report.

Navigation Beacon KX-417

Location: Kardrin Expanse Corridor

Torlan read the maintenance log carefully.

Signal stability: irregular.

Calibration drift detected.

Repair request submitted.

Repair request delayed.

Repair request resubmitted.

Alex leaned closer.

"Intermittent signal drift," she said.

Torlan nodded.

"That would affect navigation calculations."

Alex checked the dates on the report.

The beacon had begun drifting several days before the convoy incident.

"The repair crew never reached it in time," she said.

Torlan looked again at the convoy routes.

"If the beacon was transmitting incorrect position data…"

Alex finished the thought quietly.

"Ships following its signal would be given incorrect course corrections."

Torlan nodded slowly.

"That could redirect traffic into the wrong corridor."

Alex zoomed the map outward.

The Kardrin Expanse stretched across the display.

A wide, mostly empty region of space.

But several secondary trade routes passed through it.

Torlan traced one of the routes with his finger.

"The Valyra convoy entered this corridor here."

Alex nodded.

"And the Dravakar convoy approached from the opposite direction."

Torlan studied the beacon marker again.

"If both fleets relied on the same faulty beacon…"

"They could have been guided into the same corridor."

Alex leaned back slightly.

"That would explain why the routes crossed."

Torlan nodded.

"Yes."

But something about the situation still bothered him.

A simple navigation failure might explain the collision.

But it did not fully explain the war that followed.

Torlan closed the beacon report slowly.

"A malfunctioning beacon could cause confusion," he said.

"But confusion alone should not start a war."

Alex looked at the timeline again.

"No," she said.

"It shouldn't."

Torlan turned back toward the star map.

Which meant the collision was only the beginning.

Something else must have happened in that corridor.

Something that made both sides believe they were under attack.

Reconstructing the Routes

The star chart expanded across the operations wall.

Alex had layered the navigation data into several separate tracks.

Original trade corridors.

Beacon positions.

Convoy flight paths.

Torlan stepped closer to the display.

"Remove the beacon corrections," he said.

Alex nodded.

The system recalculated the routes.

Two new lines appeared.

These represented the **original planned courses** for the convoys before the navigation beacon began transmitting incorrect data.

Torlan studied the map carefully.

The difference was immediately clear.

The Valyra convoy followed a northern trade corridor.

The Dravakar cargo fleet approached along a southern route.

The two lines passed the Kardrin Expanse many thousands of kilometers apart.

Far enough that neither fleet would even detect the other.

Alex leaned forward.

"They would never have encountered each other."

Torlan nodded slowly.

"Yes."

"Now restore the beacon corrections," Torlan said.

Alex activated the second set of navigation logs.

The lines shifted.

Both routes curved inward.

Subtle course adjustments appeared along the path of each convoy.

Minor corrections.

Small directional changes.

The kind of adjustments ships make automatically when responding to navigation guidance signals.

Torlan watched the two lines move.

Until finally—

They intersected.

The collision point glowed softly on the star chart.

Alex stared at the display.

"They were both correcting their course."

Torlan nodded.

"Following the same beacon."

Alex looked again at the routes.

"They weren't intercepting each other."

Torlan folded his arms.

"No."

He studied the crossing lines again.

"They were being guided into the same corridor."

The room grew quiet.

Two convoys.

Both believing they were following safe navigation guidance.

Both slowly adjusting their course based on the same faulty beacon signal.

Until eventually—

They arrived at the same point in space.

At the same time.

Alex exhaled slowly.

"That's the collision."

Torlan nodded.

"Yes."

Alex looked back at the earlier investigation reports.

"Both governments believed the other fleet deliberately entered their route."

Torlan nodded again.

"That would appear to be the case."

"But the navigation data shows something different."

Alex watched the glowing routes crossing on the star chart.

"A guidance error."

Torlan corrected her gently.

"A beacon error."

He studied the display a moment longer.

The collision now seemed inevitable.

Two fleets.

Guided by incorrect data.

Arriving in the same narrow corridor.

Alex leaned back in her chair.

"That could explain the accident."

Torlan nodded slowly.

"Yes."

Then he added quietly,

"But not the war."

The Moment of Realization

The star chart still glowed softly across the operations wall.

Two routes crossed in the Kardrin Expanse.

A single point of light marked the place where the convoys had met.

Torlan studied the display without speaking.

Alex watched him quietly.

After a moment she said,

"Both fleets adjusted course several times."

Torlan nodded.

"Yes."

Alex zoomed in on the route corrections.

Small course changes appeared along both convoy paths.

Each adjustment looked routine.

Ships constantly made minor corrections while traveling through deep space.

But now those small corrections formed a pattern.

All of them pointed toward the same place.

The same beacon.

Torlan looked at the maintenance report again.

Beacon KX-417.

Signal drift.

Calibration error.

Repair delayed.

Alex leaned closer to the display.

"The beacon was transmitting incorrect position data."

Torlan nodded slowly.

"Yes."

He studied the routes again.

Then he said quietly,

"They were navigating by the same beacon."

Alex watched the crossing lines on the star chart.

Neither convoy had turned toward the other deliberately.

Neither had changed course to intercept.

Both had simply followed their navigation guidance.

Trusting the signal.

Trusting the system that ships had relied upon for decades.

Alex said softly,

"They never intended to meet."

Torlan nodded.

"No."

He looked again at the glowing intersection point.

"Both convoys trusted the same faulty signal."

For a moment neither of them spoke.

Two fleets.

Two civilizations.

Each believing their navigation systems were reliable.

Each adjusting course slightly as the beacon directed them.

Until finally—

Both fleets entered the same narrow corridor.

At the same time.

Alex exhaled slowly.

"That collision was inevitable."

Torlan nodded.

"Yes."

But his eyes remained on the display.

Because the accident itself was only the beginning.

The real question still remained.

What happened next?

The Debris Field

Alex adjusted the star chart again.

Another layer of information appeared across the display.

Salvage reports.

Sensor scans.

Long-range survey data.

The debris field from the convoy incident still remained scattered across a wide region of the Kardrin Expanse.

Even years later the wreckage had not completely drifted away.

Torlan studied the distribution carefully.

"How accurate are these surveys?" he asked.

Alex answered,

"Within a few kilometers."

"That's the best reconstruction available."

Torlan nodded.

"That will be enough."

The debris markers formed a wide cloud across the display.

Fragments of cargo ships.

Destroyed escorts.

Sections of hull plating.

Alex enlarged the central region.

"This is where the first impact occurred."

Torlan leaned forward slightly.

"Overlay the maneuver vectors."

Alex activated another layer.

Small directional arrows appeared beside several debris clusters.

Each arrow represented the **last recorded course correction** of the ships before they were destroyed.

Torlan studied the pattern quietly.

Several of the vectors pointed away from the collision point.

Others curved sharply to the side.

None pointed directly toward the opposing convoy.

Alex noticed it too.

"They were trying to avoid each other."

Torlan nodded slowly.

"Yes."

He traced several of the maneuver paths with his finger.

"These ships changed course suddenly."

Alex nodded.

"Emergency evasive maneuvers."

Torlan looked again at the debris pattern.

"If either fleet had been attacking…"

He gestured toward the display.

"The wreckage would show forward pursuit vectors."

Alex understood immediately.

"The debris would be concentrated along an attack path."

Torlan nodded.

"But it isn't."

The wreckage cloud spread outward in several directions.

The pattern showed ships turning away.

Turning aside.

Turning too late.

Alex leaned back slightly.

"They collided while both sides were trying to avoid the encounter."

Torlan nodded.

"Yes."

For a moment they both studied the debris field in silence.

Two fleets.

Both surprised.

Both reacting suddenly.

Both attempting defensive maneuvers in the same narrow corridor.

Alex spoke quietly.

"They thought they were under attack."

Torlan nodded.

"That would be the logical assumption."

He looked again at the shattered wreckage markers drifting across the display.

"Two convoys enter the same corridor unexpectedly."

"Both detect unknown ships."

"Both maneuver defensively."

"And in that confusion…"

He paused.

"The collision becomes unavoidable."

Torlan stepped back from the display.

Years earlier, in the quiet valley of Valaryn, Dr. Arel Ziv had once shared another lesson.

"Storms reveal the strength of a foundation."

At the time Torlan had thought Ziv was speaking about weather.

Later he understood.

When pressure comes, hidden weaknesses become visible.

Torlan looked again at the debris field.

"The foundation of this war," he said quietly,

"is misunderstanding."

Alex nodded slowly.

"Yes."

The Larger Problem

The debris field slowly faded from the display wall.

Alex closed several of the data layers.

Navigation routes.

Beacon maintenance logs.

Maneuver vectors.

For the first time since the investigation began, the pattern was becoming clear.

Torlan stood quietly near the star chart.

Two convoys.

One faulty beacon.

One tragic collision.

And a war that had followed.

Alex looked again at the timeline.

Seven years of conflict.

Battles.

Trade blockades.

Destroyed fleets.

Thousands of lives lost.

She exhaled slowly.

"If the beacon caused the collision…"

Torlan nodded.

"Yes."

"Then the war began by accident."

Torlan studied the star map.

"That appears to be the case."

Alex looked at him carefully.

"But even if we prove that…"

She gestured toward the timeline.

"The war has now lasted seven years."

Torlan nodded slowly.

"Yes."

Alex continued.

"Too many people have died."

"Too many ships have been destroyed."

"Too many leaders have committed themselves to the fight."

She paused.

"Neither government can easily admit they were wrong."

Torlan understood the problem immediately.

Wars often begin with misunderstandings.

But once blood has been shed, pride becomes stronger than truth.

Admitting a mistake becomes harder than continuing the conflict.

Torlan looked again at the star chart.

Two planets.

Valyra.

Dravakar.

Both believing the other had attacked first.

Both convinced their war was justified.

Alex leaned back in her chair.

"If the war started by accident…"

She looked toward the display again.

"Why hasn't anyone discovered this before?"

Torlan did not answer immediately.

Instead he studied the star map quietly.

Two civilizations locked in conflict.

Two histories written from opposite perspectives.

Two governments searching for evidence that supported their own beliefs.

Finally he spoke.

"Because no one was looking for peace."

The room became silent again.

Torlan reached forward and dimmed the star chart.

The intersection point in the Kardrin Expanse faded slowly.

One broken beacon.

One tragic misunderstanding.

Seven years of war.

The truth might exist.

But discovering the truth and **convincing two civilizations to accept it** were very different challenges.

Chapter 8 — No Captain Will Go

Alex Contacts Shipping Companies

Location: Operations Office

The operations office was unusually quiet that morning.

Alex sat at the long communications console reviewing a growing list of transport companies.

Cargo carriers.

Independent freighters.

Humanitarian logistics groups.

Several were known for taking difficult assignments.

Which meant they might consider Havenfall.

Alex opened the mission file she had prepared.

The request was straightforward.

Medical supplies.

Agricultural equipment.

Water drilling machinery.

The cargo itself was not unusual.

Relief missions like this happened often across the outer colonies.

The difficulty was the destination.

Havenfall.

Deep inside the Kardrin Expanse.

Alex sent the first set of inquiries.

Within minutes the responses began arriving.

One captain replied first.

"Medical relief mission? We could help."

Another carrier wrote back:

"We have cargo capacity next month."

A third message arrived moments later.

"Send the coordinates."

Alex forwarded the mission details.

Then she waited.

The tone of the replies changed quickly.

The first captain answered again.

"Havenfall?"

Another message followed.

"Kardrin Expanse corridor?"

A third response appeared shortly after.

"That region is inside the Valyra–Dravakar conflict zone."

Alex watched the incoming messages.

One by one the interested captains withdrew.

A cargo company wrote politely:

"We regret that we cannot accept operations in an active war zone."

Another carrier responded more directly.

"No captain in our fleet will enter the Kardrin Expanse right now."

A final message appeared from an independent freighter pilot.

"You're asking someone to fly straight through the middle of a war."

Alex leaned back slightly.

The pattern was already clear.

She sent additional requests anyway.

Several more carriers responded.

The results were the same.

At first they were interested.

Then they saw the destination.

And declined.

Alex finally closed the communication panel.

Across the room the mission file still glowed on the display wall.

Havenfall.

Medical shortages.

Failing agriculture systems.

Critical need for supplies.

All within a region that most captains now refused to enter.

Alex gathered the response reports.

Then she stood.

It was time to tell Torlan.

Insurance Refusal

Alex entered Torlan's office carrying a new message packet.

"I may have found a company willing to consider the mission," she said.

Torlan looked up from the star charts.

"Which company?"

"Helios Transport."

Torlan nodded slightly.

"They have a good reputation."

"Yes," Alex said. "And they operate several heavy cargo vessels capable of carrying the equipment Havenfall needs."

Torlan leaned back in his chair.

"Have they accepted?"

"Not yet," Alex replied.

"They asked to review the mission profile first."

Alex placed the report on the desk display.

Torlan read through the summary.

Cargo manifest.

Medical supplies.

Agricultural equipment.

Well drilling machinery.

Everything looked reasonable.

Then he reached the final line.

Destination: Havenfall

Sector: Kardrin Expanse

Torlan looked up.

"And?"

Alex sighed slightly.

"They didn't decline immediately."

Torlan raised an eyebrow.

"That's encouraging."

"For about twenty minutes," Alex said.

She activated the next message.

The reply from Helios Transport appeared on the screen.

Their operations director had written politely.

The mission was possible.

Their ships were capable of the journey.

Their captains were experienced.

But there was one complication.

Torlan read the next line carefully.

Insurance coverage denied.

Alex folded her arms.

"Their insurer reviewed the coordinates."

Torlan nodded slowly.

"That would be expected."

Alex opened the attached explanation.

The insurance company's response appeared in formal language.

Risk Classification Update

The Kardrin Expanse sector is now classified as an active combat region.

Recent fleet engagements between Valyra and Dravakar have increased the probability of interception or damage.

Commercial vessels entering the sector cannot be insured against loss or hostile action.

Coverage for this mission is therefore denied.

Torlan finished reading the statement.

Alex watched his reaction.

"Without insurance," she said, "no commercial company can risk the ship."

Torlan nodded.

"That is standard policy."

Alex leaned slightly against the table.

"Helios told me something else."

Torlan looked up.

"What was that?"

Alex answered plainly.

"No captain in their fleet will fly an uninsured cargo ship into a war zone."

Torlan was not surprised.

Cargo ships represented enormous investments.

Years of construction.

Millions of credits.

A captain who lost a ship without insurance could ruin an entire company.

He closed the message quietly.

"So Helios declined."

Alex nodded.

"Yes."

Torlan stood and walked to the window.

Far below, cargo shuttles moved steadily across the city's sky lanes.

Trade still flowed normally here.

But far away, in the Kardrin Expanse, the rules were very different.

Alex looked back at the mission file.

Havenfall still needed help.

Medical supplies.

Agricultural equipment.

Water systems.

But the deeper the mission entered the war zone…

The fewer captains were willing to go.

The Experienced Captain

The captain arrived precisely on time.

Alex met him at the reception desk and guided him into Torlan's office.

He was an older man with silver hair and weathered hands — the kind of hands that had spent a lifetime working with real ships instead of office consoles.

His name was **Captain Elias Rourke**.

For more than thirty years he had commanded cargo vessels across the outer systems.

If anyone might consider a difficult mission, it would be someone like him.

Torlan stood to greet him.

"Captain Rourke."

The captain shook his hand firmly.

"Mr. Arden."

Alex activated the star chart on the wall.

The Kardrin Expanse appeared across the display.

Havenfall blinked softly near the center.

Captain Rourke stepped closer to the map.

"Let's see what you're asking."

Torlan briefly described the situation.

A struggling colony.

Medical shortages.

Failing agricultural systems.

A request for humanitarian aid.

The captain listened quietly.

Then he studied the map again.

His expression slowly became more serious.

He pointed to the northern edge of the sector.

"Ion storm belts," he said.

"These drift unpredictably."

"Navigation sensors become unreliable in those regions."

His finger moved southward.

"Here you've got debris fields from fleet engagements."

"Shrapnel, broken hull sections, abandoned mines."

Alex nodded.

"We saw some of those in the survey reports."

The captain continued tracing the map.

"And these routes here…"

He tapped several patrol markers.

"Those are Valyra interception corridors."

"And Dravakar runs raider patrols along this axis."

He stepped back slightly.

"That entire region is unstable."

Torlan watched him calmly.

"Is there a safe route?"

Captain Rourke studied the map for a long moment.

"Safe?" he repeated quietly.

He shook his head.

"No."

The captain crossed his arms and looked again at the star chart.

"I've flown cargo through asteroid storms."

"I've threaded ships through collapsing jump corridors."

"I've even flown a freighter through a radiation storm once."

Alex raised an eyebrow.

"That sounds unpleasant."

The captain smiled faintly.

"Unpleasant is the polite word."

Then he pointed toward the Kardrin Expanse again.

"But that region…"

He paused.

"I'd fly through a storm before I'd fly through that."

The room became quiet.

Torlan nodded.

"I appreciate your honesty."

Captain Rourke looked at him carefully.

"You're trying to help those settlers."

"Yes."

"That's a good thing."

The captain hesitated slightly before continuing.

"But I won't take a crew into that corridor."

He extended his hand again.

"I'm sorry, Mr. Arden."

Torlan shook it calmly.

"I understand."

Captain Rourke nodded to Alex.

Then he left the office.

The star chart remained glowing on the wall.

Havenfall still blinking quietly in the middle of the war zone.

Alex looked at the empty doorway.

"That sounded like a very polite refusal."

Torlan nodded.

"Yes."

The War Zone Reality

The operations room lights were dimmed as Alex opened another group of reports.

"Shipping records from the last three years," she said.

Torlan moved closer to the display wall.

A long list of vessel names appeared.

Freighters.

Survey ships.

Relief transports.

Each entry showed the same destination region.

The Kardrin Expanse.

Alex opened the first report.

A cargo vessel named **Silver Meridian**.

Mission: agricultural equipment delivery.

Outcome: intercepted by Valyra patrol ships.

The captain's report appeared beside the star chart.

"Valyra fleet demanded immediate course change. We were escorted out of the corridor under warning fire."

Torlan read the report quietly.

"No damage?" he asked.

"Minor sensor damage," Alex replied.

"But they were forced to abandon the mission."

Alex opened another file.

Cargo ship **Talara Wind**.

Mission: medical supply delivery.

Outcome: redirected by Dravakar raiders.

The captain's statement appeared.

"Dravakar patrol insisted we leave the sector immediately. They considered all traffic suspicious."

Torlan nodded slowly.

"They assume any ship entering the region may be supporting the other side."

Alex nodded.

"Exactly."

She opened several more reports.

The pattern repeated.

Cargo vessels intercepted.

Ships forced to reroute.

Freighters escorted away from the corridor.

In several cases the captains had been ordered to change course hundreds of light years away from their original routes.

Alex pointed to the star chart.

"They're pushing neutral traffic completely out of the region."

Torlan studied the map.

"That would isolate Havenfall."

Another report appeared.

Cargo vessel **Ardent Sky**.

Mission: supply delivery attempt.

Outcome: damaged during patrol encounter.

Alex opened the captain's log.

"Weapons fire occurred during identification confusion.
Hull sustained minor impact damage.
Crew safe but mission aborted."

Torlan read the report carefully.

"That was close."

Alex nodded.

"Yes."

She opened the final file.

This report was short.

And very clear.

Mission: Havenfall resupply.

Status: unsuccessful.

Torlan looked at the timeline.

"How many ships have successfully reached Havenfall in the last year?"

Alex checked the data again.

Then she answered quietly.

"None."

The star chart glowed silently across the room.

Havenfall blinked in the center of the sector.

A small colony.

Cut off between two hostile fleets.

Torlan folded his arms.

"Which means they are running out of time."

Alex nodded.

"Yes."

Frustration Builds

The operations room had grown quiet again.

Alex had closed most of the communication windows.

Declined.

Unavailable.

Mission refused.

The messages all said the same thing in different ways.

No captain would enter the Kardrin Expanse.

Torlan stood near the star chart studying the small colony marker that represented Havenfall.

The settlement looked insignificant compared to the vast emptiness surrounding it.

Just a single blinking light in the middle of the war zone.

Alex leaned back in her chair.

"We've contacted fourteen transport companies."

Torlan nodded.

"And?"

Alex gave a small, tired smile.

"All fourteen declined."

Torlan was silent for a moment.

He was not surprised.

The reports they had reviewed made the situation clear.

Any ship attempting the journey would face serious risks.

Military patrols.

Debris fields.

Navigation hazards.

And the possibility of being mistaken for an enemy vessel.

Alex opened the mission file again.

"Havenfall's latest report arrived this morning."

Torlan turned toward her.

"What does it say?"

Alex read from the message.

"Medical supplies are already being rationed."

Torlan listened quietly.

"Water extraction systems are failing."

She continued.

"Several agricultural modules have stopped functioning."

Alex closed the report.

"If they don't receive replacement equipment soon…"

She paused.

"The colony may not survive the year."

Torlan looked again at the blinking marker on the star chart.

Havenfall.

A small settlement trying to survive between two hostile powers.

Alex watched him carefully.

"You're thinking about the timeline."

Torlan nodded.

"Yes."

Without supplies the settlers would soon face several cascading failures.

Medical shortages.

Water supply breakdown.

Agricultural collapse.

Once those systems failed, recovery would become nearly impossible.

And every day the war continued made reaching Havenfall more dangerous.

Alex sighed quietly.

"Time is running out."

Torlan remained calm.

He did not pace.

He did not show anger.

Instead he stood quietly studying the map.

Years earlier, in the valley gardens of Valaryn, Dr. Arel Ziv had once spoken a lesson that seemed simple at the time.

"Endurance outlasts power."

Torlan had learned what Ziv meant.

Many problems could not be forced into solutions.

They required patience.

Persistence.

And the willingness to keep searching when others stopped.

Torlan looked again at the star chart.

The problem was difficult.

But not impossible.

Not yet.

Alex's Question

The star chart still glowed quietly across the operations wall.

Havenfall blinked faintly in the center of the Kardrin Expanse.

Around it stretched hundreds of light-years of unstable space.

Ion storm belts.

Battle debris.

Military patrol corridors.

Alex had studied the reports all morning.

The conclusion was unavoidable.

No captain was willing to take the mission.

Alex finally broke the silence.

"If no captain will go…"

She looked again at the colony marker.

"…what happens to Havenfall?"

Torlan did not answer immediately.

Instead he continued studying the star chart.

The navigation grid slowly shifted as he adjusted several filters.

Alex noticed the change.

He was no longer looking at the usual trade routes.

Instead new layers of data appeared.

Storm movement patterns.

Patrol corridors.

Gravitational drift currents between star systems.

Alex leaned forward slightly.

"What are you doing?"

Torlan remained quiet for a moment.

His eyes moved across the display.

Studying patterns.

Distances.

Timing.

Alex watched the star map change again.

Several possible flight paths appeared briefly.

Then vanished.

Torlan erased them and tried another set of calculations.

Alex realized what he was doing.

Her expression changed.

She looked at him carefully.

"Are you trying to plan a route?"

Torlan finally spoke.

"I'm trying to see if one exists."

The star chart continued glowing in the dim room.

And somewhere inside the tangled hazards of the Kardrin Expanse…

Torlan Tarsen had begun searching for a path.

Chapter 9 — The Quiet Corridor

Star Charts

Torlan's office aboard *The Long Path* was quiet, lit only by the pale glow of the navigation console.

A broad star chart hovered above the central table, slowly rotating in the air. The **Kardrin Expanse** stretched across the display—a tangled region of storm activity, drifting debris, and the blinking patrol markers of two uneasy powers.

Torlan stood beside the console with his hands resting lightly on the edge of the table.

He had been studying the expanse for nearly an hour.

Most captains would have dismissed the region immediately. The war between **Valyra** and **Dravakar** had turned the expanse into a dangerous frontier. Patrol fleets moved constantly through the area, watching for enemy ships.

Civilian vessels simply stayed away.

Torlan reached forward and adjusted the display.

The star map shifted smoothly.

A new layer of information appeared across the projection.

Bands of luminous color slowly drifted across the region—**ion storm systems**, immense charged clouds moving through space like enormous weather fronts.

He watched their movement for several seconds before expanding the chart.

Another set of markers appeared.

Patrol routes.

Thin looping lines traced the paths taken by Valyra and Dravakar patrol ships. Small icons pulsed along the routes, showing the estimated positions of current patrol groups.

The patterns repeated, though not perfectly. Some patrols moved faster than others. Some sectors were visited more frequently.

Torlan studied the patterns without speaking.

Then he added another layer.

Gravitational drift currents.

Faint curved streams appeared across the expanse, showing the slow movement of distorted space created by ancient stellar disturbances. Navigators sometimes used these invisible currents to conserve fuel or adjust long-distance travel routes.

Most ships, however, avoided the region entirely.

Torlan leaned slightly closer to the display.

Something about the movement of the storms and patrols had caught his attention earlier.

He had not yet decided what it meant.

The door slid open quietly behind him.

Alex stepped into the office carrying a thin data pad.

"I thought you might want these," she said.

Torlan glanced back briefly.

"What are they?"

"Old navigation records," Alex replied as she walked toward the console. "Trade captains used to run the expanse years ago. Before the patrols started pushing through."

Torlan nodded once.

"Bring them up."

Alex connected the pad to the console. A moment later, a new set of faint lines appeared on the star chart.

These lines were thinner and less certain than the others—**historical navigation paths** used by civilian ships long ago.

Some of the routes cut directly through the Kardrin Expanse.

Alex folded her arms as she studied the display.

"Most of those routes were abandoned when the war started," she said. "Too many patrols. Too many storms."

Torlan said nothing.

He began adjusting the chart again.

The map zoomed slightly, centering on a cluster of storm systems drifting slowly across the region. The glowing clouds shifted position almost imperceptibly.

Alex watched him work for several moments.

"What are you looking for?" she finally asked.

Torlan considered the question.

"I'm not sure yet."

He expanded the display again.

Storm movement.

Patrol routes.

Gravitational drift currents.

Historical navigation paths.

The layers of information overlapped until the map looked like a complicated web of moving lines and glowing regions.

Most navigators would have seen only confusion.

Torlan studied the patterns patiently.

On Cyrion, he had learned that many problems could not be solved by force or speed.

Sometimes the answer appeared only after long observation.

Alex watched the rotating chart in silence.

"You've been at this for a while," she said.

Torlan nodded slightly.

"The expanse isn't random."

Alex looked at him.

"What do you mean?"

Torlan gestured toward the chart.

"The storms move in cycles. The patrols follow routes. Even the drift currents have patterns."

He paused.

"If you watch long enough, you start to see how the pieces move together."

Alex turned back toward the display.

The storm belts drifted slowly across the region.

Patrol markers pulsed along their assigned routes.

The ancient navigation lines faded quietly beneath them all.

After a moment Alex said,

"You're studying the whole system."

Torlan did not answer.

But something in the patterns was beginning to take shape in his mind.

Not a route.

Not yet.

Just a possibility.

He leaned slightly closer to the display and began adjusting the storm layer again.

Somewhere inside the chaos of the Kardrin Expanse, a pattern was waiting to be understood.

The Pattern

The star chart continued its slow rotation above the console.

Torlan adjusted the storm layer again.

The glowing bands of ion activity shifted across the Kardrin Expanse like great rivers of light. Some storms stretched for thousands of kilometers, while others appeared as dense clusters drifting through the region.

Most navigation charts treated the storms as random hazards.

Torlan was no longer certain that was true.

"Run the storm data back six weeks," he said quietly.

Alex tapped the console.

The chart changed.

The storm systems began moving in accelerated time, sliding slowly across the expanse. Their glowing shapes stretched and reformed as the simulation advanced.

Torlan watched carefully.

The storms did not drift aimlessly.

They followed subtle arcs through the region, bending around gravitational disturbances and debris fields.

Alex leaned forward slightly.

"I didn't realize they moved that predictably."

Torlan nodded.

"They don't stay in one place long enough for most navigators to notice."

He slowed the simulation.

The storm clouds drifted gradually across the display again.

"When they pass through an area," Torlan continued, "they interfere with long-range sensors."

Alex glanced at the console readouts.

"That's because of the charged particles."

"Yes."

Torlan expanded one of the storm systems on the display. A cluster of sensor interference markers appeared inside the glowing cloud.

"Anything trying to scan through this region would lose resolution," he said.

Alex studied the interference field.

"How much?"

Torlan considered for a moment.

"Depending on the density of the storm… patrol sensors could lose half their effective range."

Alex raised an eyebrow.

"That's not a small problem."

"No."

Torlan watched the storm belt slide slowly across the map.

For several seconds he said nothing.

Then he rewound the simulation slightly.

The storm drifted backward along its previous path.

Torlan slowed the motion again.

The glowing band moved steadily across the expanse.

Alex followed its movement.

"Wait," she said after a moment. "That's not random."

Torlan glanced at her.

"You see it."

"The same storm corridor passes through that region every few weeks."

Torlan nodded.

"The pattern repeats."

Alex folded her arms as she studied the chart.

"So every time that storm passes through, sensor coverage in that area drops."

"Yes."

Alex looked back at him.

"You're thinking that could hide a ship."

Torlan did not answer immediately.

Instead he expanded the map again and allowed the storm layer to continue its slow movement across the expanse.

The glowing band drifted through a section of space between the patrol corridors.

For a brief moment, the storm cloud covered a large region.

Alex watched the interference markers bloom across the display.

"That's a wide sensor shadow," she said.

Torlan nodded slowly.

"Wide enough that a ship might pass through without being seen."

Alex considered the idea.

"If the timing were right."

Torlan adjusted the chart again.

The storm continued moving across the region.

Eventually the cloud drifted away.

The interference markers faded.

Sensor coverage returned.

Alex leaned back slightly.

"So the window doesn't last long."

"No."

Torlan replayed the storm movement once more.

The cloud swept across the same region again in the simulation.

Storm.

Interference.

Clear space.

Storm again.

Alex watched the pattern repeat.

"It's like weather," she said.

Torlan nodded.

"Exactly."

Alex studied the display carefully.

"So every time that storm belt passes through… sensors weaken."

"Yes."

She turned back toward him.

"And if a ship happened to be in the right place at the right time…"

Torlan let the sentence hang in the air.

The storm cloud continued drifting across the star chart, its glowing edges washing over the patrol zones like a slow tide.

Somewhere inside that moving curtain of charged particles, Torlan suspected there might be a way through the expanse.

He had not found the path yet.

But for the first time since studying the region, the idea no longer seemed impossible.

Patrol Behavior

The storm simulation faded back to normal speed.

Torlan remained studying the display, his attention still fixed on the shifting storm belts.

Alex watched him for a moment, then tapped the console.

"Let's see how the patrols behave when those storms move through," she said.

Torlan glanced toward her.

"You have recent patrol reports?"

"A few," Alex replied. "Valyra publishes limited traffic advisories, and Dravakar interceptors show up often enough in long-range scans. It's not perfect data, but it's something."

She began pulling up another layer.

A new network of lines appeared across the star chart.

These were not the steady patrol loops Torlan had shown earlier.

Instead they showed **recorded patrol sightings**, drawn from weeks of navigation reports.

Clusters of activity marked areas where warships had frequently appeared.

Torlan leaned slightly closer.

"Overlay it with the storm layer," he said.

Alex nodded and activated the command.

The glowing storm systems returned to the display.

Now the map showed both elements together.

Storm belts drifted slowly across the region.

Patrol sightings blinked along the outer edges of the expanse.

Torlan watched silently as the simulation ran forward.

The storm clouds moved first.

A large storm belt swept through the northern half of the expanse, spreading a wide region of sensor interference.

A moment later, Alex noticed something.

"Look at the patrol markers."

Torlan's eyes moved toward the blinking icons.

The patrol ships did not follow their usual loops.

Instead, they curved away from the storm region.

Alex slowed the simulation.

The movement became easier to see.

As the storm belt advanced, the patrol paths shifted slightly outward.

Ships avoided flying directly into the charged storm fields.

Torlan nodded quietly.

"That confirms it."

Alex studied the chart.

"Their sensors must degrade too much inside the storms."

Torlan nodded again.

"A warship blind to long-range scans becomes vulnerable."

Alex watched the patrol tracks bending around the storm.

"They stay near the edges."

"Yes."

Torlan adjusted the simulation speed.

Another storm belt drifted into the region several days later in the timeline.

Again the patrol paths shifted away.

The pattern repeated.

Storm approaching.

Patrol routes adjusting.

Storm passing.

Patrol coverage returning.

Alex leaned forward slightly.

"They're avoiding the storms whenever they can."

Torlan's voice remained calm.

"Most captains would."

Alex glanced back at him.

"But someone trying to hide…"

Torlan did not answer.

He was already adjusting the display again.

He highlighted the outer edges of the storm interference zones.

Thin curved boundaries appeared where sensor disruption began.

Alex watched as Torlan marked several regions along those boundaries.

"You're mapping their avoidance zones," she said.

Torlan nodded.

"The patrol ships will rarely cross these areas."

Alex studied the display.

Storm belts.

Patrol routes.

Avoidance zones.

Slowly the map was beginning to show a clearer structure.

"What happens when the storms move deeper into the expanse?" she asked.

Torlan advanced the simulation again.

A large storm belt drifted across the central region.

As it did, the patrol routes on both sides shifted outward again, leaving a wider section of space temporarily unmonitored.

Alex saw it immediately.

"That's interesting."

Torlan said nothing.

He watched the overlapping movements carefully.

Storm movement was one thing.

Patrol behavior was another.

But together they formed something far more revealing.

Alex studied the display for several seconds.

Then she said quietly,

"You're starting to see something, aren't you?"

Torlan kept his eyes on the chart.

"Maybe."

The storms continued drifting across the map.

And with them, the patrol fleets slowly moved aside, leaving brief pockets of space where neither side was watching closely.

Torlan began marking those areas one by one.

He still did not know if they connected.

But the expanse was beginning to reveal its structure.

And hidden within that structure might be the first hint of a path.

The Overlap

Torlan stood quietly before the console, studying the web of data that now covered the star chart.

Storm belts drifted slowly across the Kardrin Expanse. Patrol sightings pulsed along the outer regions.

Between them lay a scattered network of **avoidance zones**—areas where patrol ships rarely traveled when storms approached.

Alex watched as Torlan adjusted the display again.

"What are you looking for now?" she asked.

Torlan did not answer immediately.

Instead he reached forward and activated two specific layers.

The chart simplified slightly.

Most of the older navigation data disappeared, leaving only two major elements on the display:

• ion storm movement

• patrol avoidance zones

The glowing storm systems continued drifting across the region in slow, steady motion.

Around them, the patrol paths curved outward, creating thin arcs of empty space.

Torlan slowed the simulation.

The map now moved almost imperceptibly.

Alex folded her arms as she studied the overlapping data.

"Storm interference here," she said, pointing toward one region.

Torlan nodded.

"And patrol avoidance here."

The two areas partially overlapped.

Alex leaned closer.

"That leaves a small section where neither side has good sensor coverage."

Torlan highlighted the region with a faint marker.

A narrow band of space appeared on the display.

It stretched diagonally across the expanse.

Not large.

But noticeable.

Alex studied it carefully.

"That might hide a ship," she said.

"Possibly."

Torlan continued watching the simulation.

The storm system drifted farther across the region.

As it moved, the overlap zone shifted slightly.

The corridor twisted, narrowing in some places and widening in others.

Then, after several minutes of simulated time, the storm moved past.

The overlap vanished.

Sensor coverage returned.

Alex leaned back slightly.

"That window closes fast."

Torlan rewound the simulation.

The storm drifted backward along its previous path.

He ran the simulation again.

Storm approaching.

Patrols shifting.

Overlap appearing.

Then disappearing again.

Alex watched the sequence repeat.

"How often does that happen?"

Torlan checked the timeline indicators.

"Every few weeks."

Alex's eyebrows rose.

"That frequently?"

"The storms follow repeating cycles."

Torlan expanded the map slightly.

Another feature appeared—**a scattered debris field** drifting slowly through the same region.

Fragments of asteroid rock and wreckage glimmered faintly across the display.

Alex noticed it immediately.

"That debris field crosses the overlap zone."

Torlan nodded.

"More cover."

Alex leaned closer again.

Storm interference.

Patrol avoidance.

Debris field masking.

For a brief window of time, all three elements aligned.

The result was a narrow band of space where sensors would struggle to see clearly.

Alex looked at Torlan.

"You're thinking a ship could pass through there."

Torlan did not answer right away.

Instead he adjusted the chart again, marking the boundaries of the overlap zone.

The band of space curved quietly across the expanse like a thin shadow.

Storms shifting above it.

Patrol fleets drifting around it.

Debris slowly tumbling through it.

Alex watched the line appear on the display.

It was narrow.

Unstable.

But unmistakable.

"Torlan," she said quietly.

He studied the chart for another moment.

Then he spoke.

"Mark the edges of the storm interference."

Alex entered the command.

Thin lines traced the boundaries of the charged storm field.

Torlan added the patrol avoidance zones.

Then the debris field drift path.

The layers settled together.

For several seconds neither of them spoke.

The map hovered in silence between them.

The overlapping regions formed a narrow passage through the most dangerous part of the Kardrin Expanse.

It was not obvious.

It shifted constantly as the storms moved.

But the structure was there.

Alex looked from the chart to Torlan.

"That looks like a corridor."

Torlan's voice was calm.

"Yes."

The storms continued drifting slowly across the display.

And for the first time, the chaos of the Kardrin Expanse revealed a faint and fragile shape.

A path that should not exist.

But did.

The Realization

The star chart hovered silently above the console.

Storm belts drifted in slow motion across the Kardrin Expanse. Patrol routes curved around them like cautious predators circling dangerous ground.

Between those movements, the narrow band Torlan had marked remained visible.

It was thin.

Irregular.

And constantly shifting.

Alex studied the display carefully.

"That corridor isn't stable," she said.

Torlan nodded.

"No."

The storm belt continued drifting across the map.

As it moved, the corridor narrowed slightly near the center.

A few minutes later it widened again.

Alex watched the change.

"It moves with the storms."

"Yes."

Torlan adjusted the simulation again, letting the storm layer advance several hours.

The glowing cloud slid slowly across the expanse.

The corridor bent with it.

Sometimes the passage narrowed until it nearly disappeared.

Then, as the storm shifted again, the gap reopened.

Alex leaned closer to the display.

"That's a tight window."

Torlan said nothing.

He was watching the edges of the corridor carefully.

The debris field that drifted through the region added another layer of cover, but it also created danger.

Fragments of rock and wreckage moved slowly through the same space the corridor occupied.

Alex glanced toward him.

"A ship would have to stay inside that band the entire time."

"Yes."

"And the path changes as the storm moves."

Torlan nodded again.

Alex shook her head slightly.

"That's not a route most captains would attempt."

Torlan reached forward and slowed the simulation further.

The storm belt now moved almost imperceptibly.

The corridor glowed faintly across the chart.

For several seconds he simply studied it.

Then he marked the projected path with a thin navigation line.

The line curved gently through the center of the shifting corridor.

Alex followed the motion of his hand across the display.

"You're plotting it."

Torlan finished the mark and leaned back slightly.

The line now stretched across the expanse, threading carefully between the storm edges and patrol zones.

Alex studied the route.

"It would take precise timing."

"Yes."

"If the storm moves faster than expected…"

"The corridor closes."

"And if the ship drifts outside the boundary…"

Torlan finished the thought quietly.

"Patrol sensors will see it."

Alex looked back at the map.

Storm interference.

Patrol avoidance.

Debris field masking.

Together they formed a fragile window through the most dangerous region of space between the two war planets.

For a moment the room remained silent.

The storm belt continued drifting across the display.

Torlan watched the corridor carefully.

Then he spoke.

"There is a path."

Alex looked at him.

"Through the storms?"

Torlan nodded once.

The glowing corridor shifted again as the storm moved across the expanse.

It was narrow.

Unstable.

And dangerous.

But it existed.

And for the first time since studying the region, the impossible mission to Havenfall no longer seemed beyond reach.

The Risk

For a few moments neither of them spoke.

The corridor remained glowing faintly across the star chart. Storm belts drifted slowly through the Kardrin Expanse, their charged clouds shifting the boundaries of the passage Torlan had marked.

Alex finally stepped closer to the console.

"Let's see what it would actually take to fly that route."

Torlan nodded.

"Run a navigation model."

Alex began entering commands.

The chart shifted again, converting the corridor path into a projected flight course. A thin line appeared along the route Torlan had drawn, and small timing markers began appearing along it.

The simulation started.

A small ship icon representing their cargo vessel appeared at the edge of the expanse.

It moved slowly along the projected course.

Storm interference zones glowed around the path as the simulation advanced.

Alex watched the progress carefully.

"Timing is going to be critical," she said.

Torlan folded his arms as the ship icon advanced deeper into the expanse.

"If we enter too early," Alex continued, "the patrols still have clear sensor coverage."

She pointed toward the display.

A Valyra patrol marker flashed near the northern sector.

"If we enter too late," she said, "the storm belt has already moved on."

Torlan nodded.

"Then the corridor disappears."

Alex advanced the simulation again.

The ship icon followed the curved path through the storm interference zone.

But as the storm shifted, the corridor narrowed sharply.

Alex frowned.

"That section will require constant course corrections."

Torlan studied the changing storm boundary.

"Yes."

Alex zoomed closer to the region.

Fragments of debris drifted through the path—remnants of old asteroid fragments and wreckage scattered throughout the expanse.

"That debris field crosses the route twice," she said.

Torlan nodded slightly.

"A ship would have to weave through it."

Alex shook her head.

"And while doing that, stay inside the storm interference zone."

She advanced the simulation again.

Suddenly the ship icon drifted just beyond the edge of the corridor.

A patrol sensor marker flared red.

Alex stopped the simulation immediately.

"There."

Torlan studied the display.

"If the ship drifts outside the interference zone, patrol sensors regain full resolution."

Alex nodded.

"And the moment that happens, the ship lights up like a beacon."

Torlan remained silent.

Alex leaned back slightly.

"One navigation error…"

Torlan finished the thought calmly.

"…and we appear directly inside a war zone."

Alex crossed her arms and looked again at the chart.

Storm interference.

Patrol coverage.

Debris hazards.

Every part of the corridor demanded perfect navigation.

"This route would require constant adjustments," she said.

"Yes."

"Manual piloting."

"Yes."

"And precise timing with the storm movement."

Torlan nodded again.

Alex looked back at him.

"This isn't a route normal captains would even consider."

Torlan did not argue.

He simply watched the chart as the storm belts continued their slow drift across the expanse.

The corridor shifted slightly again.

Narrow.

Fragile.

Dangerous.

Alex studied it once more.

"You'd have to fly the entire path without drifting outside the storm cover," she said quietly.

Torlan nodded.

"One mistake," Alex added, "and the patrol fleets will know someone crossed the expanse."

The room fell silent again.

The simulation continued running on the console, the ship icon moving cautiously through the shifting corridor.

The path existed.

But flying it would demand skill, patience, and nerves few pilots possessed.

Alex looked back at Torlan.

"If someone attempted this route," she said slowly, "they'd have to know exactly what they were doing."

Torlan's eyes remained on the chart.

"Yes."

Alex's Realization

The navigation simulation continued running on the console.

The small ship icon crept cautiously through the shifting corridor, staying within the storm interference zone as the glowing clouds drifted slowly across the Kardrin Expanse.

Torlan watched the movement in silence.

Alex studied the display again.

Storm edges.

Debris clusters.

Patrol coverage expanding and contracting with the storm's movement.

The corridor was real.

But it was barely wide enough for a ship to survive inside it.

Alex exhaled quietly.

"This would take constant attention."

Torlan nodded slightly.

"The storm movement would have to be monitored the entire time."

Alex stepped closer to the console and adjusted the simulation speed.

The ship icon advanced deeper into the expanse.

At one point the storm boundary shifted unexpectedly, forcing the simulated ship to adjust course to remain inside the interference zone.

Alex watched the maneuver.

"That's not autopilot flying," she said.

"No."

"Someone would have to guide the ship the entire way."

Torlan remained quiet.

Alex folded her arms as she studied the chart again.

"You'd need a pilot who could read storm movement, track patrol positions, and adjust course constantly."

Torlan did not respond.

Alex slowly turned toward him.

The room remained quiet except for the soft hum of the ship's systems.

Something about Torlan's silence suddenly began to make sense.

She looked back at the corridor on the chart.

Then back at Torlan.

"You're not just studying this," she said carefully.

Torlan's eyes remained on the display.

Alex watched him for a moment longer.

Then she asked the question that had been forming in her mind.

"Who would fly this route?"

Torlan did not answer immediately.

Instead he reached forward and marked the corridor path more clearly on the star chart.

The thin line now traced a precise route through the moving storm fields.

For a few seconds he studied the line.

Then he leaned back slightly.

The corridor glowed faintly across the expanse.

"If the route exists," Torlan said quietly, "someone can fly it."

Alex watched him.

The implication of his words settled slowly.

She tilted her head slightly.

"Do you know anyone who would try?"

Torlan finally looked up.

His expression remained calm.

"Yes."

Alex studied his face for a moment.

And then she understood.

The Quiet Corridor was not just a theoretical route through the war zone.

Torlan had already decided who would attempt it.

Chapter 10 — The Long Path

Reviewing the Corridor

Torlan's office was quiet again.

The star chart of the **Kardrin Expanse** hovered above the navigation console, its pale blue light casting soft reflections across the walls. The storm belts drifted slowly across the projection, their glowing shapes shifting almost imperceptibly as the simulation advanced.

The **Quiet Corridor** still traced a narrow path through the chaos.

Torlan stood beside the console, studying the route as if seeing it for the first time.

Across the room, Alex worked at the secondary terminal, reviewing a set of calculations that had been running through the ship's navigation system for most of the morning.

She finally exhaled softly.

Torlan glanced toward her.

"Something wrong?"

Alex shook her head.

"Not wrong," she said. "Just… precise."

She turned the terminal display toward him.

"I reran the navigation model using updated storm data."

Torlan stepped closer.

A series of timing markers appeared along the corridor path. Each point marked the predicted position of the storm interference zones over the next several days.

Alex tapped one of the markers.

"The storm belt that creates the corridor will pass through this sector in about seventy-two hours."

Torlan nodded slowly.

"And the patrol routes?"

Alex brought up another layer.

Valyra patrol markers pulsed along the northern edge of the expanse. Dravakar interceptors appeared farther south, their movement patterns forming irregular arcs across the region.

"The patrol fleets still avoid the heavy storm regions," Alex said. "That part of the model hasn't changed."

She expanded the display slightly.

"But the corridor itself…" she continued, "…is even narrower than we thought."

Torlan studied the chart carefully.

The storm interference zone drifted across the map like a moving curtain. The corridor formed only where that interference overlapped with the patrol avoidance zones.

Alex highlighted the boundaries.

"The safe passage window lasts about six hours," she said.

Torlan raised an eyebrow slightly.

"Six?"

Alex nodded.

"Possibly less."

She advanced the simulation.

The storm belt shifted gradually across the expanse. The corridor appeared, widened briefly, then narrowed again before disappearing entirely.

Alex watched the sequence repeat.

"If a ship enters too early," she said, "the patrol sensors are still active."

Torlan nodded.

"And too late?"

"The storm moves past the corridor," Alex replied. "Sensor coverage returns."

Torlan folded his arms as he studied the display again.

The corridor was there.

But it was fragile.

A narrow ribbon of opportunity drifting through one of the most dangerous regions of space between the two war planets.

Alex leaned against the console slightly.

"I also ran navigation drift calculations," she said.

Torlan glanced toward her.

"The storm interference affects guidance systems slightly."

"How much?"

"Enough that the ship would need constant adjustments to remain inside the corridor."

Torlan considered that.

"So the pilot can't rely entirely on automation."

Alex shook her head.

"Not safely."

She paused.

"A computer could assist with the calculations, but someone would have to monitor the course continuously."

Torlan returned his attention to the star chart.

The storm belt continued drifting across the expanse.

For a brief moment, the corridor widened slightly.

Then it narrowed again.

Alex watched him study the map.

"The route is possible," she said quietly.

Torlan nodded once.

"Yes."

Alex hesitated for a moment before adding the rest.

"But only if everything happens at exactly the right time."

Torlan did not respond immediately.

The storm systems moved slowly across the chart.

Patrol markers pulsed along their distant routes.

Between them, the narrow corridor continued its quiet movement through the expanse.

Possible.

But unforgiving.

Torlan watched the shifting passage for several seconds.

Then he said quietly,

"Run the simulation again."

Alex nodded and restarted the model.

The corridor formed once more inside the moving storm belt.

And once again, it offered a brief and dangerous path through the Kardrin Expanse.

The Final Obstacle

The simulation ended.

The storm belt drifted beyond the corridor region and the narrow passage vanished from the chart.

For a moment the star map showed only the familiar dangers of the Kardrin Expanse—storm activity, scattered debris fields, and the pulsing patrol markers of Valyra and Dravakar.

The path was gone.

Alex rested her hands lightly on the edge of the console.

"Well," she said quietly, "that confirms it."

Torlan looked toward her.

"The corridor exists."

"Yes."

Alex gestured toward the map.

"But only for a few hours."

Torlan nodded once.

"That is enough."

Alex studied him for a moment.

"You're certain?"

Torlan looked back at the display.

The storm simulation restarted automatically, slowly advancing toward the moment when the interference field would form again.

"The timing is precise," he said.

Alex gave a small smile.

"That's a polite way of saying unforgiving."

Torlan did not disagree.

Alex folded her arms and watched the chart again.

"The navigation problem is difficult," she said, "but it's not the real obstacle."

Torlan glanced toward her.

"No?"

Alex shook her head slightly.

"The real problem is much simpler."

She paused, then said the question that had been quietly waiting between them.

"Even if the route works… who will fly it?"

The room grew still again.

The star chart rotated slowly above the console.

Patrol markers pulsed along their distant paths.

Storm belts drifted across the expanse.

Torlan did not answer.

Alex watched him carefully.

"You know as well as I do," she continued, "no commercial captain will take that job."

Torlan said nothing.

Alex continued calmly.

"A cargo captain entering a war zone would risk being mistaken for a spy."

She pointed toward the northern patrol routes.

"Valyra would stop the ship for inspection."

Then she gestured toward the southern sectors.

"And Dravakar would probably intercept it before that."

Torlan nodded slightly.

Alex continued.

"Even if a captain were willing to attempt the corridor, their insurance company would cancel the contract before the ship cleared orbit."

Torlan allowed himself the faintest hint of a smile.

"That seems likely."

Alex returned the small smile, but it faded quickly.

"Besides," she added, "most captains would refuse simply because of the storms."

Torlan looked back at the chart.

Ion storms.

Debris fields.

Military patrols.

A shifting corridor that existed for only a few hours.

Alex studied his expression.

"This is the point where most plans end," she said.

Torlan remained quiet.

Alex leaned slightly against the console.

"The route is real," she said. "But there's no one who would take it."

Torlan's eyes remained on the map.

The storm simulation advanced again.

The glowing belt approached the central region of the expanse.

Slowly the corridor began to form once more.

Alex followed its movement.

For a moment neither of them spoke.

Then she said quietly,

"So the question still remains."

Torlan looked at her.

"Which one?"

Alex met his gaze.

"Who flies the mission?"

The Decision

The star chart continued its slow rotation above the console.

The storm simulation advanced quietly, the glowing belt drifting toward the point where the **Quiet Corridor** would appear once again.

Torlan stood watching it.

Alex remained beside the secondary terminal, her arms folded as she studied both the chart and Torlan's expression.

For several seconds neither of them spoke.

The room felt calm, but the question she had asked remained suspended in the air.

Who flies the mission?

The corridor began to form again on the map.

A narrow band of storm interference appeared between the patrol zones. The passage widened slightly, then stabilized for a brief stretch across the expanse.

Torlan watched the corridor carefully.

He had studied the region for hours.

Storm movement.

Patrol behavior.

Drift currents.

Every piece of the puzzle had been examined again and again.

There were still risks.

Many risks.

But the pattern was clear.

The corridor existed.

Alex finally spoke again.

"No captain will accept a contract like that," she said quietly.

Torlan nodded.

"I know."

"Even if the pay were extraordinary."

Torlan gave the faintest hint of a smile.

"It would not matter."

Alex looked back at the star chart.

Storm belts drifted slowly through the expanse.

The corridor glowed faintly for a few moments longer before beginning to narrow again.

"If no one takes the mission," she said, "Havenfall will have to survive on its own."

Torlan said nothing.

The corridor on the map disappeared again as the storm moved past.

Sensor coverage returned.

Patrol routes reoccupied the region.

The expanse once again looked impossible to cross.

Torlan studied the chart for several seconds.

Then he reached forward and deactivated the simulation.

The storm belts froze.

The patrol markers stopped moving.

The Quiet Corridor vanished from the display entirely.

For a moment the console showed only the static star map of the Kardrin Expanse.

Alex watched him.

"You're done studying it?"

Torlan considered the question.

"Yes."

He reached forward again and closed the chart.

The room grew slightly darker as the projection faded away.

Alex looked at him.

"You've made a decision."

Torlan nodded once.

"Prepare a ship."

Alex did not move for a moment.

"You're serious."

Torlan met her gaze calmly.

"If no captain will go…"

He paused briefly.

"…we will."

The words were spoken without drama.

Just a simple statement of fact.

Alex studied him for several seconds.

She had suspected this might be where the conversation was leading.

Still, hearing him say it made the mission suddenly real.

The Quiet Corridor was no longer a theoretical path across the expanse.

It was the route they intended to fly.

Alex finally nodded slowly.

"All right," she said.

Then she glanced toward the darkened console where the star chart had been only moments before.

"We'd better start preparing."

Alex's Reaction

For a moment the office remained quiet.

The star chart had faded, leaving only the soft ambient lighting of the room and the steady hum of the ship's systems.

Alex leaned lightly against the console, studying Torlan.

She was not shocked.

Not exactly.

After watching him analyze the corridor for so long, she had begun to suspect where his thinking would lead. Still, there was a difference between **considering an idea** and **committing to it**.

Torlan had just crossed that line.

Alex exhaled slowly.

"All right," she said at last. "Let's assume we do this."

Torlan nodded slightly.

Alex straightened and began pacing slowly across the office, thinking aloud.

"The Kardrin Expanse contains three things that make navigation difficult."

She raised one finger.

"Ion storms."

A second finger.

"Debris fields."

Then a third.

"And two military patrol fleets that will assume any unidentified ship is hostile."

Torlan listened without interrupting.

Alex turned back toward him.

"That corridor might hide us from sensors," she said, "but it doesn't remove the other problems."

Torlan nodded.

"I know."

Alex studied him carefully.

"You're planning to fly the ship yourself."

Torlan did not deny it.

"Yes."

Alex tilted her head slightly.

"Do you know how to fly a cargo vessel through that environment?"

Torlan considered the question.

Then he answered honestly.

"Not yet."

Alex blinked once.

"That is not especially reassuring."

Torlan's expression remained calm.

"It will be."

Alex watched him for a moment.

There was no trace of arrogance in his voice—only quiet certainty.

Torlan was not claiming to already possess the necessary skills.

He was simply confident that they could be learned.

Alex shook her head slightly, though a faint smile tugged at the corner of her mouth.

"That may be the most optimistic statement I've heard all week."

Torlan allowed the smallest hint of humor to reach his expression.

"Navigation is a skill."

Alex nodded.

"Yes."

"And skills can be learned."

Alex considered that.

"True."

She walked back toward the console and rested her hands lightly on its edge.

"If we're going to attempt this," she said, "we'll need time to train."

Torlan nodded.

"Agreed."

"Storm navigation."

"Yes."

"Debris avoidance."

"Yes."

"And we'll need to study the patrol patterns in much more detail."

Torlan nodded again.

Alex glanced toward the darkened star chart projector.

Then back at Torlan.

"You do realize," she said, "most people would consider this plan extremely dangerous."

Torlan did not disagree.

"It is."

Alex folded her arms.

"And you're still determined to do it."

Torlan met her gaze calmly.

"Havenfall needs help."

Alex held his gaze for a moment longer.

Then she nodded slowly.

"All right," she said.

"If we're going to fly into a war zone, we should probably start learning how."

Cyrion Reflection

The room grew quiet again after Alex's last words.

Torlan remained standing near the console, his hands resting lightly on its edge. The navigation display was dark now, but the patterns of the **Kardrin Expanse** still lingered clearly in his mind.

Storm movement.

Patrol routes.

The narrow passage through the storms.

Alex returned to her terminal and began reviewing the navigation calculations again, but Torlan's attention drifted elsewhere for a moment.

He stepped slowly toward the wide viewport at the far end of the office.

Beyond the glass, the quiet lights of the orbital station stretched across the darkness. Transport ships drifted slowly between docking arms, their running lights gliding silently through space.

Peaceful.

Orderly.

Very different from the region they were preparing to enter.

Torlan stood there for several seconds.

The decision he had spoken aloud only moments earlier had not been sudden. The thought had been forming since he first learned of Havenfall's situation.

But saying it had made the path forward unmistakably clear.

His thoughts returned to a memory from Cyrion.

Years earlier, he had once asked **Dr. Ziv** why some choices in life seemed so difficult.

Ziv had smiled in that patient way he often did.

"Because the easy road rarely leads anywhere important," he had said.

Torlan remembered the quiet courtyard where the conversation had taken place, the soft wind moving through the tall trees of Valaryn Valley.

Ziv had continued:

"On Cyrion we sometimes speak of the *long path*."

Torlan had asked what that meant.

Ziv had gestured toward the distant mountains that rose beyond the valley.

"The long path is the road that asks the most of us," he explained. "It is rarely comfortable. It requires patience, courage, and often sacrifice."

Torlan had listened quietly.

Ziv had added one final thought.

"But when you find yourself standing at a crossroads, and one path serves only convenience while the other serves something greater… the choice is not truly difficult."

Torlan stood quietly by the viewport now, remembering those words.

The mission to Havenfall would be difficult.

There would be storms.

Military patrols.

A corridor through space that existed only for a few fragile hours.

But the purpose was clear.

Havenfall needed help.

Behind him, Alex finished reviewing another set of calculations.

She glanced toward Torlan, noticing his quiet reflection.

"Still thinking about the corridor?" she asked.

Torlan turned slightly from the viewport.

"In a way."

Alex waited.

Torlan looked back out toward the station lights again.

"Dr. Ziv once spoke about something he called the long path," he said.

Alex tilted her head.

"That sounds philosophical."

"It was."

Torlan smiled slightly.

"He said the long path is often the most difficult road a person can choose."

Alex considered that.

"And you think this mission is one of those."

Torlan nodded once.

"Yes."

Alex studied him for a moment.

Then she said quietly,

"Well… if we're going to walk the long path, we should probably start preparing for it."

Torlan turned back toward the room.

"Yes," he said.

"I believe we should."

Naming the Ship

Alex returned to the console and began opening several new data windows.

"If we're serious about this," she said, "the first thing we need is a ship."

Torlan walked back toward the console.

"A ship capable of long-range travel," Alex continued, "large cargo capacity, and enough structural strength to handle heavy storm turbulence."

She pulled up the station's registry of available transport vessels.

A long list appeared across the display.

Freight haulers.

Survey ships.

Old cargo transports.

Most of them were designed for routine commercial routes between stable systems.

Alex began filtering the list.

"We'll need something built for frontier supply work," she said. "Those ships are designed to operate in unpredictable environments."

Torlan nodded.

"Agreed."

Alex entered a few more search parameters.

The list narrowed.

Several ships remained.

She opened the first record.

A large bulk freighter appeared on the display.

"Too slow," she said after a moment.

She moved to the next.

"Not enough maneuverability."

Another vessel appeared.

"Too fragile for storm turbulence."

Torlan studied the changing entries quietly as Alex continued reviewing them.

Eventually the list narrowed to a handful of ships.

Alex opened another file.

A mid-sized cargo vessel appeared on the display.

The ship's design was practical and compact, with reinforced hull plating and powerful maneuvering thrusters designed for frontier resupply missions.

Alex scanned the specifications.

"This one's interesting."

Torlan stepped closer.

"What is it?"

"Frontier cargo transport," Alex said. "Designed for supply routes in unstable systems."

She highlighted several details.

"Reinforced frame. Good maneuvering thrusters. Strong environmental shielding."

Torlan studied the schematic carefully.

The ship was not elegant.

It was built for endurance rather than appearance.

"Range?" he asked.

"Excellent."

"Cargo capacity?"

"Enough to carry the supplies Havenfall will need."

Torlan nodded slowly.

Alex scrolled further down the vessel's registry.

Then she paused.

"What?" Torlan asked.

Alex smiled faintly.

"You might appreciate this."

She highlighted the ship's name on the registry.

Torlan read it.

For a moment he said nothing.

Then a small smile appeared.

The ship's name was **The Long Path**.

Alex glanced toward him.

"That seems appropriate."

Torlan looked again at the name on the display.

The memory of Dr. Ziv's words returned quietly.

Walk the long path.

He nodded once.

"Yes," he said.

"I think it does."

Alex saved the ship's file.

"I'll begin the transfer request," she said.

Torlan watched the schematic of the vessel rotating slowly above the console.

The ship was not impressive.

It was not a warship.

But it was built for difficult journeys.

Exactly the kind of journey they were preparing to undertake.

Torlan studied the image for another moment.

Then he said quietly,

"That will be our ship."

Preparations Begin

The decision changed everything.

Within minutes the quiet planning room had transformed into a place of activity.

Alex moved quickly between consoles, opening communication channels and accessing the station's logistics network. Several new data windows appeared across the display as she began organizing the mission.

Torlan watched as the work began to unfold.

"What's first?" he asked.

Alex didn't look up from the terminal.

"Confirm the ship assignment."

She entered the authorization request for the cargo vessel.

A moment later the station registry responded. The transfer process began immediately.

"The ship is currently docked in Hangar Four," Alex said. "It's scheduled for a routine inspection tomorrow morning."

Torlan nodded.

"That works in our favor."

Alex continued entering commands.

"Next we'll need to assemble supplies."

She opened a cargo planning window.

"Havenfall will need agricultural equipment, medical kits, water purification systems, and spare habitat components."

Torlan studied the growing list.

"Add structural repair materials."

Alex nodded and added the request.

"Good idea. If their dome systems are failing, they'll need reinforcement supports."

Another message window appeared.

Alex opened it quickly.

"That's the docking authority," she said. "They're approving our access to the ship."

Torlan allowed himself a small nod.

"Good."

Alex continued working.

"Next problem," she said. "Crew."

Torlan raised an eyebrow slightly.

"We will need help."

Alex glanced toward him.

"You plan to pilot the ship yourself."

"Yes."

"But a cargo vessel still requires more than one person to operate safely."

Torlan nodded.

"Then we will recruit a crew."

Alex opened another data file.

"We'll need people who can handle long-distance operations."

She began listing positions as she spoke.

"Engineering support."

Torlan nodded.

"Yes."

"Navigation assistance."

"Agreed."

"And at least one person who understands agricultural systems."

Torlan smiled slightly.

"That will help when we reach Havenfall."

Alex finished the preliminary planning list.

The mission outline now filled the main console.

Locate the ship.

Prepare supplies.

Recruit crew.

Train for corridor navigation.

Torlan studied the growing plan.

Only an hour earlier the mission had been a possibility.

Now it was becoming real.

Alex closed several of the planning windows and finally stepped back from the console.

"We should see the ship," she said.

Torlan nodded.

"That would be wise."

A few minutes later they stood in the observation gallery overlooking **Hangar Four**.

Below them the cargo vessel rested quietly inside the massive docking bay.

It was not large compared to the heavy freighters that sometimes passed through the station.

Its design was simple and practical.

Reinforced hull plating.

Strong maneuvering thrusters.

Cargo compartments built for frontier supply work.

Alex studied the ship carefully.

"That's the one."

Torlan nodded.

"Yes."

The vessel sat quietly beneath the hangar lights.

Not a warship.

Not an explorer.

Just a working cargo vessel designed for difficult journeys.

Exactly the kind of ship their mission required.

Alex rested her hands lightly on the railing.

"When do we leave?" she asked.

Torlan watched the ship for a moment before answering.

"As soon as we are ready."

The Long Path waited quietly in the hangar below them.

And the journey to Havenfall had begun.

Chapter 11 — Assembling the Crew

The Crew List

Torlan's office was quieter than it had been the previous day.

The star charts of the Kardrin Expanse were no longer filling the room. Instead, the console now displayed a far simpler document—one that would determine whether the mission to Havenfall could actually happen.

Alex stood beside the console reviewing the list.

Torlan sat across from her, reading the same information in silence.

The heading at the top of the display was straightforward:

Crew Requirements — The Long Path

Beneath it, several positions were listed.

Alex tapped the screen lightly.

"We've secured the ship," she said. "But a cargo vessel isn't something two people can operate safely, especially not on a mission like this."

Torlan nodded.

"I agree."

Alex scrolled down the list.

"First position," she said.

Pilot / Navigation

Torlan studied the line for a moment.

"That will be important."

Alex gave him a quick look.

"That may be the understatement of the week."

She continued.

"The corridor is going to require constant adjustments. Whoever handles navigation will have to track storm movement, drift currents, and patrol zones all at the same time."

Torlan nodded.

"Continue."

Alex highlighted the next line.

Engineering

"We need someone who understands cargo systems and structural mechanics," she said. "The ship will be operating inside storm turbulence for hours. If anything breaks, we'll want someone who can fix it immediately."

Torlan agreed quietly.

"That would be wise."

Alex scrolled again.

Medical Officer

Torlan looked up slightly.

"For Havenfall?"

"Yes," Alex said. "Frontier colonies usually operate with limited medical infrastructure. If their supplies are failing, they'll need immediate help."

Torlan nodded.

"Add medical supplies to the cargo manifest as well."

"Already done," Alex replied.

She continued down the list.

Communications / Sensors

Alex tapped the display again.

"This position might be even more important than the others."

Torlan raised an eyebrow slightly.

"Explain."

"If the ion storms behave the way we expect," Alex said, "sensor coverage in the corridor will be unstable."

Torlan nodded.

"Yes."

"We'll need someone who can interpret partial sensor readings," she continued. "Someone who understands signal interference, storm behavior, and military detection systems."

Torlan considered the idea for a moment.

"That will help us remain unseen."

Alex nodded.

"That's the goal."

The list ended there.

Four positions.

Not a large crew.

But enough to operate the ship safely.

Alex looked at Torlan.

"How many people do you want aboard?"

Torlan studied the list again.

A pilot.

An engineer.

A medical officer.

A communications specialist.

Each one would play a critical role once the ship entered the Kardrin Expanse.

For a moment he remained silent.

Then he answered calmly.

"Only the ones who believe the mission matters."

Alex watched him for a moment.

"That may narrow the candidate list."

Torlan allowed the faintest hint of a smile.

"That would not be a disadvantage."

Alex nodded slowly.

"Fair enough."

She began opening several personnel databases on the console.

"All right," she said.

"Let's find some people who care about Havenfall."

The Pilot

Later that afternoon, Torlan and Alex met their first candidate in one of the station's smaller briefing rooms.

The man who entered carried himself with the relaxed confidence of someone who had spent most of his life in flight.

Captain **Mateo Rios** was tall, with weathered features and dark hair that had begun to gray slightly at the temples. His movements were unhurried, but there was nothing careless about them.

He nodded politely as he stepped into the room.

"You wanted to see me."

Alex gestured toward the display table.

"Thank you for coming, Captain."

Mateo sat down across from them, his eyes already moving toward the star chart hovering above the table.

Torlan activated the projection.

The **Kardrin Expanse** appeared between them, its storm belts and patrol markers drifting slowly across the map.

Mateo studied the display without speaking.

After a few seconds he leaned forward slightly.

"That region looks familiar."

Torlan nodded.

"You've flown near it before."

Mateo gave a short smile.

"Near it, yes."

He glanced toward Alex.

"Most cargo captains prefer to stay well outside that particular neighborhood."

Alex folded her arms lightly.

"That's generally considered wise."

Mateo's attention returned to the chart.

Torlan expanded the display and highlighted the **Quiet Corridor**.

The narrow band appeared across the storm field.

Mateo's expression changed slightly.

"What's that?"

Torlan answered calmly.

"A storm interference corridor."

Mateo leaned closer.

Torlan brought up the storm simulations and patrol avoidance zones.

The corridor shifted slowly as the simulation ran.

Mateo watched the patterns carefully.

Storm movement.

Sensor interference.

Patrol coverage bending away from the storms.

The narrow path appeared again.

Mateo said nothing for a long moment.

Alex and Torlan waited.

Finally Mateo leaned back in his chair.

"That route is dangerous."

Torlan nodded.

"Yes."

Mateo studied the chart again.

"You're planning to fly through the storm belt while both war fleets are operating nearby."

Torlan did not argue.

"That is correct."

Mateo's eyes returned to the corridor.

Another quiet pause followed.

Then, slowly, a small smile appeared.

"Good," he said.

Alex blinked.

"Good?"

Mateo nodded.

"I dislike boring flights."

Alex glanced briefly at Torlan.

Torlan remained calm.

Mateo leaned forward again and pointed at the corridor.

"The storm movement will require precise timing."

"Yes," Torlan said.

"And the ship will have to remain inside the interference zone the entire way."

"Yes."

Mateo nodded thoughtfully.

"Interesting navigation problem."

Alex studied him carefully.

"You're not concerned about the patrol fleets?"

Mateo shrugged lightly.

"If the corridor works the way you think it does, they won't see us."

Torlan met his gaze.

"That is the plan."

Mateo sat quietly for another moment, then extended his hand across the table.

"When do we start?"

Torlan shook his hand.

"Immediately."

Mateo nodded once.

"Good."

He looked back at the chart.

"I've always wanted to try something that hasn't been done before."

Alex allowed herself a small smile.

It appeared they had found their pilot.

The Engineer

Hangar Four was louder than the quiet offices above the station.

Maintenance crews moved steadily across the vast docking bay, their equipment carts humming softly as they passed between the parked vessels. Overhead lights cast long reflections across the polished metal floor.

At the center of the hangar rested **The Long Path**.

The cargo vessel looked sturdy rather than impressive. Its reinforced hull plating showed the subtle wear of years spent on frontier supply routes, but the ship's structure was solid.

Torlan and Alex stood near the landing ramp as their next candidate slowly circled the vessel.

Owen Tark was a compact man with broad shoulders and permanently grease-stained hands. A small diagnostic scanner rested in his grip as he moved methodically along the hull.

He paused beside one of the maneuvering thrusters and tapped the casing lightly.

The sound echoed through the hangar.

Tark frowned.

He knelt down and ran the scanner along the thruster assembly.

Alex leaned closer to Torlan.

"Is he always this quiet?" she whispered.

Torlan watched the engineer continue his inspection.

"I believe he prefers machines to conversations."

Alex smiled faintly.

"That could be useful."

Tark stood again and continued walking slowly around the ship.

He inspected the landing gear.

Then the cargo hatch.

Then several exposed maintenance panels near the engine housing.

For nearly five minutes he said nothing.

Finally he returned to where Torlan and Alex were standing.

He glanced once more at the ship.

Then he delivered his assessment.

"Technically speaking," Tark said, "the ship flies."

Alex raised an eyebrow.

"Technically?"

Tark nodded once.

"Technically."

A short pause followed.

Alex waited.

Tark continued.

"The hull frame is solid. Thrusters are functional. Engine output is stable."

He tapped the hull lightly with the scanner again.

"But the ship hasn't been pushed through serious turbulence in a while."

Torlan nodded.

"We will be traveling through ion storms."

Tark looked at him directly for the first time.

"Yes. I noticed that part of the mission description."

Alex folded her arms.

"So what would the ship need?"

Tark considered the question.

"Reinforced navigation stabilizers."

He raised one finger.

"Additional shielding around the primary sensor array."

Another finger.

"And a few upgrades to the maneuvering control systems."

Alex smiled slightly.

"That sounds manageable."

Tark shrugged.

"It will help the ship survive."

Torlan studied him.

"Can you make those modifications?"

Tark glanced back toward the vessel.

"Yes."

He paused.

"But I would prefer to supervise the work personally."

Alex tilted her head.

"You want to come with us."

Tark gave a small shrug.

"If I'm responsible for the upgrades, I should also be responsible for keeping them working."

Torlan nodded.

"That would be acceptable."

Tark looked back toward **The Long Path** again.

"Besides," he added, "someone should make sure the ship continues to fly."

Alex smiled.

"Technically speaking."

Tark nodded once.

"Technically speaking."

Torlan allowed himself a small smile.

It appeared they had found their engineer.

The Medical Officer

The medical wing of the station was far quieter than the hangar.

Soft lighting reflected from the polished walls, and the steady hum of diagnostic equipment filled the air with a gentle background rhythm. Medical staff moved calmly through the corridors, their work precise and unhurried.

Torlan and Alex waited just outside one of the consultation rooms.

A moment later the door slid open and **Dr. Lila Chen** stepped into the hallway.

She removed a pair of medical gloves as she walked toward them, dropping them neatly into a disposal unit along the wall.

"Captain Tarsen," she said with a small nod.

Torlan returned the greeting.

"Doctor."

Alex offered a polite smile.

"Thank you for meeting with us."

Dr. Chen gestured toward the nearby seating area.

"I have a few minutes before my next patient."

They sat together at a small consultation table.

Dr. Chen folded her hands calmly.

"So," she said, "what sort of medical assistance do you require?"

Alex activated a small data pad and displayed a short report.

"Havenfall Colony."

Dr. Chen read the name and her expression immediately sharpened with interest.

"I've heard of Havenfall," she said. "Frontier agricultural settlement."

Torlan nodded.

"They are experiencing supply failures."

Alex added a few details.

"Medical shortages as well. Their supply ships stopped arriving once the war patrols moved into the Kardrin Expanse."

Dr. Chen read through the report carefully.

Her calm expression shifted slightly as she reached the section describing the colony's current medical inventory.

"Antibiotic reserves are nearly exhausted," she said.

Alex nodded.

"And their surgical equipment is outdated."

Dr. Chen looked up.

"How many people live there?"

"Approximately eight hundred," Alex replied.

Dr. Chen leaned back slightly, thinking.

"A colony that size will eventually face injuries, infections, and childbirth complications."

Torlan nodded.

"Yes."

Dr. Chen studied the report for another moment.

Then she closed the file and looked directly at them.

"You're planning to deliver supplies."

"Yes," Torlan said.

Dr. Chen tilted her head slightly.

"How?"

Alex exchanged a brief glance with Torlan.

Then she answered honestly.

"By flying through the Kardrin Expanse."

Dr. Chen raised an eyebrow.

"That's… ambitious."

Alex smiled faintly.

"That's one way to describe it."

Dr. Chen leaned forward again.

"What sort of ship?"

"A cargo transport," Torlan said. "The *Long Path*."

Dr. Chen nodded slowly.

"And you're assembling a crew."

"Yes."

She looked again at the Havenfall report.

The numbers were not encouraging.

Limited medical infrastructure.

A population large enough that even minor illnesses could quickly become serious.

Finally she looked back at Torlan and Alex.

"You had me at 'medical supplies.'"

Alex smiled.

"We were hoping you might say that."

Dr. Chen stood and picked up a small tablet from the table.

"I'll need to assemble a portable medical unit," she said. "Surgical kits, antibiotics, trauma supplies, and diagnostic equipment."

Torlan nodded.

"That would be very helpful."

Dr. Chen began walking toward the supply room.

"I'll also want to review Havenfall's medical records before we leave," she added.

Alex blinked.

"We?"

Dr. Chen glanced back over her shoulder with a calm smile.

"If a colony has medical shortages, someone should go help."

She tapped the tablet thoughtfully.

"Besides," she added, "I've spent most of my career working in well-equipped stations like this."

She gestured toward the quiet medical wing.

"It might be refreshing to practice medicine where it actually matters."

Torlan nodded respectfully.

"Welcome aboard."

Dr. Chen smiled slightly.

"Thank you."

It appeared they had found their doctor.

Communications Specialist

Later that evening, Torlan and Alex met their final candidate in the station's **sensor analysis lab**.

The room was dim except for the glow of several large displays. Data streams flowed steadily across the screens, mapping nearby traffic lanes, weather patterns in surrounding systems, and long-range sensor readings from the Kardrin Expanse.

A man stood near the main console studying a complex chart.

Samir Haddad was lean and thoughtful, with dark hair and a calm, attentive expression. He did not look up immediately when Torlan and Alex entered; instead he continued watching the display, as if he were already deep inside the problem.

After a moment he spoke.

"You're the ones planning to cross the expanse."

Alex smiled faintly.

"That rumor is spreading quickly."

Samir finally turned toward them.

"It tends to," he said calmly. "Especially when someone asks the sensor lab for storm interference models."

Torlan stepped forward.

"You've reviewed the data."

Samir nodded and gestured toward the main display.

The **Kardrin Expanse** appeared again, with the familiar storm belts drifting slowly across the map.

But Samir had added several new layers.

Sensor interference gradients.

Electromagnetic turbulence.

Long-range detection probabilities.

Alex studied the new information with interest.

"You've been busy."

Samir shrugged lightly.

"You asked for storm behavior analysis. I thought it would be useful to examine the sensor effects as well."

Torlan watched the display.

The Quiet Corridor appeared faintly across the storm belt.

Samir traced the path with a finger.

"If the ion storms behave the way your model predicts," he said, "this corridor will degrade long-range sensor resolution significantly."

Alex nodded.

"That's what we were hoping."

Samir zoomed in on the storm layer.

Charged particle clouds flickered across the display.

"These storms scatter active sensor pulses," he explained. "Military patrol ships will have difficulty resolving objects inside the interference zone."

Torlan studied the shifting patterns.

"That allows a ship to remain unseen."

Samir nodded.

"Possibly."

Alex tilted her head.

"Possibly?"

Samir adjusted the chart again.

"Storm behavior is rarely perfect," he said. "There will still be moments when the interference weakens."

Alex crossed her arms.

"So we could still be detected."

"Yes."

Samir zoomed the map outward again.

"But if the timing is precise," he continued, "the corridor will reduce the detection range enough to slip through."

Torlan nodded slowly.

"That is our intention."

Samir studied the route for another moment.

Then he looked at Torlan.

"You will need someone monitoring the sensor spectrum the entire time."

Torlan nodded.

"That is why we are here."

Samir gave a small thoughtful smile.

"I assumed as much."

Alex studied him carefully.

"You don't seem particularly surprised by the plan."

Samir shrugged slightly.

"I've worked in communications and sensor systems for many years."

He gestured toward the storm patterns.

"Storm interference like this is rare, but not impossible to use."

Torlan met his gaze.

"Will you join the mission?"

Samir considered the question for a moment.

Then he nodded.

"Yes."

Alex raised an eyebrow.

"That was quick."

Samir smiled faintly.

"From a technical perspective, this is an interesting problem."

Torlan watched him.

"And from a humanitarian perspective?"

Samir glanced toward the Havenfall colony marker on the chart.

"A colony cut off from medical supplies and food shipments will not survive long."

He turned back toward them.

"I believe helping them is worth the risk."

Torlan nodded.

"Welcome aboard."

Samir returned his attention to the chart.

"If the storm models remain accurate," he said calmly, "we might remain invisible long enough to reach Havenfall."

Alex smiled.

"That's exactly what we're hoping."

It appeared they had found their communications specialist.

The First Crew Meeting

The cargo hold of *The Long Path* had been converted into a temporary briefing room.

Several crates of newly delivered supplies were stacked neatly along the bulkheads—medical containers, repair materials, and agricultural equipment awaiting final loading. In the center of the compartment, a portable display table projected a rotating star chart of the **Kardrin Expanse**.

The entire crew stood around the display.

For the first time, the people who would attempt the journey were together in one place.

Torlan stood at the head of the table.

Beside him was **Alex**, reviewing navigation data on a small tablet.

Across from them stood the rest of the crew.

Captain Mateo Rios, relaxed but attentive, watched the storm patterns with quiet interest.

Owen Tark, arms folded, leaned slightly against one of the cargo crates as if already evaluating the ship's systems in his mind.

Dr. Lila Chen stood calmly near the table, her tablet already displaying a list of medical supplies for Havenfall.

And **Samir Haddad** studied the sensor interference patterns projected above the display.

Torlan activated the star chart.

The familiar storm belts drifted across the Kardrin Expanse.

"This," Torlan said calmly, "is the Quiet Corridor."

The narrow band appeared across the storm field.

Mateo studied the shifting path.

"That's the route," he said.

"Yes."

Torlan continued.

"The mission is simple in principle."

He pointed toward the small marker representing **Havenfall.**

"We will transport supplies to the colony."

Dr. Chen nodded slightly.

"They need them."

Torlan continued.

"To reach Havenfall, we must cross the Kardrin Expanse without being detected by either patrol fleet."

Samir studied the storm interference zones.

"The ion storms should reduce sensor resolution," he said.

"That is the expectation," Torlan replied.

Mateo leaned closer to the display.

"The timing window is narrow."

Alex nodded.

"Approximately six hours."

Owen Tark glanced at the corridor.

"And if we drift outside the storm interference?"

Samir answered calmly.

"Both war fleets will see us."

Tark nodded once.

"Good to know."

Torlan looked around the group.

"I will not hide the risks," he said.

"The corridor is unstable. Storm movement may shift the boundaries unexpectedly. Patrol ships may change their routes."

Mateo smiled faintly.

"That's the interesting part."

A few of the others smiled slightly.

Torlan continued.

"But the colony at Havenfall has limited supplies. If we do not reach them soon, they may not survive."

Dr. Chen nodded firmly.

"That is reason enough."

Torlan looked at the crew for a moment before speaking again.

"On Cyrion," he said quietly, "there is a saying."

The group waited.

"A village stands because its people stand."

Samir tilted his head slightly.

"Meaning?"

Torlan met their eyes.

"This mission will succeed only if we work together."

No one spoke for a moment.

Then Mateo leaned over the display again, studying the corridor carefully.

He traced the route slowly with his finger.

After a long pause he looked up.

"You realize something."

Torlan waited.

Mateo smiled slightly.

"No one has ever flown through this corridor."

Torlan nodded once.

"Then we will be the first."

The crew exchanged glances.

The mission that had begun as a theory was now becoming a shared reality.

The journey to Havenfall was no longer an idea.

It was about to begin.

Chapter 12 — Preparing the Ship

"The quiet mind sees the farthest."
Calm thinking reveals paths that panic cannot see.
— Wisdom of Cyrion

First Walkthrough of *The Long Path*

The docking hangar was alive with quiet activity.

Maintenance crews moved between ships with tool carts and diagnostic scanners, their voices echoing softly beneath the tall ceiling of the station's main bay. Overhead lights reflected across the polished hull of **The Long Path**, casting long silver lines across the cargo vessel's weathered plating.

Up close, the ship looked practical rather than elegant.

Its hull carried the marks of many frontier supply runs—small repair welds, reinforced panels, and faded registry numbers that had clearly been repainted more than once. But the vessel had a sturdy, dependable appearance.

The kind of ship built to work.

Torlan stood near the landing ramp with the rest of the crew.

"This," he said calmly, "is our transport."

Captain **Mateo Rios** looked up toward the bridge section and nodded approvingly.

"She's not pretty," he said.

Engineer **Owen Tark** folded his arms.

"Pretty ships break too easily."

Mateo smiled.

"Good point."

Alex gestured toward the open ramp.

"Let's take a look inside."

The crew moved up the ramp and into the cargo hold.

Inside, the air smelled faintly of machine oil and recently cleaned metal. The hold itself was large enough to carry several dozen cargo containers, though most of the space was still empty while final loading preparations continued.

Torlan led the group forward.

"Cargo storage," he said.

Owen Tark had already begun scanning the room with his diagnostic unit.

He walked to a nearby wall panel and tapped it lightly.

The sound echoed hollowly through the metal.

He frowned slightly.

Then he opened the panel and inspected the wiring behind it.

"This system is twenty years old," he said.

Alex looked over.

"Is that bad?"

Tark considered the question carefully.

"Only if you enjoy arriving alive."

Mateo chuckled.

"Good to know."

They continued deeper into the ship.

A narrow corridor led forward toward the **bridge**.

The bridge itself was compact but efficient. Two pilot stations faced a wide forward viewport, while several smaller control panels surrounded the navigation console.

Mateo stepped toward the pilot's chair and ran a hand across the control surface.

"Manual controls are still intact," he said with approval.

Alex leaned against the doorway.

"That's unusual?"

Mateo nodded.

"Most cargo ships rely heavily on autopilot systems."

He tapped the controls.

"I prefer to fly my ships."

Torlan studied the navigation displays.

"They will require recalibration for storm interference."

Samir Haddad stepped forward and examined the sensor panel.

"I'll handle that."

The group moved again.

Next came **engineering**.

The engine room was louder than the rest of the ship. Power regulators hummed steadily while coolant systems circulated through thick pipes along the bulkheads.

Owen Tark immediately disappeared into the machinery.

Within seconds he had opened two access panels and was studying the components inside.

"These stabilizers will need reinforcement," he muttered.

He glanced briefly at Torlan.

"Storm turbulence will push this ship hard."

Torlan nodded.

"Make the improvements you believe are necessary."

Tark seemed satisfied with that answer.

"Good."

Further down the corridor they reached the **medical bay**.

The room was small but well designed. A single treatment bed stood in the center while diagnostic equipment lined the walls.

Dr. **Lila Chen** stepped inside and examined the equipment carefully.

"This will work," she said.

She began mentally organizing where additional medical supplies would be stored.

Finally the group reached the **crew quarters**.

Six small sleeping compartments surrounded a shared common area. The space was simple but comfortable enough for a long voyage.

Mateo looked around.

"Not luxurious."

Alex smiled.

"We're not running a cruise line."

Samir leaned lightly against the wall.

"For a mission like this, simple is probably best."

Torlan nodded.

"Yes."

Behind them, a metallic clang echoed from the engineering compartment.

Owen Tark's voice followed.

"This power regulator is outdated!"

Alex glanced down the corridor.

"That didn't take long."

Torlan allowed himself a small smile.

"No."

The crew had begun learning the ship.

And the ship had begun revealing its problems.

Engineering Upgrades

Engineering quickly became the busiest place on *The Long Path*.

Panels were open across half the engine compartment, revealing wiring bundles, coolant lines, and control circuits that had not been inspected closely in years. Portable work lights illuminated the machinery, casting sharp reflections across the metal surfaces.

At the center of the activity stood **Owen Tark**.

The engineer moved from system to system with intense concentration, a diagnostic scanner in one hand and a tool kit resting open on the floor beside him.

Torlan stood nearby, observing quietly.

Tark tapped one of the navigation stabilizer housings with a small wrench.

The hollow sound made him shake his head.

"These stabilizers were designed for standard cargo routes," he said. "Not ion storm turbulence."

Torlan nodded.

"What modifications would you recommend?"

Tark pointed toward a nearby control module.

"First, reinforcement brackets around the stabilizer mounts."

He raised a second finger.

"Second, a secondary control loop for the navigation dampers."

Torlan studied the system diagram displayed on a nearby console.

"That would reduce oscillation during storm drift."

Tark glanced up at him.

"Yes."

Torlan stepped closer to the console and began reading through the engineering specifications.

For a few minutes the room was filled only with the low hum of machinery and the occasional sound of tools striking metal.

Then Tark noticed something.

Torlan had moved on to a different technical manual on the console.

Another few minutes passed.

Then another.

Finally Tark spoke.

"You read engineering manuals often?"

Torlan did not look up from the display.

"Occasionally."

Tark watched him turn several more pages.

"You're reading that rather quickly."

Torlan closed the manual and stepped back from the console.

"That section describes the stabilizer control architecture."

Tark frowned slightly.

"Yes."

Torlan pointed toward the control module.

"The secondary loop you mentioned should connect through the existing power relay."

Tark blinked once.

"That's correct."

Torlan continued calmly.

"If the relay remains inside the primary circuit, it may introduce a timing delay."

Tark crossed his arms thoughtfully.

"Yes."

Torlan tapped the diagram.

"You may want to reroute the loop through the auxiliary regulator instead."

The engineer studied the display again.

After a moment he nodded slowly.

"That would stabilize the control cycle."

Torlan inclined his head slightly.

"That was my thought."

Tark looked at him with new interest.

"You just read the control manual."

"Yes."

Tark glanced back at the console.

"Did you just finish that manual?"

Torlan considered the question.

"Mostly."

Tark let out a short breath.

"Well."

He picked up his wrench again.

"That makes my job easier."

Torlan looked toward the open engine panels.

"How long will the upgrades require?"

Tark glanced around the compartment.

"Several hours."

He tapped the stabilizer housing again.

"Maybe less if you keep reading manuals."

Torlan smiled faintly.

"That can be arranged."

The engineer returned to work, already reorganizing several components in his mind.

For the first time since meeting him, Tark appeared quietly impressed.

Cargo Loading

By mid-afternoon the docking hangar had become a steady stream of cargo activity.

Automated loaders rolled across the floor carrying large supply containers toward the open ramp of **The Long Path**. Workers guided the machines carefully, aligning each crate with the ship's cargo grid.

Inside the hold, **Alex** stood beside a handheld logistics console, checking each delivery against the mission manifest.

One by one the containers were moved into position and secured.

She read the labels as they passed.

"Medical supplies… antibiotics… surgical kits…"

Dr. **Lila Chen**, standing nearby, nodded approvingly.

"Those will help."

Another crate rolled up the ramp.

Alex checked the label.

"Portable diagnostic equipment."

Dr. Chen made a note on her tablet.

"Place that near the medical bay access."

The loader operator nodded and guided the crate into position.

A second wave of cargo arrived.

Large reinforced containers marked:

AGRICULTURAL SYSTEMS

Alex watched as they were lifted into the hold.

Torlan stepped beside her.

"These will help the colony restore crop production."

Alex nodded.

"They should."

She checked another item on the manifest.

"Water drilling equipment."

Torlan studied the crate.

"Havenfall's water table is unstable."

Alex looked over.

"You've studied the colony reports."

"Yes."

The next container rolled forward.

Alex leaned closer to read the label.

It read:

AGRICULTURAL MISCELLANEOUS

She frowned slightly.

"What exactly does that mean?"

The supplier standing near the loader glanced at the label.

"Seeds."

Alex blinked.

"That's… a large crate for seeds."

The supplier shrugged.

"Farmers prefer options."

Torlan allowed himself a small smile.

"That seems reasonable."

More cargo followed.

Replacement **power units**.

Additional **water filtration systems**.

Emergency **ration packs**.

Each container was secured carefully inside the hold.

Samir Haddad walked through the cargo area studying the placement.

"You're keeping the heavier containers near the center of mass."

Alex nodded.

"That will make Mateo's life easier during turbulence."

Samir looked toward the engineering corridor.

"Owen will approve."

As if summoned by the comment, Owen Tark stepped into the hold, wiping his hands on a cloth.

He glanced at the cargo arrangement.

Then nodded once.

"This layout will work."

Alex smiled slightly.

"High praise."

Tark shrugged.

"It won't make the ship unstable."

Torlan looked across the growing stacks of supplies.

For the first time the mission's purpose felt tangible.

These crates were more than cargo.

They were medicine.

Food.

Water.

The tools a colony would need to survive.

Torlan spoke quietly.

"Havenfall will need all of this."

Alex looked around the hold.

"And more."

Torlan nodded.

"Then we should not delay."

Outside the hangar, more cargo vehicles were already approaching.

The ship was beginning to look like a lifeline rather than a transport.

Navigation Planning

The bridge of *The Long Path* was dim except for the glow of the navigation displays.

Several star charts floated above the central console, layered with storm simulations, debris field projections, and patrol route estimates. The **Kardrin Expanse** stretched across the display like a shifting ocean of charged clouds.

Captain Mateo Rios leaned over the navigation table studying the patterns carefully.

Beside him stood **Torlan.**

Mateo adjusted the simulation controls and the storm belts began drifting slowly across the map.

"Let's run it again," Mateo said.

The computer reset the model.

Ion storms rolled through the expanse in slow cycles. As each storm passed through a sector, the projected sensor interference zones expanded and contracted around it.

Torlan watched the patterns without speaking.

After a moment he pointed toward the display.

"There."

Mateo paused the simulation.

The **Quiet Corridor** appeared again, a narrow pathway forming between two large storm bands.

Mateo nodded slowly.

"That's the window."

He zoomed the map closer.

Storm turbulence flickered across the corridor's edges.

"If the storm cycle shifts by even a few minutes," Mateo said, "the corridor could close before we reach the midpoint."

Torlan studied the timing indicators.

"We will need to enter the corridor at exactly the correct moment."

Mateo leaned back slightly.

"Exactly."

He ran another simulation.

This time the display added **debris drift patterns**.

Small clusters of wreckage—remnants from earlier battles in the war zone—moved slowly through the storm belts.

Mateo traced their paths.

"These debris fields might actually help us."

Torlan looked up.

"Explain."

Mateo highlighted several clusters.

"Patrol ships tend to avoid areas with heavy debris," he said. "It's risky for navigation."

Torlan nodded.

"That would reduce patrol density."

Mateo smiled slightly.

"Exactly."

He ran the model again, this time overlaying **patrol detection ranges**.

Red sensor cones extended outward from several simulated patrol ships.

As the storms intensified, the cones shrank.

Torlan watched the change carefully.

"The storms disrupt their sensors."

"Yes," Mateo said.

He studied the corridor again.

"If the interference remains strong enough, their detection range drops by nearly seventy percent."

Torlan nodded thoughtfully.

"That should allow us to pass through the corridor unseen."

Mateo folded his arms.

"Should."

Torlan glanced at him.

Mateo smiled faintly.

"I like plans with a small amount of uncertainty."

Torlan allowed a small smile in return.

"That may be fortunate."

Mateo ran the simulation one final time.

Storm movement.

Debris drift.

Patrol avoidance zones.

The narrow corridor opened again.

For a few seconds the path looked almost peaceful.

Mateo leaned forward and studied the route carefully.

Finally he spoke.

"You've spent a lot of time studying this region."

Torlan nodded.

"Yes."

Mateo glanced at him.

"Most people would never notice this pattern."

Torlan looked back at the display.

"The storms reveal the path."

Mateo studied him for a moment, impressed.

Then he nodded slowly.

"Well," he said, straightening slightly.

"I think this might actually work."

The bridge fell quiet again as the simulation continued running.

Outside the viewport, the docking hangar lights glowed softly across the station walls.

But soon those lights would disappear behind them.

And the ship would be flying into the storms.

Medical Preparation

The small medical bay aboard *The Long Path* had quickly transformed into a carefully organized supply center.

Portable medical cases lined the walls, each one neatly labeled and secured inside storage brackets. Diagnostic scanners rested beside sealed containers of antibiotics, trauma kits, and surgical tools.

At the center of the room, **Dr. Lila Chen** reviewed her inventory tablet.

She moved methodically from container to container, verifying that each item had been delivered correctly.

"Antibiotics… sterile dressings… surgical clamps…"

She opened a crate beside the treatment table.

Inside were several sealed cases of injectable medications.

She nodded with quiet approval.

"These will help."

Alex stepped into the doorway.

"Do you have everything you need?"

Dr. Chen looked up briefly.

"For the moment."

She tapped the tablet again and reviewed the remaining list.

"Portable diagnostic scanner… emergency trauma kits… pediatric medications…"

Alex raised an eyebrow.

"Pediatric?"

Dr. Chen nodded.

"Frontier colonies always have children."

Alex smiled faintly.

"That's a good point."

Dr. Chen finished her inventory and closed the final container.

Then she paused for a moment, studying the medical reports displayed on her tablet.

The files described Havenfall's medical infrastructure.

It was… limited.

Very limited.

Only basic diagnostic equipment.

A small clinic.

Minimal surgical capability.

And almost no remaining pharmaceutical supplies.

Dr. Chen leaned back slightly in her chair.

"They've been rationing antibiotics."

Alex stepped closer.

"That bad?"

"Yes."

Dr. Chen scrolled through the report.

"If an infection outbreak occurs, they would struggle to treat it."

Alex nodded quietly.

"That's why this mission matters."

Dr. Chen looked around the small medical bay again.

The room was well stocked now.

Enough supplies to stabilize a colony's medical system—at least for a while.

She closed the tablet.

"How long is the journey?"

Alex answered.

"If everything goes according to plan, we should reach Havenfall within two days."

Dr. Chen nodded.

"Good."

She secured the last medical container inside its bracket.

"Then we may arrive before their situation becomes critical."

Alex leaned lightly against the doorframe.

"You've worked on frontier colonies before."

Dr. Chen smiled slightly.

"Yes."

She glanced at the supplies again.

"Colonies like Havenfall survive because people help each other."

Alex nodded.

"That's what Torlan believes."

Dr. Chen stood and adjusted the medical equipment around the treatment bed.

"Well," she said calmly, "let's make sure we arrive in time to help."

Outside the medical bay, the ship's internal systems hummed quietly.

Preparations were nearly complete.

Soon the mission would begin.

The Crew Bond

Later that evening, the activity aboard *The Long Path* finally began to slow.

Most of the major preparation work had been completed. Cargo was secured, engineering upgrades were nearly finished, and the navigation simulations had been run more times than anyone could count.

For the first time that day, the crew found themselves with a few quiet minutes.

They gathered in the ship's small **mess area**, a simple room near the crew quarters with a narrow table and several built-in seats along the walls.

A pot of station coffee sat in the center of the table.

Mateo poured himself a cup.

Owen Tark sat nearby, leaning back slightly with his arms folded. His hands were still smudged with grease from hours spent in engineering.

Dr. Chen reviewed a few notes on her tablet while Samir Haddad studied a sensor display projected from his handheld device.

Alex sat at the end of the table.

Torlan stood near the doorway, quietly observing the group.

For a moment no one spoke.

Then Samir finally broke the silence.

"So let me make sure I understand the plan."

Mateo looked up.

"That sounds dangerous already."

Samir continued calmly.

"We are flying into an active war zone…"

He held up one finger.

"…through an ion storm corridor…"

A second finger.

"…that no one has ever attempted to navigate before."

He paused.

"…while avoiding detection from two military fleets."

The room was quiet for a moment.

Then Mateo nodded thoughtfully.

"When you say it like that," he said, "it sounds reckless."

Owen Tark glanced toward the bridge corridor.

"Technically speaking, it is."

Alex smiled slightly.

Torlan stepped forward.

"It is calculated."

Samir looked at him.

"Calculated?"

Torlan nodded.

"We have studied the storm cycles, the patrol routes, and the sensor interference patterns."

Mateo took another sip of coffee.

"And if those calculations are wrong?"

Torlan met his gaze calmly.

"Then we adjust."

Dr. Chen smiled slightly.

"That seems optimistic."

Torlan considered the comment.

"Preparation improves the probability of success."

Owen tapped the table lightly.

"And reinforced stabilizers improve the probability of surviving the trip."

Mateo nodded.

"I like those odds better."

The crew shared a quiet moment of laughter.

After a moment Torlan spoke again.

"When I was studying on Cyrion," he said quietly, "my teacher often reminded me of something important."

The others looked toward him.

"Observe first," Torlan continued.

"Act second."

Samir nodded thoughtfully.

"That explains the last two days."

Torlan inclined his head slightly.

"Everything we have done has been preparation."

Mateo set his cup down.

"Well," he said, "we're about to see whether the preparation was enough."

Alex checked the time display on her tablet.

"The storm cycle begins soon."

The room grew slightly quieter.

The moment they had been preparing for was approaching.

Torlan looked around the table at the small crew who had chosen to join the mission.

"Thank you," he said simply.

Mateo smiled faintly.

"Let's get Havenfall their supplies."

Torlan nodded.

Soon the ship's systems would begin their final preflight sequence.

And *The Long Path* would leave the safety of the station behind.

Chapter 13 — Into the Kardrin Expanse

Departure

The docking hangar lights reflected softly across the hull of **The Long Path**.

The cargo vessel rested quietly inside the orbital platform, its systems now fully powered. The ship's running lights glowed faintly along the length of the hull, casting pale reflections across the polished docking deck.

Inside the **bridge**, the crew sat at their stations.

The atmosphere was calm, but focused.

Final preparations were underway.

At the engineering console, **Owen Tark** reviewed the system diagnostics scrolling across his display.

Power output stable.

Navigation stabilizers reinforced and operational.

Shield emitters functioning within normal parameters.

Owen tapped a few final commands into the console.

"All systems operational," he announced.

He paused briefly, then added in his usual practical tone:

"At least the important ones."

Alex glanced toward him from the navigation console.

"That is reassuring."

Owen shrugged slightly.

"It should be."

At the pilot's station, **Captain Mateo Rios** adjusted the flight controls and checked the ship's thruster response.

The console lights reflected across the forward viewport.

Beyond the glass, the massive docking bay stretched outward, with dozens of other ships resting in their assigned berths.

Mateo nodded once to himself.

"Flight controls responding normally."

Samir Haddad monitored the communication systems.

"Station traffic control confirms departure clearance."

Alex checked the final cargo logs on her tablet.

"Cargo secure."

Torlan stood quietly behind the pilot's chair.

For a moment he looked through the viewport at the station around them.

The structure had been their safe harbor during the last several days of preparation.

But the mission required them to leave that safety behind.

Torlan spoke calmly.

"Release docking clamps."

A quiet mechanical sound echoed through the ship as the external clamps disengaged.

Mateo placed his hands on the controls.

"Thrusters ready."

He applied a small amount of thrust.

The ship moved slowly forward.

Outside the viewport, the docking platform began to slide backward as **The Long Path** drifted gently away from the station.

The ship cleared the docking bay doors and entered open space.

For a moment no one spoke.

The stars stretched endlessly ahead.

Behind them, the orbital station grew smaller as the ship moved farther away.

Mateo glanced toward the navigation display.

"Course plotted."

Torlan nodded.

"Begin acceleration."

The engines responded with a low, steady vibration through the ship.

The vessel slowly gained speed.

Far ahead in the distance, a faint glow flickered across space.

The outer storms of the **Kardrin Expanse**.

Alex studied the display.

"Storm activity detected."

Samir monitored the sensors.

"Interference levels increasing."

Mateo adjusted the heading slightly.

The ship continued forward.

The quiet safety of the station was now behind them.

Ahead waited the war zone.

The mission had begun.

Over the next several days, The Long Path pushed steadily outward from Earth's orbit, its engines building speed as it crossed the quiet regions of open space.

Routine checks filled the hours, but the destination ahead never left their thoughts.

Leaving Safe Space

The steady glow of the orbital station slowly faded behind them.

From the bridge of *The Long Path*, the stars ahead appeared calm and distant, but the navigation display told a different story. The edge of the **Kardrin Expanse** stretched across the forward sensors like a dark, shifting tide.

Mateo increased engine output slightly.

The ship responded with a deeper vibration through the deck.

"Acceleration steady," he said.

Torlan stood beside the pilot's station, watching the sensor data begin to fill the displays.

Samir Haddad leaned forward at the communications console, studying the incoming readings.

"Electromagnetic interference increasing," he reported.

The sensor screens flickered faintly as charged particles from the outer storm bands began disturbing long-range signals.

Alex watched the navigation map.

"We're approaching the outer boundary."

Small warning indicators began appearing along the display.

Fragments of metallic debris—too small to threaten the ship directly—drifted through the region ahead. Remnants of earlier battles slowly spiraled through the gravitational currents of the expanse.

Samir adjusted the sensor filters.

"Debris density increasing."

Mateo glanced toward him.

"Anything large?"

"Not yet."

A faint ripple passed across the main sensor screen.

Samir studied it carefully.

Then he frowned slightly.

"Storm activity ahead… heavier than predicted."

Mateo looked briefly toward Torlan.

The glow of the storm belts was now faintly visible through the forward viewport—dim streaks of blue-white energy flashing across distant clouds of charged particles.

Torlan stepped closer to the sensor display and reviewed the incoming data.

The storm intensity was indeed slightly stronger than the models had suggested.

He studied the readings quietly for a moment.

Then he nodded once.

"Within acceptable range."

Mateo gave a small smile.

"I was hoping you would say that."

The ship continued accelerating.

Behind them, the quiet safety of civilized space had disappeared completely.

Ahead, the storm-filled darkness of the **Kardrin Expanse** waited.

And they were now committed to entering it.

The First Storm Edge

The first flashes of storm energy appeared across the forward viewport like distant lightning.

At first they were faint—thin streaks of blue-white light flickering across the darkness of space. But as *The Long Path* moved closer to the storm belt, the flashes grew brighter and more frequent.

The ship crossed the boundary of the **outer ion storm field**.

Immediately the sensor displays began to flicker.

Samir adjusted several controls on his console.

"Electromagnetic turbulence increasing," he reported. "Signal stability dropping."

Mateo leaned forward at the pilot's station.

"I see it."

The navigation display trembled slightly as charged particle waves rippled through the region.

Torlan watched the storm patterns carefully.

Outside the viewport, glowing arcs of ionized energy twisted slowly through space, illuminating clouds of charged particles drifting through the expanse.

The ship began to shudder lightly as the first waves of turbulence reached them.

Mateo tightened his grip on the controls.

"Entering storm edge."

He adjusted the ship's attitude slightly, guiding the vessel through a calmer region between two turbulent bands.

The deck vibrated softly beneath their feet.

Owen Tark's voice came across the bridge intercom from engineering.

"Shield emitters holding."

The ship rocked again as another wave of charged particles brushed past the hull.

"Stabilizers responding," Owen added.

Mateo nodded approvingly.

"Your upgrades are working."

Owen's voice returned through the intercom.

"Good."

There was a brief pause.

Then he added casually:

"If anyone hears strange noises… that's probably normal."

Alex looked up from the navigation console.

"That is not comforting."

Owen replied without hesitation.

"Comfort is not part of the engineering package."

Mateo smiled slightly as he guided the ship through another turbulent patch.

Outside, the storm flashes illuminated the darkness again.

The glowing arcs of energy stretched across space like massive electrical currents flowing through the void.

Torlan watched the patterns carefully.

The storm currents were strong—but predictable.

For now.

Mateo adjusted their heading again.

"Storm turbulence increasing."

Torlan nodded calmly.

"Maintain course."

The ship continued forward, deeper into the glowing storm belt.

And the Kardrin Expanse began to close around them.

The Debris Field

The storm turbulence gradually settled as *The Long Path* moved deeper into the ion belt.

The glowing arcs of charged energy still flickered across space, but the immediate turbulence had lessened. The ship now traveled through a strange region of dim light and drifting particles, the storm clouds glowing faintly around them.

Samir adjusted the sensor filters again.

"Picking up solid objects ahead," he reported.

Mateo glanced at the display.

"Debris?"

Samir nodded.

"Multiple fragments."

The navigation screen filled with small markers.

As the ship moved closer, the shapes outside the viewport began to resolve in the storm-lit darkness.

Fragments of **wreckage**.

A large section of torn hull plating drifted slowly past the ship, its edges jagged where explosive forces had ripped it apart. The metal surface was blackened and scarred by weapons fire.

Nearby, the twisted frame of an engine assembly spun slowly through space.

Mateo reduced speed slightly.

"Easy now."

The ship glided carefully between the drifting fragments.

More wreckage appeared ahead.

Broken cargo containers.

Fragments of communication arrays.

The skeletal remains of what might once have been a small patrol craft.

No one spoke for a moment.

The storm flashes illuminated the debris field in brief bursts of cold light.

Dr. Lila Chen studied the scene through the viewport.

"Seven years of war," she said softly.

Torlan stood quietly beside the pilot's station.

The drifting wreckage told its own story.

Battles fought here.

Ships destroyed.

Lives lost.

The fragments moved slowly through the storm currents, silent reminders of the conflict that had turned this region into a dangerous frontier.

Samir watched the sensor display carefully.

"These wrecks have been drifting for years."

Mateo nodded.

"The storms keep them moving."

He guided the ship gently around a massive hull section floating ahead.

The torn metal structure rotated slowly, its internal framework exposed like the bones of a skeleton.

Alex studied the debris field on her console.

"There must have been dozens of battles here."

Torlan nodded slightly.

"The expanse became a natural battlefield."

Mateo steered the ship through a narrow gap between two drifting fragments.

Outside the viewport, another burst of storm energy illuminated the debris field.

For a moment the broken ships shone brightly in the stormlight.

Then the darkness returned.

Mateo glanced ahead.

"Debris density decreasing."

Samir confirmed the reading.

"Clear path forming."

The ship continued forward.

Behind them, the silent graveyard of the war slowly faded back into the storm clouds.

Ahead lay deeper regions of the Kardrin Expanse.

And the patrol fleets that still guarded it.

Patrol Signal

The storm clouds around *The Long Path* glowed faintly as the ship continued deeper into the Kardrin Expanse.

Charged particles drifted past the viewport like glowing mist, occasionally flashing with brief arcs of energy as the storm currents shifted around them.

Inside the bridge, the crew remained focused.

Samir watched the sensor console carefully, filtering through the interference created by the storm.

The readings flickered constantly.

Storm noise.

Debris reflections.

Ion turbulence.

Then a small signal appeared.

Samir leaned forward.

"Contact."

Mateo immediately reduced engine output.

"What kind?"

Samir studied the signal pattern.

"Military patrol beacon… long range."

The bridge became very quiet.

Torlan stepped closer to the sensor display.

"Distance?"

Samir adjusted the filters again.

"Approximately forty thousand kilometers."

Mateo lowered the engine power further.

The steady vibration of the ship softened as the thrust dropped.

"We'll drift for a while."

Alex studied the navigation map.

"The storm interference should mask our emissions."

Samir nodded.

"Assuming the interference remains strong."

Outside the viewport, a bright flash of storm energy illuminated the surrounding clouds.

Torlan watched the sensor readings carefully.

"Maintain minimal power."

Mateo nodded.

"Understood."

The ship drifted quietly through the storm corridor.

The engines produced only the faintest thrust, barely enough to maintain their heading.

Samir tracked the patrol signal.

"It's moving across our sector."

The signal strength increased slightly.

Alex folded her arms.

"That's closer than I would prefer."

Mateo kept his hands lightly on the controls.

"If they're scanning through this storm, they'll be fighting their own sensors."

Samir nodded.

"Storm interference is heavy."

Torlan remained calm.

"Hold position within the corridor."

The ship continued drifting through the charged particle clouds.

For several long moments the patrol signal remained on the sensors.

Then slowly…

It began to fade.

Samir watched the readings carefully.

"Signal strength decreasing."

Mateo allowed himself a small breath.

"Looks like they're moving away."

A few seconds later the signal disappeared completely.

Samir leaned back slightly.

"Contact lost."

The tension on the bridge eased.

Mateo increased engine output again.

The ship resumed its slow forward movement through the storm corridor.

Alex glanced at Torlan.

"That was close."

Torlan nodded once.

"The storms are working as expected."

Outside the viewport, the glowing storm clouds continued to shift and swirl around the ship.

For now, the corridor still hid them.

But deeper inside the expanse, more patrols would be waiting.

The Corridor

The storm currents thickened around *The Long Path.*

Outside the forward viewport, glowing clouds of charged particles drifted slowly past the ship, illuminated by flashes of ion lightning deep within the storm belt. The region felt almost like a living ocean of light and shadow.

On the bridge, the navigation displays shifted as the storm patterns continued to evolve.

Samir adjusted the sensor filters again.

"Storm interference increasing," he reported. "Signal resolution is dropping."

Mateo leaned forward at the pilot's station.

"That's good news for us."

The navigation display began highlighting new storm boundaries forming ahead.

Torlan studied the patterns carefully.

The shifting storm bands moved almost exactly as his models had predicted.

He pointed toward a narrow region forming between two expanding storm currents.

"There."

Mateo zoomed the navigation map closer.

The passage appeared clearly now.

A narrow **storm shadow** where the charged particle density created heavy sensor distortion.

Mateo smiled slightly.

"You were right."

The corridor had formed.

Alex studied the display.

"It's even narrower than the simulation suggested."

Torlan nodded.

"Yes."

Mateo placed both hands firmly on the controls.

"All right."

He gently adjusted the ship's heading.

"Let's stay inside the storm shadow."

The ship slid deeper into the glowing corridor.

Outside the viewport, the storm clouds intensified, swirling slowly around the vessel like luminous fog.

The sensors flickered constantly as electromagnetic interference flooded the systems.

Samir monitored the displays carefully.

"We're nearly invisible in this interference."

Mateo nodded.

"That's the idea."

Torlan watched the storm currents carefully.

Everything was unfolding exactly as he had hoped.

For the moment.

Then Samir suddenly leaned forward.

"New signal detected."

The bridge fell silent.

Mateo glanced toward the sensor console.

"Another patrol?"

Samir studied the data.

The signal strength increased rapidly.

He adjusted the filters again.

His expression tightened.

"Multiple signals."

Alex looked up.

"How many?"

Samir watched the display for a moment.

Then he answered quietly.

"Several."

Mateo frowned.

"They shouldn't be this deep inside the storm belt."

Samir shook his head slightly.

"They're ahead of us."

Torlan stepped closer to the display.

"Distance?"

Samir answered without looking away from the screen.

"Closing."

The storm corridor ahead no longer looked empty.

Somewhere beyond the glowing clouds, several **patrol vessels** were moving through the expanse.

And *The Long Path* was heading directly toward them.

Chapter 14 — The Storm Corridor

Entering the Corridor

The storm clouds around *The Long Path* thickened as the ship pushed deeper into the Kardrin Expanse.

Outside the viewport, arcs of blue-white energy flickered across enormous clouds of charged particles. The glowing storms shifted slowly, like great tides moving through space.

Inside the bridge, the displays were alive with movement.

Sensor readings fluctuated constantly as electromagnetic interference washed through the ship's instruments.

Samir Haddad leaned forward at the sensor console.

"Storm density increasing," he reported. "Signal interference levels are climbing."

Mateo studied the navigation screen.

The storm fronts appeared as vast drifting walls of charged particles, their boundaries constantly shifting as currents moved through the expanse.

He glanced toward Torlan.

"Where exactly is the corridor?"

Torlan stepped closer to the central display.

He compared the live storm readings with the storm cycle models he had memorized days earlier.

Two massive storm fronts were slowly moving toward one another.

Between them was a narrow region of lower turbulence.

Torlan pointed calmly at the display.

"Between the storm fronts."

Mateo leaned closer.

The highlighted region appeared only as a thin band across the navigation map.

"That space is very narrow."

Torlan nodded.

"Yes."

Alex watched the display carefully.

"If the storms shift even slightly, that corridor could close."

Torlan studied the storm patterns again.

The currents were moving exactly as he had predicted.

For the moment.

Mateo placed both hands firmly on the flight controls.

"All right."

He adjusted the ship's heading slightly.

The nose of *The Long Path* turned toward the narrow opening between the glowing storm fronts.

Outside the viewport, the charged clouds brightened as the ship approached.

Electric arcs flashed through the storm, illuminating the darkness in brief bursts of light.

Samir monitored the sensors.

"Interference increasing rapidly."

Mateo nodded.

"That means we're in the right place."

Torlan watched the storm movement with steady concentration.

"Maintain position between the fronts."

Mateo guided the ship carefully into the narrow corridor.

The moment the vessel crossed the invisible boundary, the sensors flickered violently as the storm interference intensified.

But the patrol detection systems outside the storm would now have great difficulty seeing them.

The ship slid deeper into the storm shadow.

The **Quiet Corridor** had opened.

And *The Long Path* was now inside it.

Turbulence

The moment *The Long Path* entered the corridor, the ship began to shudder.

Not violently at first—just a steady vibration through the hull as waves of charged particles rolled through the storm belt.

Outside the viewport, bright arcs of ion energy flashed across the clouds, briefly lighting the cockpit in pale blue light.

Mateo tightened his grip on the flight controls.

"Storm turbulence increasing."

The navigation display flickered again as the storm interference intensified.

Samir worked quickly at the sensor console.

"Signal distortion rising. I'm filtering out storm noise."

Alex held the navigation display steady as the data shifted across her screen.

"Course drifting half a degree port."

Mateo corrected immediately.

"Adjusting."

The ship responded with a slight roll as he steered through a calmer band between two turbulent currents.

The deck vibrated beneath their feet.

In engineering, Owen Tark's voice came over the intercom.

"Power levels fluctuating."

Mateo glanced toward the engineering display.

"How bad?"

"Manageable," Owen replied. "For now."

Another wave of charged particles swept across the ship.

The lights on the bridge dimmed briefly, then returned to normal.

Samir leaned closer to his console.

"If storm intensity increases any further, we may lose sensors completely."

Alex frowned.

"That would make navigation… difficult."

Torlan stood quietly behind the pilot's station, studying the storm patterns flowing across the displays.

He watched the shifting movement of the charged clouds.

The turbulence had increased exactly as expected.

But the pattern was already beginning to stabilize.

Torlan spoke calmly.

"It will stabilize in eight minutes."

Mateo glanced at him.

"You sound confident."

Torlan nodded once.

"The storm currents are aligning."

Another jolt ran through the ship.

Mateo guided the vessel carefully between two bright arcs of electrical discharge that flashed across the viewport.

"Let's hope you're right."

The crew watched the storm readings carefully.

Outside the ship, the glowing clouds churned with restless energy.

Inside the bridge, the ship continued forward—shaking, flickering, and pushing through the turbulent corridor.

Eight minutes suddenly felt like a very long time.

Debris Hazard

The turbulence gradually eased, but the sensor displays remained unstable.

The storm corridor around *The Long Path* glowed with shifting bands of charged particles. Every few seconds the viewport flashed with pale light as arcs of ion energy rippled through the clouds.

Samir adjusted the sensor filters again.

"New contacts ahead."

Mateo glanced at the display.

"Storm reflections?"

Samir shook his head.

"No. Solid objects."

Alex leaned closer to her console.

"How many?"

Samir expanded the scan.

The screen filled with small markers.

"Multiple fragments."

Torlan studied the pattern.

"Debris field."

Mateo frowned slightly.

"That figures."

The navigation display projected the drifting wreckage ahead.

Fragments of destroyed warships floated slowly through the storm currents.

Broken hull plates.

Twisted structural beams.

Sections of engine housings.

The storm had scattered them across the corridor like silent obstacles.

Mateo reduced speed slightly.

"Everyone keep an eye out."

Outside the viewport, the first piece of wreckage drifted past.

A jagged section of hull plating, scorched black and torn open by weapons fire, rotated slowly through the glowing storm light.

Samir tracked the objects carefully.

"Debris density increasing."

Mateo guided the ship slightly to starboard.

The vessel slid past another fragment—this one the twisted remains of a communications array.

Alex gripped the edge of the navigation console as a large shape drifted suddenly across the forward view.

Mateo reacted instantly.

He rolled the ship gently to avoid the spinning object.

The fragment passed just beneath the hull.

Alex exhaled slowly.

"Please tell me that wasn't important."

Owen's voice came over the intercom from engineering.

"It used to be."

A faint smile passed across the bridge.

The moment of humor eased the tension briefly.

But the debris field continued to thicken.

Another massive piece of wreckage appeared ahead—an entire engine structure drifting sideways through the storm.

Mateo adjusted the ship's attitude again.

"Hold steady."

The ship slipped through a narrow opening between two floating fragments.

For a moment the storm light illuminated the broken shapes around them.

A silent graveyard of war.

Torlan watched the wreckage carefully.

Each fragment moved slowly through the charged clouds, pushed by the storm currents that had carried them here.

Samir checked the sensors again.

"Debris density decreasing ahead."

Mateo nodded.

"Good."

The ship cleared the last cluster of wreckage and returned to open space inside the storm corridor.

But the storm currents were still shifting.

And the path ahead remained uncertain.

Patrol Ships Nearby

The storm corridor grew darker as the charged clouds thickened around *The Long Path*.

Outside the viewport, glowing currents of ionized particles drifted slowly past the hull, occasionally erupting into bright flashes of electrical discharge that illuminated the ship for an instant before fading back into shadow.

Inside the bridge, the crew remained focused on the sensors.

Samir watched the signal filters carefully as waves of electromagnetic interference swept across the instruments.

Then a faint pattern appeared.

He leaned forward.

"Contact."

Mateo glanced toward the console.

"Storm reflection?"

Samir shook his head slowly.

"No."

He adjusted the filters again.

The signal strengthened slightly.

"Multiple signals."

The bridge grew quiet.

Alex studied the navigation display.

"How close?"

Samir expanded the scan area.

Several faint markers appeared across the sensor map.

"Military patrol vessels."

Mateo frowned.

"That's sooner than I expected."

Torlan stepped closer to the display.

"Distance?"

"Approximately thirty thousand kilometers."

Mateo reduced engine output immediately.

The steady vibration of the ship softened as thrust dropped.

"Dropping to minimal power."

Torlan nodded.

"Good."

Alex watched the navigation display.

"We'll drift inside the storm shadow."

Outside the ship, the glowing storm clouds thickened as the corridor narrowed around them.

Samir continued monitoring the patrol signals.

"They're scanning nearby sectors."

Mateo rested his hands lightly on the controls, allowing the ship to glide forward with minimal thrust.

"Let's hope the storms are as blinding to them as we expect."

Another flash of ion lightning lit the viewport.

The ship drifted silently through the glowing clouds.

Seconds passed.

Then minutes.

Samir watched the signal strength carefully.

The patrol markers moved slowly across the display.

One of them shifted slightly closer.

Alex held her breath.

Mateo kept the ship perfectly steady.

No sudden movements.

No strong engine emissions.

Just drifting inside the storm's interference field.

Finally Samir spoke again.

"Signal strength decreasing."

The patrol markers began moving away across the map.

Another minute passed.

Then another.

Samir leaned back slightly.

"They're leaving the sector."

The tension on the bridge eased.

Mateo slowly increased engine output again.

The ship resumed its careful forward movement through the corridor.

Torlan watched the storm patterns quietly.

The corridor had protected them once.

But deeper inside the expanse, the storms would grow stronger.

And the patrol fleets would grow more numerous.

The Corridor Narrows

The storm corridor ahead began to change.

On the navigation display, the two massive storm fronts that formed the corridor slowly drifted closer together. What had been a narrow but manageable path was now becoming something far tighter.

Mateo leaned forward, studying the display.

"That's not ideal."

Alex glanced at the shifting map.

"The corridor is closing."

Outside the viewport the storm clouds thickened, glowing with streaks of blue-white lightning that flashed across the charged particles surrounding the ship.

The vessel shuddered slightly as another turbulent wave brushed the hull.

Samir watched the sensors carefully.

"Storm intensity increasing again."

Mateo adjusted the ship's course slightly to remain inside the corridor.

But the available space was shrinking.

"We're running out of room."

Torlan stepped closer to the navigation display.

The storm fronts were shifting faster now.

Charged particle currents were bending the corridor into a narrow curve that did not match the original navigation model.

Alex frowned.

"The route we planned won't hold."

Torlan studied the patterns rapidly.

His eyes moved across several storm simulations on the display.

He compared them with the storm movement cycles he had memorized during his days of preparation.

Several possible outcomes flashed through his mind.

Storm drift patterns.

Electromagnetic current flows.

The position of nearby debris clusters.

Most of the possible paths collapsed immediately.

But one possibility remained.

Torlan pointed at the display.

"Alter course two degrees starboard."

Mateo glanced at the new path.

"That puts us closer to the storm wall."

"Yes."

Mateo studied the shifting currents again.

The path was extremely narrow—but it existed.

"All right."

He adjusted the controls.

The ship shifted slightly to starboard, sliding closer to the glowing storm front.

Outside the viewport, arcs of energy flashed dangerously close to the hull.

The storm clouds swirled around the vessel like a river of light.

Samir monitored the sensors.

"Interference levels rising."

Mateo nodded.

"That means we're still hidden."

The ship continued forward through the tightening corridor.

For several long moments no one spoke.

Then slowly, the storm fronts began drifting apart again.

Alex exhaled quietly.

"The corridor is widening."

Mateo relaxed slightly at the controls.

"That was close."

Torlan continued watching the storm patterns.

The path had held.

For now.

Inside his thoughts, he remembered something Dr. Ziv had once told him during a difficult navigation exercise.

"The quiet mind sees the farthest."

Panic closed the mind.

Calm observation revealed the path.

And for the moment, the path still existed.

Emerging From the Storm

The storm turbulence began to fade.

Gradually the violent flickering on the sensor displays settled into steady readings again. The charged clouds around *The Long Path* still glowed faintly, but the violent electrical arcs that had filled the sky moments earlier were now growing more distant.

Mateo eased his grip on the flight controls.

"Storm intensity dropping."

Outside the viewport the dense clouds of charged particles slowly thinned. The glowing storm wall drifted behind the ship as the corridor widened into calmer space.

Samir ran a fresh sensor sweep.

"Electromagnetic interference decreasing."

Alex studied the navigation map.

"We're clearing the storm belt."

Another minute passed.

Then the sensor displays stabilized completely.

Samir leaned back slightly.

"No debris fields detected ahead."

Mateo exhaled quietly.

"That's a welcome change."

The ship emerged fully from the glowing storm corridor.

Behind them, the massive ion storm front continued to roll slowly through the Kardrin Expanse like a distant ocean of light.

Mateo glanced toward Torlan.

"I think we made it."

Torlan studied the star map carefully.

The storm belt now lay behind them.

But the journey was not finished.

He shook his head slightly.

"We are halfway."

Alex looked at the display.

"Havenfall is still several hours away."

Mateo leaned back in his seat.

"Well," he said, "halfway through a war zone is still progress."

The crew allowed themselves a brief moment of relief.

Then Samir ran a long-range scan of the forward sector.

The sensors swept through the dark space ahead.

He frowned slightly.

Mateo noticed.

"Something wrong?"

Samir adjusted the scan again.

A faint signal appeared on the display.

"I'm detecting a transmission."

Mateo looked toward him.

"Another patrol?"

Samir studied the signal pattern carefully.

Then he shook his head.

"No."

A small smile crossed his face.

"A colony beacon."

Alex leaned forward.

"Havenfall?"

Samir nodded.

"That's the signal."

For the first time since entering the Kardrin Expanse, the crew could see their destination clearly on the navigation display.

They had crossed the storm corridor.

They had avoided the patrol fleets.

And now, somewhere ahead in the darkness, the settlers of **Havenfall** were waiting.

Chapter 15 — Havenfall

First View of Havenfall

The faint signal of the **Havenfall colony beacon** pulsed steadily on the sensor display.

After hours inside the storms of the Kardrin Expanse, the signal felt almost comforting.

Samir adjusted the long-range scanner.

"Beacon confirmed," he said. "Signal strength increasing."

Mateo leaned forward in the pilot's chair.

"That means we're close."

Outside the viewport, a pale green world slowly grew larger.

The planet turned quietly beneath them, clouds drifting across wide continents of forest and open plains.

Torlan stepped closer to the forward window.

"Bring us into orbital approach."

Mateo nodded and adjusted the ship's course.

The ship descended through the upper atmosphere, and the planet's surface began to sharpen into clear detail.

Samir switched the display to a visual scan.

"There," he said.

A marker appeared across the landscape.

The bridge lights dimmed slightly as the forward display magnified the view.

Below them stretched a broad valley surrounded by distant mountain ridges. A river wound across the plains like a silver ribbon, cutting through deep forests that spread across the land.

It was a beautiful world.

Quiet.

Untouched.

But as the display zoomed further, the colony itself came into view.

The settlement was small.

A handful of structures clustered around a rough landing field.

Several greenhouses stood nearby, their transparent domes reflecting sunlight. A few narrow roads wound between the buildings, connecting the farms to the central settlement.

Compared to the vast wilderness surrounding it, Havenfall looked fragile.

Mateo studied the view silently.

"They really are alone out here."

No neighboring cities.

No orbital stations.

Just one small colony surrounded by thousands of kilometers of wilderness.

Torlan watched the valley below.

For a moment he said nothing.

Then he spoke quietly.

"Not anymore."

The ship continued its slow descent toward the valley.

Below them, the settlers of Havenfall were about to learn that help had arrived.

Landing at the Colony

The valley of Havenfall grew larger beneath *The Long Path* as the ship descended through the lower atmosphere.

The broad landing field came into view—a flattened stretch of packed earth just beyond the main cluster of buildings. Several small cargo pads had been marked out with faded guide lights, though only one of them appeared to have been used recently.

Mateo studied the approach carefully.

"Landing field looks stable," he said. "But not exactly busy."

Alex glanced at the surface scanners.

"That may change in a moment."

Samir zoomed the forward camera slightly.

Movement appeared near the colony structures.

Doors opened.

Several settlers stepped outside.

More followed.

Mateo smiled faintly.

"They see us."

Torlan watched the growing crowd through the viewport.

People were gathering near the landing area, shielding their eyes from the sunlight as they looked toward the sky.

Some stood still in disbelief.

Others pointed upward.

The ship's engines shifted tone as Mateo adjusted the descent.

Dust began to swirl across the landing field.

The settlers moved closer, forming a loose group near the center of the pad.

As the ship dropped lower, more people arrived from the nearby buildings.

Some carried tools.

A few wore worn work jackets covered in dust from the fields.

Children appeared among them as well, standing slightly behind the adults but staring upward with wide curiosity.

Mateo eased the ship lower.

"Final descent."

The landing thrusters engaged with a deep rumble.

Dust and loose soil lifted into the air as the engines slowed the ship's fall.

For several seconds the settlers stood perfectly still.

Watching.

Waiting.

Then *The Long Path* touched down.

The landing struts absorbed the impact with a gentle thud.

The engines powered down gradually, their rumble fading into quiet.

Outside the viewport, the dust cloud slowly settled across the landing field.

For a moment the valley was silent.

The settlers stared at the ship as if confirming that it was real.

Then someone began cheering.

Others joined.

The sound spread across the landing field as relief and excitement swept through the crowd.

Alex smiled as she watched them.

"They knew what that ship meant."

Torlan nodded quietly.

"Yes."

Outside, the settlers of Havenfall celebrated.

Help had arrived.

Meeting Mara Ellison

The cargo ramp of *The Long Path* lowered slowly with a soft mechanical hum.

Outside, the settlers waited just beyond the base of the ramp. The dust stirred by the landing thrusters had settled now, leaving the small landing field quiet again except for the low ticking sounds of the ship's cooling engines.

Torlan stepped forward first.

Behind him came Alex, Mateo, Dr. Chen, Samir, and Owen Tark.

The settlers watched carefully as the crew reached the bottom of the ramp.

For a moment no one spoke.

Then one woman stepped forward from the group.

She carried herself with the steady confidence of someone used to making difficult decisions. Her clothing was practical—work boots, a weathered jacket, and gloves tucked into her belt.

Her eyes studied the ship and the crew with calm focus.

"Mara Ellison," she said.

Torlan inclined his head politely.

"Torlan Tarsen."

She glanced briefly at the ship behind them.

"You made it through the Kardrin Expanse."

Her tone held quiet respect more than surprise.

Torlan nodded once.

"Yes."

For a moment Mara simply studied him.

Frontier settlements learned quickly that promises meant little until work began.

But the cargo vessel standing behind Torlan told its own story.

She looked toward the open cargo bay.

"You brought supplies."

Alex stepped forward.

"Medical equipment, agricultural systems, water drilling equipment, replacement power units."

Mara exhaled slowly.

"That will help."

She looked back at the gathered settlers.

Relief showed on several faces now, though most remained quiet and composed.

Frontier people had learned long ago not to celebrate too early.

Mara turned back toward Torlan.

"We weren't sure anyone could reach us."

Torlan glanced across the valley.

"The storms created an opportunity."

Mara nodded.

"Then we are grateful you saw it."

Behind her, several settlers were already looking toward the cargo ramp with cautious hope.

Mara stepped aside and gestured toward the settlement.

"You should see Havenfall."

Torlan nodded.

"We would be glad to."

As the group began walking toward the colony buildings, the settlers followed closely behind.

The ship had arrived.

Now the real work could begin.

The Colony Tour

Mara Ellison led Torlan and Alex along a narrow dirt road that wound through the center of the settlement.

Up close, Havenfall looked even smaller than it had from orbit.

A cluster of sturdy but weathered buildings stood around the central landing field—storage sheds, a few living quarters, and several utility structures connected by worn pathways.

The air smelled faintly of soil and growing crops.

Beyond the buildings stretched long rows of farmland where settlers worked quietly among the fields.

But signs of strain were visible everywhere.

One of the colony's **water tanks** stood near the main well structure. The metal casing showed several recent patch repairs, and a small maintenance platform had been assembled beside it.

Mara noticed Torlan studying it.

"That system has been giving us trouble."

Alex looked closer.

"How serious?"

Mara folded her arms.

"Serious enough that we've been rationing water."

Torlan nodded thoughtfully.

They continued walking.

A short distance away stood several **greenhouse domes**. The transparent panels glowed softly in the afternoon sunlight, though several sections had been patched with mismatched materials.

"Storm damage?" Alex asked.

"Last season," Mara replied.

"We repaired what we could."

Inside one of the greenhouses, settlers worked carefully among rows of young plants. The crops were healthy, but the equipment supporting the irrigation system looked old and worn.

Mara continued toward a smaller building near the center of the colony.

"This is our clinic."

The door opened as they approached.

Dr. Lila Chen had already arrived ahead of them.

Inside the clinic, several settlers stood nearby while she unpacked medical supplies from one of the cargo containers that had already been delivered.

The room was modest—one treatment bed, a small diagnostic scanner, and a few shelves containing medical supplies.

Most of those shelves were nearly empty.

Dr. Chen looked up as Torlan entered.

"You arrived just in time."

Mara nodded toward the shelves.

"That's what we were afraid of."

Torlan studied the room quietly.

The colony had survived so far.

But just barely.

Outside again, they continued along the path toward a cluster of agricultural machines parked beside the fields.

Several pieces of equipment sat idle.

One harvester had been partially dismantled for repairs.

Another irrigation unit looked as though it had been patched together from spare parts.

Mara rested her hands on the railing beside the equipment.

"We've been keeping everything running as best we can."

Alex glanced toward the distant fields.

"How close were you to shutting things down?"

Mara considered the question carefully.

"Another year without supplies…"

She looked across the valley.

"…and we might not have made it."

Torlan followed her gaze.

The valley was beautiful.

But survival here required more than beauty.

It required tools.

Supplies.

And people willing to keep going even when conditions grew difficult.

Now, at least, Havenfall had help.

Cargo Unloading

Back at the landing field, the cargo ramp of *The Long Path* had become the center of activity.

The first supply containers were already moving down the ramp.

Settlers worked alongside the ship's crew, guiding the heavy crates onto small transport carts that rolled across the packed earth toward the colony buildings.

Alex stood near the cargo bay entrance with a logistics tablet in her hand.

"Medical supplies first," she said.

Two settlers carefully lifted a sealed container marked **CLINICAL EQUIPMENT** onto a cart.

Dr. Chen appeared beside them almost immediately.

"That one goes to the clinic."

The settlers nodded and quickly pushed the cart toward the medical building.

Another crate followed.

ANTIBIOTIC STORAGE

Dr. Chen watched it disappear across the landing field.

"That will help."

Behind them, Owen Tark supervised the unloading of several large mechanical crates.

He studied the labels carefully.

"Water drilling equipment," he said.

A group of settlers gathered around the container with interest.

One of them ran a hand across the metal casing.

"We haven't had equipment like this since the original supply ships stopped coming."

Owen nodded.

"Well, you do now."

Nearby, a second loader lowered a large container onto the ramp.

The label read:

AGRICULTURAL SYSTEMS

Mara Ellison stepped closer.

"What's inside?"

Alex glanced at her tablet.

"Replacement irrigation pumps, soil monitors, and new planting equipment."

Mara allowed herself a small smile.

"That will save us weeks of repairs."

The unloading continued steadily.

Crates of **water filtration units**.

Replacement **power generators**.

Emergency **ration packs**.

Each one disappeared quickly into the hands of settlers who had been waiting months for these supplies.

Torlan stood near the base of the ramp, watching the work.

The activity across the landing field had transformed the mood of the colony.

Where earlier there had been cautious uncertainty, now there was visible relief.

One of the older settlers paused beside Torlan.

The man studied the cargo containers being unloaded.

"We thought we might not make it through the year."

Torlan looked toward the busy landing field.

The settlers worked quickly but carefully, treating every crate as something valuable.

"You have survived this long," Torlan said quietly.

The man nodded.

"Barely."

He looked toward the cargo ramp again.

"But now we might actually have a chance."

Torlan watched the settlers continue their work.

The supplies they had carried through the storms of the Kardrin Expanse were already changing the future of Havenfall.

The mission had reached its destination.

And the valley was beginning to breathe again.

Evening at Havenfall

Evening settled gently across the valley.

The sun dipped behind the distant mountains, casting long golden shadows across the fields surrounding Havenfall. A soft breeze moved through the grasslands, carrying the scent of soil and growing crops.

From the ridge above the settlement, the colony looked peaceful.

Small lights began appearing one by one as the settlers powered up their homes and work buildings. The warm glow spread slowly across the valley floor like scattered stars.

Torlan stood quietly near the edge of the ridge, watching the colony below.

Beside him, Alex folded her arms against the cooling evening air.

The sounds of the settlement carried faintly up the hillside.

Voices.

The distant rumble of machinery.

Laughter.

Work was still continuing even as darkness approached.

Alex studied the lights below.

"For the first time in months," she said softly, "they probably feel like they can breathe again."

Torlan nodded.

"Yes."

Down in the valley, settlers moved between the buildings carrying equipment and supplies from the ship. The arrival of the cargo had turned the entire settlement into a place of activity.

Alex watched the scene quietly.

"Do you think the war fleets will come here?"

Torlan looked toward the distant horizon where the mountains rose against the fading sky.

"If they do," he said calmly, "we will be ready."

Alex considered that for a moment.

Then she nodded.

Below them, the small colony continued its work beneath the evening sky.

Havenfall had survived because its people refused to give up.

Torlan thought of something Dr. Ziv had once told him during his years of study on Cyrion.

"A village stands because its people stand."

The settlers of Havenfall had stood together through months of hardship.

Now, at last, they had help.

Footsteps approached from behind them.

Mara Ellison walked up the ridge path and joined them.

She studied the valley for a moment before speaking.

"The supplies are already making a difference."

Torlan nodded.

"I'm glad."

Mara crossed her arms thoughtfully.

"There's one more problem we haven't solved."

Alex glanced toward her.

"What's that?"

"Our communications system."

Mara looked toward the valley floor.

"It was damaged months ago during a storm."

Torlan listened carefully.

"We've repaired what we could," Mara continued, "but the long-range transmitter never worked properly again."

Alex frowned slightly.

"That means you have no early warning."

Mara shook her head.

"If someone came here… we wouldn't know until they arrived."

Torlan considered the valley below.

Then he looked toward the ridge where they stood.

"Is there high ground nearby?"

Mara gestured toward the hills surrounding them.

"This ridge is the highest point overlooking the valley."

Torlan nodded once.

"Then tomorrow we build an antenna."

Mara looked at him with quiet appreciation.

"That would help."

Torlan studied the valley one last time.

The settlers of Havenfall had fought hard to survive.

Now the colony would become stronger.

And tomorrow, they would begin building something new.

Chapter 16 — Helping Havenfall

The Medical Clinic

The small clinic at Havenfall had never been so busy.

Inside the modest building, settlers waited quietly along the walls while **Dr. Lila Chen** organized the newly delivered medical supplies. Containers that had arrived only hours earlier were now opened across the room—rows of sealed antibiotic kits, sterile surgical instruments, and compact diagnostic scanners.

The clinic's shelves, once nearly empty, were slowly filling again.

Dr. Chen moved quickly but calmly between the tables.

"Next patient," she said.

An older settler stepped forward, removing his worn hat as he approached the examination table.

Dr. Chen checked the portable scanner and ran it slowly across his arm.

The screen displayed a clear infection reading.

She nodded.

"That's treatable."

The man exhaled in relief.

"For weeks they've been telling me to just keep it clean and hope."

Dr. Chen prepared a small injection.

"You were rationing antibiotics."

He nodded.

"We had to."

She administered the medicine carefully.

"That will begin working within a few hours."

The man studied the rows of newly delivered medical supplies behind her.

Then he looked at her with quiet gratitude.

"You arrived just in time."

Dr. Chen smiled gently.

"That's what we were hoping."

Across the room, several settlers were assisting her by organizing equipment and preparing examination areas for the next patients.

The clinic had transformed from a nearly empty room into a functioning medical center again.

Torlan stepped quietly into the doorway, observing the activity.

Alex stood beside him.

"It looks different in here already."

Torlan nodded.

"Yes."

Inside the room, the tension that had once filled the clinic was slowly giving way to relief.

Settlers who had postponed treatment for weeks were finally receiving care.

Dr. Chen moved to the next patient.

A young mother holding a small child stepped forward.

The child had been coughing heavily.

Dr. Chen ran the diagnostic scanner across the child's chest.

"Respiratory infection," she said gently.

She prepared a small dose of medication and handed the mother a sealed container.

"Use this tonight. The fever should break by morning."

The woman nodded gratefully.

"Thank you."

Torlan watched quietly from the doorway.

The supplies they had carried through the storms of the Kardrin Expanse were already changing lives.

Alex looked around the clinic.

"This is only the first day."

Torlan nodded.

"And already it matters."

Outside the clinic, the colony continued its work.

But inside, Havenfall had begun to heal.

Repairing Agricultural Systems

The fields of Havenfall stretched across the valley floor in long green rows.

From a distance the farms looked healthy, but up close the strain on the colony's equipment was obvious. Several irrigation pipes had been patched repeatedly, and one of the small tractors sat partially dismantled beside a storage shed.

A group of settlers had gathered around a large **irrigation pump assembly** that had stopped working weeks earlier.

Torlan knelt beside the machinery while Owen Tark examined the replacement components from the cargo shipment.

Owen wiped his hands on a cloth and pointed toward the pump housing.

"The motor's burned out," he said. "We'll replace the whole unit."

One of the farmers nodded.

"We've been rotating the fields just to keep the crops alive."

Alex checked the supply manifest on her tablet.

"The new pumps should double your water flow."

The farmer looked relieved.

"That would save the harvest."

Owen opened the replacement crate and removed the new pump motor.

It was heavier than it looked.

Two of the settlers stepped forward to help move it into position beside the irrigation frame.

They lifted together.

The motor shifted slightly—but barely moved.

One of the farmers frowned.

"Hold on."

Torlan stepped forward.

"Allow me."

He bent down, grasped the base of the pump housing, and lifted one side of the heavy unit smoothly into place.

The farmers paused.

The motor had weighed enough that two of them had struggled to move it.

Torlan held it steady while Owen secured the mounting bolts.

"Easy," Owen said, tightening the fasteners.

The farmers exchanged surprised glances.

One of them finally spoke.

"You're the company owner?"

Torlan nodded calmly.

"Yes."

The farmer studied him for a moment.

Then he asked,

"And you're helping install irrigation pumps?"

Torlan stepped back once the motor was secured.

"Today I'm a laborer."

A few of the farmers smiled.

Owen finished tightening the final bolt and stood up.

"All right," he said.

He tapped the control switch.

The pump motor hummed to life.

Water surged through the irrigation pipes and flowed across the fields again.

The farmers watched the water spreading through the channels.

One of them laughed softly.

"That sound is beautiful."

Torlan looked across the fields.

The crops would survive now.

And Havenfall's future looked a little more secure.

The Water Wells

The drilling site sat near the edge of the valley where the ground sloped gently toward a line of low hills.

Several settlers had already cleared the area, and the new **water drilling equipment** from *The Long Path* had been assembled into a sturdy metal frame above the test site.

Engineer **Owen Tark** stood beside the control unit studying the assembly.

"This will work," he said. "But we'll need to anchor the frame properly before we begin drilling."

A few settlers carried heavy support brackets into position while others secured the power lines running back toward the colony generators.

Torlan stepped forward and helped guide one of the large stabilizing beams into place.

The metal frame rose slowly as the supports locked into position.

Owen checked the alignment using a handheld scanner.

"Good," he said.

He looked toward the drilling tower above them.

"Havenfall's current wells are shallow."

One of the settlers nodded.

"We hit rock before we reached a stable water layer."

Owen pointed toward the new drill assembly.

"This unit can go deeper."

He ran a few quick calculations on the control panel.

"If the geological readings are accurate, we should reach a stronger aquifer."

Torlan studied the surrounding terrain.

The valley floor had clearly been shaped by ancient water flows long ago. The deeper groundwater reserves were likely still there—hidden beneath layers of rock.

"Begin drilling," Owen said.

The drill motor powered up with a low mechanical rumble.

The long drill shaft began turning slowly as it pressed into the earth.

Dust and small fragments of rock spilled away from the drilling head as the machine pushed deeper into the ground.

The settlers watched carefully.

For months they had worried about the long-term survival of their water supply.

Now, for the first time, they had equipment capable of solving the problem.

Owen monitored the drilling speed.

"Rock layer starting."

The drill vibrated slightly as it cut through the harder material.

Torlan stepped forward and helped stabilize one of the support braces as the machine pushed deeper.

Owen glanced toward him.

"I should hire you for engineering work."

Torlan smiled faintly.

"I prefer simpler jobs."

Several of the settlers laughed quietly.

The drill continued its slow descent.

Minutes passed.

Then suddenly the drill shaft shuddered.

A low gurgling sound echoed from deep below the surface.

Owen watched the pressure gauge.

"Water layer."

The drill punched through the final rock barrier.

A surge of groundwater flowed upward through the bore shaft and spilled across the containment basin.

The settlers erupted in cheers.

One of them leaned over the edge of the basin, watching the fresh water filling the reservoir.

"We haven't seen flow like that in years."

Torlan watched the water rising slowly in the basin.

Havenfall had survived through determination.

Now it had something even more important.

Security for the future.

The Community Meal

That evening the settlers gathered near the center of the colony.

A long wooden table had been assembled beside the main storage building, and several lanterns hung from nearby posts, casting a warm glow across the open space. The air carried the smell of simple cooking—fresh bread, roasted vegetables, and stew simmering slowly over portable heaters.

It was not a grand meal.

But it was shared gladly.

Members of the crew from *The Long Path* sat among the settlers as food was passed along the table.

Mateo Rios accepted a bowl of stew and examined it with interest.

"This smells better than most station food."

One of the settlers laughed.

"That's because it didn't come from a machine."

Mateo took a bite and nodded approvingly.

"I believe you're right."

Across the table, Dr. Lila Chen spoke with several settlers who had visited the clinic earlier that day. The new medical supplies had already allowed her to begin treatments that had been impossible only a day before.

Nearby, Owen Tark was deep in conversation with two farmers about irrigation systems and pump maintenance.

At the center of the table, Mara Ellison sat with Torlan and Alex.

The settlers had begun sharing stories.

"How long ago did you arrive here?" Alex asked.

One of the older settlers leaned back thoughtfully.

"Almost nine years now."

He gestured toward the valley.

"When we first landed, this place was nothing but wilderness."

Another settler nodded.

"No roads. No wells. Just the landing field and a few supply crates."

Mara added quietly,

"We built everything else."

Alex looked out across the dark valley.

The scattered lights of Havenfall glowed softly beneath the evening sky.

"That must have taken courage."

One of the farmers smiled.

"More stubbornness than courage."

Laughter moved around the table.

Torlan listened quietly as the settlers continued describing their early years.

Storms that damaged the first shelters.

Equipment failures that forced them to improvise repairs.

Months when supply ships arrived late—or not at all.

But through every story, one theme remained constant.

They had refused to abandon the colony.

Alex leaned slightly toward Torlan.

"These people are remarkable."

Torlan nodded.

"Yes."

Across the table, Mara watched the crew carefully.

"You didn't have to come here," she said.

Torlan met her gaze calmly.

"But we did."

For a moment Mara studied him.

Then she nodded once.

"And Havenfall is better for it."

The meal continued beneath the lantern light.

For the first time in months, the settlers of Havenfall were able to relax.

Not because their problems had disappeared.

But because they were no longer facing them alone.

The Communications Problem

The evening meal ended slowly as the settlers drifted back toward their homes and work areas. The lanterns continued to glow softly around the small gathering space while the valley grew quiet again.

Torlan, Alex, and Mara Ellison walked together toward the edge of the settlement.

From there the valley could be seen clearly even in the fading light. Small farm lights dotted the fields where settlers continued tending irrigation lines and equipment.

Mara folded her arms as she studied the distant hills.

"There's one problem we haven't solved yet."

Torlan listened.

"Our long-range communications system failed several months ago," she continued. "A storm destroyed the main relay tower."

Alex looked surprised.

"You have no early warning system?"

Mara shook her head.

"None."

She pointed toward the valley floor where several farming areas stretched outward from the colony center.

"If ships approach the planet, we won't know until they enter the atmosphere."

Torlan considered this quietly.

"That means you cannot warn settlers working in distant fields."

"Exactly," Mara said.

"And we cannot contact nearby trade routes either. Even if help passed nearby, we would have no way to signal them."

Alex glanced back toward the colony buildings.

"How were you managing before the tower failed?"

"We had a ridge antenna," Mara explained. "High ground above the valley allowed us to broadcast across the entire region."

She pointed toward a steep ridge rising beyond the settlement.

The dark outline of the rocky ridge cut across the skyline.

"The storm damaged the tower completely. The winds up there are stronger than anything down here."

Torlan studied the ridge carefully.

The height would allow wide signal coverage.

The winds would make construction difficult.

But not impossible.

"Is there access to the top?" he asked.

"A narrow trail," Mara said. "It's steep, but it's the only path."

Alex followed Torlan's gaze up the slope.

"That would be a difficult place to build anything."

Torlan nodded slowly.

"Perhaps."

He continued studying the terrain, mentally measuring distances and angles the way he had studied star charts earlier in the journey.

A ridge antenna could solve several problems at once.

Early warning.

Regional communication.

Emergency signaling.

Mara watched him carefully.

"You're thinking of rebuilding it."

Torlan turned toward her.

"Yes."

She looked surprised.

"That would take equipment we don't have."

Torlan gestured toward the landing field where *The Long Path* rested.

"We brought more than supplies."

Alex smiled slightly.

"Quite a lot more."

Torlan looked once more toward the ridge.

The wind moved across the upper rocks even now, visible in the shifting tree lines along the slope.

"A signal tower built there could monitor the entire valley," he said.

Mara nodded slowly.

"It could."

Torlan turned back toward the colony.

"Then tomorrow we begin planning."

The problem that had worried Havenfall for months suddenly seemed solvable.

The Ridge Plan

The next morning began early.

Soft sunlight spread across the valley as Torlan and Alex stood outside the operations building with a portable display unit. The screen projected a simple topographic map of the surrounding terrain.

Mara Ellison joined them a moment later.

"The ridge trail begins just beyond the northern fields," she said, pointing toward the map. "It's about a two-hour climb."

Torlan adjusted the display and zoomed in on the ridge.

The height advantage was clear. From that position a communications antenna could transmit signals across the entire valley and well beyond Havenfall's immediate region.

Alex studied the elevation lines.

"The signal range would be excellent."

Mara nodded.

"That's why we built the original tower there."

Torlan reviewed the terrain quietly.

The ridge rose sharply above the valley floor. Strong winds swept along the exposed rock formations near the summit. Any structure built there would need to be anchored securely.

"We'll need a lightweight tower frame," Torlan said.

Alex tapped the cargo inventory displayed on her tablet.

"We brought modular antenna sections and signal amplifiers. Those were originally intended for colony communications upgrades."

Torlan nodded.

"They will serve this purpose well."

Mara looked between them.

"You're certain the equipment can survive the winds?"

Torlan studied the ridge again.

"Yes."

Alex smiled slightly.

"That sounds like a Cyrion answer."

Torlan returned the faint smile.

"Perhaps."

He began sketching a rough construction layout on the display.

"The antenna tower can be anchored between these rock formations."

He marked several points on the ridge map.

"The natural stone will provide additional stability."

Mara studied the design carefully.

"If we can get the equipment up there."

Torlan looked toward the distant ridge rising above the valley.

"That is tomorrow's challenge."

Alex followed his gaze.

The slope looked steeper in the morning light.

"That climb won't be easy," she said.

Torlan answered calmly.

"Most worthwhile things are not."

The wind moved across the ridge again, bending the trees along the summit line.

Tomorrow the crew and settlers would climb that ridge together.

And Havenfall would gain the protection it had been missing.

Chapter 17 — The Ridge Antenna

"Every valley hides a purpose."
What appears ordinary may hold great value when carefully observed.
— Wisdom of Cyrion

The Climb Begins

Morning light spread slowly across the valley of Havenfall.

The air was cool and clear, and a steady wind moved through the tall grass surrounding the settlement. Above the colony the ridge rose sharply, its rocky slopes catching the early sunlight.

At the base of the trail a small group gathered beside a stack of equipment cases.

The antenna components had been divided into manageable loads. Metal frame sections, signal amplifiers, and power units were secured onto **utility carriers** and heavy pack frames.

Mara Ellison checked the straps on one of the carriers.

"That ridge looks closer from the valley floor," Owen Tark said, squinting upward.

Alex followed his gaze.

From this angle the climb looked far steeper than it had the day before.

The narrow trail wound upward between outcroppings of rock before disappearing into a line of wind-bent trees near the summit.

Mara turned toward the group.

"The path stays narrow most of the way," she said. "Watch your footing."

Torlan lifted one of the largest equipment cases from the ground and secured it onto his shoulder harness.

The case held the **primary antenna control unit**—one of the heaviest pieces of equipment they had brought.

Alex noticed immediately.

"That's the control module," she said. "It's the heaviest one."

Torlan adjusted the straps calmly.

"It is manageable."

Owen raised an eyebrow.

"That case weighs more than my tool kit."

Torlan nodded slightly.

"It appears well constructed."

The settlers nearby exchanged amused glances.

Alex stepped closer.

"You know we could share that load," she said.

Torlan looked at her for a moment.

"We are."

She smiled despite herself.

Mara started up the trail.

"Let's move before the wind picks up."

The group followed her onto the rocky path.

Loose gravel shifted beneath their boots as they began the climb. The trail curved upward along the ridge face, sometimes narrowing to only a few feet wide.

Below them the colony quickly began to shrink.

The rooftops of Havenfall appeared smaller with every step.

The landing field where **The Long Path** rested gleamed faintly in the morning light.

Owen adjusted the straps on his tool pack.

"You realize," he said, breathing a little harder as they climbed, "this is exactly the sort of terrain engineers prefer to avoid."

Alex glanced back down the slope.

"Too late now."

Torlan continued climbing steadily at the front of the group.

The heavy equipment case did not seem to slow him.

Above them the ridge summit stood against the bright sky, where the wind moved constantly through the rocks and trees.

Somewhere up there they would build the antenna that Havenfall had been missing.

And the climb had only just begun.

Fighting the Wind

The trail grew steeper as the group climbed higher along the ridge.

Loose stones shifted beneath their boots, and the wind that had felt gentle in the valley now pushed steadily against them. The higher they climbed, the stronger it became.

Mara led the way with practiced confidence, stepping carefully along the narrow path.

"Stay close to the rock wall," she called back over her shoulder. "The wind is stronger near the outer edge."

The trail curved around a jagged outcrop where the ridge dropped sharply into the valley below.

Alex paused for a moment and glanced down.

From this height Havenfall looked small—just a cluster of buildings surrounded by green fields and winding streams.

Torlan continued climbing steadily behind Mara, the large equipment case balanced securely against his back.

Owen Tark adjusted the straps of the tool pack he carried.

"I'm beginning to see why your first antenna didn't survive the storm," he said.

Mara smiled slightly.

"That tower stood for five years."

Owen looked toward the ridge summit where the wind bent the trees sideways.

"I admire its optimism."

A powerful gust swept across the ridge just then.

The group instinctively leaned toward the rock wall as the wind roared past them.

Loose gravel rattled down the slope.

Samir steadied one of the equipment carriers as it shifted under the pressure of the wind.

"Maybe we should have installed the antenna down in the valley," he said.

Owen shook his head.

"Signals need height."

He looked up toward the summit again.

"Unfortunately, so does wind."

They continued climbing.

The path narrowed further, forcing them to move single file along a ledge where jagged stone rose on one side and open air stretched on the other.

Several times they stopped to secure the equipment straps or catch their breath.

Even with the cool morning air, the climb demanded steady effort.

Torlan remained calm and unhurried, placing each step carefully as the wind moved across the ridge.

Alex noticed that despite carrying the heaviest case, he seemed no more tired than when they had begun.

Another strong gust swept across the slope.

Everyone braced themselves again.

Owen wiped dust from his hands and looked up toward the summit.

"Perfect place for a communications tower," he muttered.

He paused.

"Terrible place to build one."

Alex laughed softly.

"That seems to be the theme of today."

The ridge above them rose another few hundred meters.

But now the summit was clearly visible.

They were getting close.

Reaching the Summit

The final stretch of the climb was the steepest.

The trail narrowed to little more than a rough line of stones leading upward between wind-twisted trees. The sound of the wind grew louder as the group approached the top of the ridge.

Mara reached the summit first and stepped onto a broad shelf of exposed rock.

She turned and waited while the others climbed the final few meters.

One by one they pulled themselves onto the ridge.

The wind struck them immediately.

Up here it moved in steady, powerful gusts that rushed across the rocks and bent the nearby trees almost sideways.

Owen set down his tool pack and took a deep breath.

"Well," he said, looking around, "the wind is exactly as advertised."

Alex stepped closer to the edge of the ridge.

The view stopped her for a moment.

The entire Havenfall valley spread out below them.

Rivers curved through green plains and patches of forest stretched across the distant hills. The colony itself appeared small from this height—just a handful of buildings clustered near the landing field.

The silver hull of *The Long Path* glinted faintly in the morning sunlight.

Mateo would be able to see the ridge from the ship's bridge.

Samir set down one of the equipment cases and opened a portable sensor unit.

He checked the signal readings carefully.

After a moment he smiled.

"This location is perfect."

He turned the display so the others could see.

"Signal strength from here will cover the entire valley—and several hundred kilometers beyond."

Mara looked relieved.

"That's exactly what we need."

Torlan walked slowly across the summit area, studying the terrain.

Large rock formations surrounded the ridge top, forming natural anchor points where the antenna structure could be secured.

He nodded once.

"This will work."

Owen crouched beside the equipment crates and began unpacking the antenna components.

Metal frame sections clanged lightly against the stone as he laid them out.

"Alright," he said, already slipping into his usual work rhythm. "Let's build ourselves a tower."

The group quickly organized the equipment.

Support braces were assembled.

Signal amplifiers were placed near the base location.

Power cables were uncoiled and prepared for connection.

Above them the wind continued to sweep across the ridge.

But the view made it clear why the original antenna had been placed here.

From this height Havenfall could finally see the stars again.

And any ship approaching the valley would now be visible long before it arrived.

The Tower Problem

The antenna structure rose slowly above the ridge.

Owen directed the assembly like a careful engineer conducting an orchestra.

"Support brace there… tighten that bolt… not that one, the other one."

Metal frame sections were locked together piece by piece until the tower mast lay across the rock surface, ready to be lifted into position.

The wind pushed constantly across the summit, tugging at loose cables and rattling the unfinished structure.

Owen studied the base anchors drilled into the rock.

"Alright," he said. "When we lift this, we do it together."

He pointed to the tower frame.

"Slow and steady. No sudden moves."

The group gathered around the mast.

Torlan took position near the center support beam.

Alex and two settlers moved to the base frame while Owen and Samir positioned themselves near the upper section.

"Ready," Owen said.

"Lift."

The antenna mast rose slowly from the rock.

For a moment everything seemed stable.

Then a powerful gust of wind rushed across the ridge.

The tower frame shuddered violently.

The upper section swung sideways.

"Hold it!" Owen shouted.

The metal structure lurched dangerously toward the edge of the ridge.

One of the base supports slipped across the rock.

Alex grabbed the frame to steady it, but the wind pushed again.

The tower began tipping.

Before anyone else could react, Torlan climbed quickly onto the support frame itself, gripping the central beam with both hands.

His weight shifted the structure back toward balance.

"Secure the base!" he called calmly.

Owen and the settlers immediately drove the anchor bolts deeper into the rock brackets.

Samir tightened the stabilizing cables as fast as his hands could move.

Another gust struck the ridge.

But this time the tower held.

Alex braced herself against the frame and shouted over the wind, "This was definitely not in the job description!"

Torlan steadied the mast as the final anchor bolts were secured.

"We can revise the description later," he replied calmly.

Owen finished tightening the last bracket.

"Tower base secured!"

Torlan stepped carefully down from the support beam.

The antenna mast now stood upright against the sky.

The wind still pulled against it, but the rock anchors held firm.

Owen wiped dust from his hands and looked up at the tower.

"Well," he said.

"That was exciting."

Alex looked at Torlan.

"You realize most people would have stepped away from a falling antenna tower."

Torlan adjusted the straps of his harness.

"That seemed inefficient."

Several of the settlers laughed.

Above them the newly raised tower swayed slightly in the wind.

But it stood solid against the ridge.

And Havenfall's new communications system was almost ready.

Activation

With the tower finally secured, the work shifted from construction to calibration.

Samir knelt beside the base console and opened the antenna control panel. A series of small indicator lights flickered to life as he connected the power units.

"Power routing… good."

He attached the final cable to the signal amplifier and looked toward Owen.

"Engineering, ready for system start."

Owen wiped dust from his hands and checked the tower braces one more time.

"All structural supports are holding."

He stepped back and nodded.

"Bring it online."

Samir tapped the activation panel.

For a moment nothing happened.

Then the antenna mast emitted a soft hum as current moved through the system. Small directional plates along the tower slowly adjusted themselves, aligning with orbital relay frequencies and deep-space scanning bands.

Samir watched the display closely.

"Signal amplification stabilizing… now."

The screen filled with data as the system began scanning the surrounding region.

Torlan stepped closer.

"What range are we receiving?"

Samir zoomed the display outward.

"Scanning across the valley… now expanding to upper atmosphere."

A few seconds passed.

Then new signals began appearing on the screen.

Orbital reflections.

Background radiation.

Faint distant transmissions from passing trade routes far beyond the system.

Samir smiled.

"Communications online."

The settlers standing nearby broke into cheers.

Mara Ellison stepped forward and looked up at the antenna tower swaying gently in the wind.

"For the first time since the storm," she said, "we can see what's coming."

Samir continued adjusting the signal filters.

"Early detection range should be several hundred kilometers."

He tapped the console again.

"If a ship enters this sector, you'll know long before it reaches the valley."

Mara turned to Torlan.

"That changes everything."

Torlan nodded quietly.

The antenna now stood against the bright sky, its signal spreading across the region.

Below them Havenfall continued its quiet work in the valley, unaware that the colony had just gained something it had been missing for months.

Time.

Time to prepare.

Time to respond.

Time to survive.

The ridge wind continued to move across the summit as the new communications system began its silent watch.

Torlan's Observation

While the others continued adjusting the antenna controls, Torlan stepped a short distance away from the tower.

From the summit the entire Havenfall valley lay open beneath him.

The morning sun had risen higher now, casting long bands of light across the plains and forests below. Rivers glinted between clusters of trees, and the colony buildings appeared small against the wide landscape.

For several minutes Torlan simply observed.

His mind worked the way it always had—quietly connecting details others often overlooked.

Something in the valley drew his attention.

Along the southern fields he noticed clusters of plants growing in long patches near the riverbanks. Even from this height their color stood out.

Amber.

The plants formed dense, low-growing fields that shimmered slightly in the sunlight.

Torlan studied them carefully.

A memory surfaced.

Months earlier he had read a technical briefing about industrial supply shortages affecting **Dravakar's manufacturing sector**. One of their major chemical catalysts came from a rare biological compound extracted from plants with a similar amber coloration.

He looked again.

The pattern of growth.

The leaf structure.

The color.

It was remarkably similar.

Torlan's gaze shifted toward the northern edge of the valley.

Along the cliffs where the ridge descended, layers of exposed rock cut through the hillside. In several places the sunlight reflected off metallic surfaces embedded within the stone.

Torlan crouched and examined the rock beneath his boots.

The mineral composition of the ridge matched the formations below.

Another memory surfaced.

A report from **Valyra's defense archives** describing a crystalline mineral used in the energy shielding systems that protected their orbital fleets.

The structure of the rock beneath Havenfall looked almost identical.

Behind him the others continued celebrating the successful antenna installation.

Torlan remained still, studying the valley.

Two rare resources.

Two civilizations at war.

And both might exist in the same place.

Footsteps approached behind him.

Mara Ellison joined him near the edge of the ridge.

"You're studying the valley," she said.

Torlan nodded slightly.

He pointed toward the amber-colored patches near the river.

"Do you harvest those plants?"

Mara followed his gesture.

She shook her head.

"No. They grow wild near the waterbanks."

She looked puzzled.

"We assumed they were useless."

Torlan considered this.

Then he pointed toward the exposed rock layers along the valley wall.

"And those mineral formations?"

Mara glanced at the cliffs.

"Common ridge stone," she said. "We've used it for basic construction."

Torlan remained quiet.

His photographic memory compared what he was seeing with the technical documents he had studied earlier.

The resemblance was too precise to ignore.

Behind them the antenna tower hummed softly in the wind.

But Torlan was no longer thinking about communications.

He was thinking about something much larger.

The Realization

The wind moved steadily across the ridge.

Behind them the antenna tower hummed softly as Samir continued calibrating the system. The settlers were still talking excitedly near the equipment crates, relieved that Havenfall would finally have an early-warning system again.

Torlan remained at the edge of the ridge, studying the valley below.

Alex walked over and stopped beside him.

She had noticed the same quiet concentration she had seen earlier when Torlan studied star charts. It meant his mind was working through something important.

"What are you thinking?" she asked.

Torlan did not answer immediately.

Instead he pointed toward the riverbanks where the amber-colored plants grew in thick clusters.

"Those plants," he said.

Alex followed his gesture.

"I saw them earlier near the farms."

"Do the settlers use them?"

"Apparently not."

Torlan nodded slowly.

"In Dravakar industrial systems, a chemical catalyst is required for several major manufacturing processes."

Alex frowned slightly as she thought.

"Yes… I remember reading something about that during the trade briefings."

Torlan continued.

"The catalyst is extracted from a rare plant species."

Alex looked again toward the valley.

"Those?"

"Possibly."

He then pointed toward the rocky cliffs along the valley wall.

Sunlight glinted off the exposed mineral layers.

"And the rock formations?"

Alex studied the ridge more carefully.

"The structure looks crystalline."

Torlan nodded.

"Valyra uses a similar mineral in its defensive shield technology."

For a moment Alex said nothing.

She slowly looked across the valley again.

The plants.

The minerals.

The colony sitting quietly between two civilizations locked in war.

Her eyes widened slightly.

"You're saying Havenfall may contain resources that both planets need."

Torlan nodded once.

Alex turned toward him.

"If that's true…"

She stopped mid-sentence as the realization settled in.

Torlan finished the thought quietly.

"Havenfall may be more valuable than anyone realizes."

The wind moved across the ridge again.

Alex studied the valley below in a completely different way now.

Not just as a struggling colony.

But as a place that might change the balance of an entire war.

"Valuable how?" she asked softly.

Torlan looked across the valley once more.

"Valuable enough," he said,

"to end a war."

Below them Havenfall continued its quiet work, unaware that the small colony might hold the key to peace between two worlds.

Chapter 18 — The Discovery

Samples Collected

The morning after the ridge antenna was completed, Torlan returned to the southern edge of the valley.

Mist still hung lightly above the riverbanks where narrow streams fed into Havenfall's main water channel. The ground there was damp and rich with plant growth.

Clusters of the **amber-colored plants** Torlan had noticed from the ridge grew thick along the water's edge.

Alex walked beside him carrying a small field kit from *The Long Path*.

"You're certain these are the plants you saw from above?"

Torlan knelt beside one of the clusters.

"Yes."

Up close the plants were even more distinctive. Their leaves were narrow and translucent, with faint amber veins running through them like threads of gold.

Torlan carefully cut a small section from one stem and placed it into a sealed sample container.

Alex opened her tablet and began cataloging the entry.

"Sample one," she said.

"Valley riverbank plant species."

Torlan collected several additional samples from nearby clusters.

"These plants grow only in specific soil conditions," he said.

Alex glanced toward the valley cliffs where the exposed rock formations shimmered faintly in the sunlight.

"You think the minerals in the soil might be connected?"

"Possibly."

He sealed another container.

Alex studied the plant more closely.

"What exactly do you think they contain?"

Torlan stood and brushed dust from his hands.

"A catalytic compound."

Alex looked at him.

"Important to whom?"

Torlan answered calmly.

"Dravakar."

Alex's eyebrows lifted slightly.

"The industrial catalyst used in their manufacturing systems?"

Torlan nodded.

"I read several technical reports while studying the war archives."

He gestured toward the valley plants.

"The structure of these leaves is similar to the species used to produce that compound."

Alex slowly began to understand why Torlan had been studying the valley so carefully from the ridge.

"You're saying Havenfall might be sitting on something extremely valuable."

Torlan did not answer immediately.

Instead he looked toward the cliffs rising along the edge of the valley.

Sunlight glinted off the exposed mineral layers.

"That possibility must be confirmed."

Alex closed the sample case.

"Which means we're not finished collecting."

Torlan nodded once.

"Not yet."

They moved toward the base of the cliffs where fragments of the ridge rock had broken away and scattered across the ground.

Torlan picked up a piece of the stone and turned it slowly in the sunlight.

The crystalline structure inside the rock caught the light with a faint metallic shimmer.

Alex watched him carefully.

"Let me guess," she said.

"You've seen that mineral somewhere before."

Torlan placed the rock fragment into another sealed container.

"Yes."

Alex waited.

Torlan looked back across the valley of Havenfall.

"In Valyra's defensive systems."

The implications of that statement hung quietly in the morning air.

Alex looked across the valley again.

For the first time she began to see Havenfall the same way Torlan did.

Not just as a struggling colony.

But as a place that might hold something both sides of a war desperately needed.

Laboratory Examination

Later that afternoon, several sealed sample containers sat on the analysis table inside the small laboratory aboard *The Long Path.*

The room was compact but well equipped. Diagnostic scanners lined one wall, and a portable chemical analyzer hummed quietly as its systems warmed up.

Owen Tark leaned over the console, arms folded.

"You know," he said, glancing at the sample trays, "when I signed on for this mission I expected engine repairs and storm navigation."

He tapped one of the sealed plant containers.

"Not botanical research."

Dr. Lila Chen smiled slightly as she prepared the first sample.

"Science often appears when you least expect it."

Torlan stood nearby reviewing the ship's data display while Alex organized the field notes they had recorded earlier in the valley.

Dr. Chen carefully placed a small section of the amber plant into the analyzer chamber.

The machine sealed itself with a soft click.

"Beginning chemical scan," she said.

A moment later the screen began filling with data lines.

Molecular structures appeared across the display as the analyzer mapped the plant's internal compounds.

Owen studied the screen.

"That's an unusually dense chemical structure for a simple plant."

Torlan stepped closer.

"Yes."

The analysis continued for several seconds.

Then the scanner highlighted one compound cluster in bright amber.

Dr. Chen leaned forward.

"Well," she said.

"That is interesting."

Alex looked up from her tablet.

"What did you find?"

Dr. Chen expanded the molecular diagram on the display.

"This plant contains a catalytic compound with extremely high reaction stability."

Torlan nodded slowly.

"The same compound used in Dravakar industrial systems."

Owen looked impressed.

"You mean the catalyst used in their heavy manufacturing complexes?"

"Yes," Torlan replied.

Alex crossed her arms thoughtfully.

"So Havenfall has something Dravakar industries desperately need."

Dr. Chen removed the plant sample and placed the mineral fragment into the analyzer.

"Let's see what the rocks say."

The scanner hummed again as it began its second analysis.

Layers of crystalline structure appeared across the display.

Dense mineral lattices formed a repeating geometric pattern inside the rock sample.

Owen leaned closer.

"That's no ordinary stone."

Torlan watched the display carefully.

His photographic memory compared the crystalline pattern with technical diagrams he had studied months earlier.

He pointed to the screen.

"Magnify that section."

Dr. Chen adjusted the image.

The crystalline layers became clearer.

Torlan nodded once.

"Shieldstone."

Alex looked at him.

"The defensive mineral used by Valyra?"

Torlan confirmed.

"Yes."

Owen whistled softly.

"So this valley contains a rare industrial catalyst *and* the mineral used in Valyra's defense technology."

Dr. Chen shut down the analyzer and removed the rock sample.

"Well," she said, placing the fragment back on the table.

"That explains why Torlan wanted to run these tests."

Alex looked down at the samples spread across the laboratory table.

Plants needed by one civilization.

Minerals needed by the other.

And both resources sitting quietly in the same remote valley.

Slowly the implications began to take shape in her mind.

Alex Connects the Idea

The laboratory grew quiet after the scans finished.

The amber plant samples and the mineral fragments rested on the table between them, each labeled and cataloged. The diagnostic screens still displayed the molecular structures and crystalline patterns revealed by the analysis.

Alex studied the data carefully.

For several moments she said nothing.

Torlan remained calm beside the console, allowing her time to think. He had learned long ago that good conclusions were stronger when people reached them themselves.

Alex slowly walked around the table, reviewing the results again.

"The plants contain the catalyst Dravakar's factories require," she said quietly.

Torlan nodded.

"And the rock formations contain shieldstone similar to the material used by Valyra."

Torlan nodded again.

Alex folded her arms.

"If Havenfall has both resources…"

She paused as the idea began forming in her mind.

Torlan watched her carefully.

Alex turned toward the laboratory window where the Havenfall valley could be seen in the distance.

The farms.

The rivers.

The ridge they had climbed that morning.

"This colony sits directly on top of resources both war planets need," she said slowly.

Torlan answered simply.

"Yes."

Alex looked back toward the sample table.

"That means both sides would want access to this valley."

"Yes."

Her expression grew more serious.

"But if either side tried to take it by force…"

She stopped again as the next part of the idea became clear.

Torlan finished the thought quietly.

"The colony would be destroyed."

Alex nodded.

"And if that happens, neither side gains anything."

Torlan gestured lightly toward the samples.

"These resources are valuable only if the valley remains intact."

Alex leaned back against the console.

The logic was suddenly very clear.

"Which means neither side can afford to fight over Havenfall."

Torlan gave a small nod.

The valley had changed in her mind.

It was no longer just a struggling colony on the edge of the war zone.

It had become something far more significant.

A place that both sides needed—but neither side could safely claim.

Alex looked at Torlan again.

"And you realized this while standing on the ridge."

Torlan answered calmly.

"I suspected it."

Alex smiled slightly.

"You always say that when you've already solved the problem."

Torlan allowed the faintest hint of a smile.

"The problem is not solved yet."

Alex glanced back at the laboratory table.

"No," she said.

"But I think we just found the beginning of the answer."

The Trade Possibility

Alex remained leaning against the laboratory console, still looking at the samples spread across the table.

The more she thought about it, the clearer the situation became.

Two resources.

Two civilizations.

One small colony sitting between them.

She turned back toward Torlan.

"If Havenfall has both of these resources," she said slowly, "then both sides will eventually discover it."

Torlan nodded.

"Yes."

"And if they discover it during the war…"

She didn't finish the sentence.

Torlan did.

"They will attempt to claim it."

Alex walked toward the laboratory window and looked down toward the valley again.

Fields stretched along the riverbanks where the amber plants grew naturally. The rocky cliffs along the valley edge shimmered faintly with the mineral deposits they had just confirmed.

"Neither side would tolerate the other controlling this place," she said.

Torlan joined her at the window.

"That is correct."

Alex folded her arms.

"So the colony becomes a battlefield."

Torlan remained quiet for a moment.

"Unless," he said.

Alex turned toward him.

"Unless what?"

Torlan spoke calmly.

"Havenfall must belong to neither side."

Alex studied him carefully.

"Neutral."

Torlan nodded.

"If the valley remains independent, both sides could gain access to the resources without destroying them."

Alex's mind immediately began working through the implications.

"You mean a trade agreement."

"Yes."

Torlan continued.

"If both war planets agree to recognize Havenfall as a neutral world…"

He gestured toward the samples on the table.

"…then both sides gain what they need."

Alex finished the thought.

"And the settlers gain stability."

Torlan nodded.

"The colony could export the catalyst plants to Dravakar."

He pointed to the mineral samples.

"And the shieldstone to Valyra."

Alex slowly began to see the elegance of the idea.

"You're not just solving Havenfall's problems."

Torlan remained calm.

"No."

Alex looked out across the valley again.

"You're creating a reason for the war to stop."

Torlan gave a slight nod.

"Wars often end when cooperation becomes more valuable than conflict."

Alex considered the idea carefully.

If both sides depended on Havenfall's resources…

Then destroying the colony would become the worst possible outcome for both.

Which meant protecting the colony would suddenly become everyone's priority.

She turned back toward Torlan.

"That might actually work."

Torlan studied the valley quietly through the window.

"Yes."

For the first time since arriving on Havenfall, the future of the colony no longer depended only on survival.

It might soon depend on diplomacy.

Confirming the Evidence

The laboratory lights dimmed slightly as the ship's systems shifted to evening power mode.

Outside the window, the valley of Havenfall had grown quiet again. Small lights glowed from the colony buildings, and the ridge antenna they had installed earlier now blinked softly against the dark sky.

Inside the laboratory, Torlan continued studying the data.

Several diagnostic screens displayed the results of the plant and mineral analyses. Charts and molecular structures filled the displays as Torlan reviewed them carefully.

Alex sat nearby with her tablet, organizing the information into a clear report.

"You're checking the results again," she said.

"Yes."

Alex smiled faintly.

"You already know what they say."

Torlan nodded slightly.

"Confirmation is important."

He adjusted one of the displays and enlarged the catalyst compound identified in the plant samples.

"The chemical stability matches the industrial catalyst used in Dravakar manufacturing systems."

Alex glanced at the screen.

"And the mineral?"

Torlan switched to the geological scan.

Layered crystalline structures appeared across the display.

"The lattice density closely matches the shieldstone used by Valyra."

Alex leaned back in her chair.

"So both resources are real."

"Yes."

Torlan opened a third data display showing the survey results from the valley.

The amber plants appeared across several regions near the riverbanks.

"They grow naturally in large quantities," he said.

Alex studied the map.

"That's not a small field."

"No."

Torlan highlighted the mineral deposits along the valley cliffs.

"These formations extend along most of the northern ridge."

Alex nodded slowly.

"So the resources aren't rare samples."

"They are abundant."

Torlan paused, reviewing the final data points.

Three conclusions now stood clearly before him.

He spoke them aloud.

"First: Havenfall's resources are significant."

Alex nodded.

"Second: both war planets require them."

Alex nodded again.

"And third," Torlan said quietly, "neither side can obtain them without risking destruction of the colony."

Alex closed her tablet.

"That's the key."

Torlan looked toward the valley through the laboratory window.

"Yes."

If either civilization attempted to seize Havenfall through force, the colony—and its valuable resources—would almost certainly be destroyed.

Which meant something unusual had become true.

For the first time in seven years of war, both sides shared the same interest.

Preserving Havenfall.

The Key Question

Night had settled over Havenfall.

From the laboratory window aboard *The Long Path*, the valley appeared peaceful beneath the stars. Small lights from the colony buildings glowed faintly across the fields, and the newly installed ridge antenna blinked steadily on the distant ridge.

Inside the laboratory, Alex studied the star map projected across the central display.

The Kardrin Expanse stretched across the holographic chart, with Havenfall marked quietly between the two war regions.

Valyra's territory lay on one side.

Dravakar's on the other.

Alex folded her arms.

"If your plan works," she said slowly, "Havenfall could become the most important place in this entire region."

Torlan stood beside the display reviewing the navigation data from their journey through the Expanse.

"Yes."

Alex turned toward him.

"But there's still one problem."

Torlan looked at her.

"How do we convince them?"

The question hung quietly in the room.

Seven years of war had hardened both sides.

Entire fleets had been lost.

Trust between the two civilizations had long since vanished.

Torlan considered the question calmly.

Then he spoke.

"We show them the truth."

Alex tilted her head slightly.

"Which truth?"

Torlan turned toward the valley outside the window.

"Both truths."

Alex waited.

Torlan continued.

"First, how the war began."

Alex nodded slowly.

The destruction of the royal convoy.

The accusation.

The retaliation that followed.

Years of conflict built on a single unresolved event.

"And the second truth?" she asked.

Torlan gestured toward the valley below.

"What Havenfall offers."

Alex looked again at the star map.

If both sides understood what existed here—

If they understood that the colony could provide what each of them needed—

Then the logic of cooperation might become stronger than the instinct to fight.

She looked back at Torlan.

"You're asking two enemies to sit at the same table."

Torlan answered calmly.

"Yes."

Alex studied him for a moment.

"You realize neither side will trust the other."

Torlan nodded.

"That is true."

Alex raised an eyebrow.

"So why would they listen?"

Torlan reached toward the communications console.

"Because we will speak to both."

He entered two destination codes into the transmission system.

One signal routed toward the government network of **Valyra**.

The other toward the command authority of **Dravakar**.

Alex watched the transmission panel activate.

"You're contacting them both at the same time."

Torlan nodded once.

"That is necessary."

The communications system confirmed signal lock with both distant networks.

Torlan prepared the outgoing message.

Alex read the transmission text as it appeared on the screen.

It was simple.

Direct.

And impossible to ignore.

"I believe I have found a way to end your war."

Torlan transmitted the message.

The signal left Havenfall and raced outward across the stars.

Toward two civilizations that had been enemies for seven years.

And toward a decision that could change everything.

Chapter 19 — The Plan

Reviewing the Discovery

Morning light filtered through the windows of the conference room aboard *The Long Path.*

The room had been converted temporarily into a planning space. Charts and data displays filled the central table, and several screens projected the results of the laboratory analyses from the previous night.

Alex stood beside the display reviewing the information once again.

On the left side of the screen appeared the molecular diagram of the **catalytic compound** extracted from the amber plants growing along Havenfall's riverbanks.

On the right side appeared the crystalline lattice structure from the **mineral samples** collected along the ridge cliffs.

Torlan studied both sets of data calmly.

The evidence had now been confirmed several times.

There was no longer any doubt.

Alex folded her arms.

"The plants produce the catalyst Dravakar needs for its manufacturing systems."

Torlan nodded.

"And the ridge minerals match the shieldstone used in Valyra's defensive technology."

"Yes."

Alex looked down at the map of Havenfall displayed beneath the data screens.

Amber plant clusters marked the river valleys.

Shieldstone deposits marked the northern cliffs.

The two resources overlapped directly beneath the colony.

She shook her head slowly.

"Either planet would fight to control this valley."

Torlan remained quiet for a moment.

Then he said calmly,

"Which is why neither of them must control it."

Alex looked up at him.

That statement had become the foundation of the entire strategy.

If one side seized Havenfall, the other would attack to reclaim it.

The valley would become a battlefield.

And the colony would almost certainly be destroyed.

But if neither side owned Havenfall…

Then both sides might benefit.

Alex walked around the table, studying the resource map again.

"The settlers don't even realize what's beneath their farms."

Torlan nodded.

"They built their colony on a place others would consider extremely valuable."

Alex looked toward the valley outside the window.

Havenfall appeared peaceful in the morning sunlight.

Farm fields stretched along the riverbanks.

Small utility vehicles moved slowly between buildings.

To the settlers below, life was continuing as it had the day before.

Unaware that their home might soon become the focus of an interstellar negotiation.

Alex turned back toward Torlan.

"If your plan works," she said, "Havenfall becomes the most important neutral world in the Kardrin Expanse."

Torlan studied the map quietly.

"Yes."

Alex watched him for a moment.

"You're not just solving the colony's problems."

Torlan met her gaze.

"No."

Alex nodded slowly as the full scope of the idea settled in.

"You're trying to end a war."

Protecting Havenfall

Later that afternoon, Torlan and Alex walked across the colony square toward the small operations building where Havenfall's council held its meetings.

The building was simple—constructed from reinforced panels and local stone—but it served as the center of the colony's planning and decision-making.

Inside, several settlers were already gathered around a long wooden table.

Mara Ellison stood at the head of the room.

Beside her were several members of the colony council—farmers, engineers, and technicians who had helped build Havenfall from the ground up.

They all looked curious, and a little concerned.

Mara nodded as Torlan and Alex entered.

"You said you had something important to discuss."

Torlan placed a portable display unit on the table and activated it.

A map of the Havenfall valley appeared in the air above the projector.

Several settlers leaned forward immediately.

Torlan spoke calmly.

"While installing the ridge antenna yesterday, I observed several unusual features in the valley."

He enlarged the display, highlighting the amber plant clusters along the riverbanks.

"These plants contain a catalytic compound used in Dravakar industrial manufacturing."

The room grew quiet.

One of the settlers frowned.

"You mean those weeds by the river?"

Torlan nodded.

"They are not weeds."

He adjusted the map again.

Now the northern cliffs appeared on the display, with several sections glowing faintly where mineral deposits had been identified.

"These rock formations contain crystalline minerals similar to the shieldstone used by Valyra."

The council members exchanged uneasy glances.

One of the farmers leaned forward.

"So both war planets would want what's here."

"Yes," Torlan said.

The realization moved slowly through the room.

Another settler spoke quietly.

"If those fleets find out about this…"

He didn't finish the sentence.

Everyone in the room already knew the ending.

"Havenfall becomes the battlefield," he said at last.

Torlan remained calm.

"Only if the information is revealed without a solution."

Mara studied him carefully.

"You already have one."

Torlan nodded slightly.

"Havenfall must become a neutral trade world."

Several settlers looked surprised.

Torlan continued.

"The colony would remain independent."

He gestured toward the valley map.

"These resources could be exported through peaceful agreements."

"To both sides," Alex added.

The room grew thoughtful.

One of the council members spoke again.

"You're saying the two planets would agree not to fight here."

"Yes."

Torlan looked around the table.

"If both civilizations depend on Havenfall's resources, then protecting the colony becomes more valuable than destroying it."

Mara leaned back slowly in her chair.

For years the settlers had fought simply to survive.

Now the valley beneath their farms might hold something powerful enough to change the future of two civilizations.

She looked at Torlan.

"And you think they'll agree to this?"

Torlan answered calmly.

"They will consider it."

The settlers around the table exchanged uncertain looks.

For the first time since Havenfall had been founded, the fate of the colony might soon be decided by forces far beyond their valley.

But for the first time, they also had something they had never possessed before.

Leverage.

The Two Truths

That evening the planning room aboard *The Long Path* was quiet again.

The settlers had returned to their work across the valley, and the crew had settled into their normal routines. Outside the windows, Havenfall's lights glowed softly beneath the dark sky.

Inside the room, the central display projected a star map of the Kardrin Expanse.

Alex stood beside it, studying the positions of the two war regions.

Valyra's territory lay to the north.

Dravakar's lay to the south.

Havenfall rested quietly between them.

Torlan adjusted several data panels and enlarged the region surrounding the colony.

Alex watched the map for a moment before turning toward him.

"So this is the plan."

Torlan nodded.

"It must be presented carefully."

Alex folded her arms.

"Start from the beginning."

Torlan considered the display.

"There are two truths that must be understood."

Alex waited.

Torlan raised one finger.

"The first truth concerns the beginning of the war."

He activated a second display showing the reconstructed flight path of the destroyed convoy.

The beacon malfunction.

The navigation error.

The collision.

All the evidence they had uncovered.

"The destruction of the royal convoy was an accident," Torlan said quietly.

Alex nodded.

"And both sides have been fighting for seven years over a misunderstanding."

"Yes."

Torlan raised a second finger.

"The second truth concerns Havenfall."

He switched the display back to the valley resource map.

Amber plant fields.

Shieldstone deposits along the ridge.

"These resources benefit both civilizations."

Alex studied the map again.

"Which means both sides gain something if peace is established."

Torlan nodded.

Alex walked slowly around the display table.

"You're giving them a reason to stop fighting."

Torlan answered calmly.

"Yes."

Alex stopped beside the window and looked out toward the valley.

Lights from the colony farms stretched across the fields below.

"But that's not the difficult part," she said.

Torlan waited.

Alex turned back toward him.

"The difficult part is pride."

Torlan nodded slightly.

"For seven years both sides have believed the other was responsible."

Alex leaned against the console.

"If they suddenly admit the war started by accident, someone looks weak."

Torlan met her gaze.

"That is why both truths must be presented together."

Alex thought about that.

"The accident explains the past."

Torlan nodded.

"And Havenfall explains the future."

Alex slowly smiled.

"You're giving them a way to stop fighting without losing honor."

Torlan answered quietly.

"Yes."

The room fell silent again as the star map of the Kardrin Expanse rotated slowly above the table.

Somewhere beyond those stars two civilizations still believed they were enemies.

Soon they would be asked to reconsider everything.

Preparing the Message

Later that night, the communications room aboard *The Long Path* glowed softly with the light of the transmission consoles.

Samir Haddad had already prepared the long-range communication channels, leaving Torlan and Alex alone to compose the message that would travel across the Kardrin Expanse.

The central screen displayed two destination markers.

Valyra — Royal Command Network

Dravakar — Chancellor's Office

Alex leaned against the console while Torlan reviewed the transmission format.

"You're inviting both leaders to the same place," she said.

"Yes."

Alex considered that.

"That alone will get their attention."

Torlan began entering the message text slowly and carefully.

The wording mattered.

Every phrase needed to be precise.

Alex watched the message take shape on the display.

Torlan avoided accusations.

He avoided conclusions.

Instead, he described what he had discovered in simple, factual terms.

Information that could resolve the conflict.

Information that affected both civilizations.

Information that required discussion.

Alex read the message quietly.

"You're not explaining everything."

Torlan shook his head slightly.

"Not yet."

Alex tapped the console lightly.

"We already have the proof about the convoy beacon malfunction."

Torlan nodded.

The reconstructed navigation data still rested in the ship's archives.

"If we include that evidence," Alex said, "they might believe you immediately."

Torlan looked at the message again.

"That evidence must be revealed when both leaders are present."

Alex understood the reasoning immediately.

"If one side learns the truth first…"

"They might attempt to control the outcome," Torlan said.

Alex nodded slowly.

"You want them both hearing the same information at the same time."

"Yes."

Torlan finished typing the final line of the transmission.

The message was short.

Respectful.

Direct.

Alex read it again from the screen.

I have discovered information that may resolve the conflict between your civilizations.

The information concerns the origin of the war and a development on Havenfall that affects both sides.

I request a meeting to present the evidence and a proposal that may bring peace.

Alex looked at him.

"That will definitely get their attention."

Torlan saved the transmission draft.

But he did not send it yet.

"There is still one thing to consider," Alex said.

Torlan waited.

"What happens if one of them decides not to come?"

Torlan studied the star map projected above the console.

"That possibility must be accepted."

Alex nodded slowly.

The risk of failure was still very real.

But now the message was ready.

And the next step would place Havenfall directly between two war leaders who had not spoken to each other in seven years.

The Risk

The communications room grew quiet after the message draft was completed.

Outside the observation window the night sky stretched across Havenfall, filled with distant stars. Somewhere beyond that darkness lay the territories of Valyra and Dravakar—two civilizations that had spent seven years destroying one another.

Alex studied the message still glowing on the screen.

"It's a bold invitation," she said.

Torlan nodded slightly.

"Yes."

Alex turned toward him.

"But it also carries a risk."

Torlan waited.

Alex crossed her arms thoughtfully.

"What if one of them sends a fleet instead of coming themselves?"

Torlan considered the possibility calmly.

"That outcome must be considered."

Alex walked toward the window and looked out over the quiet valley.

"If either side decides Havenfall is strategically valuable," she said, "they might try to secure it immediately."

Torlan joined her at the window.

"Yes."

Alex watched the scattered lights of the colony below.

Farm vehicles moved slowly along the roads, and a few settlers could still be seen working late near the agricultural systems.

"They have no defenses," she said quietly.

"No," Torlan agreed.

Alex turned back toward him.

"So if a fleet arrives…"

Torlan finished the thought.

"Havenfall becomes the battlefield they feared."

For a moment neither of them spoke.

The risk was real.

Alex thought for a moment longer.

"And what if neither leader comes?"

Torlan answered calmly.

"Then the war continues."

Alex sighed softly.

"That's not exactly reassuring."

Torlan remained thoughtful.

"Peace always carries risk."

Alex studied him.

"You're asking two enemies who have been fighting for seven years to trust you."

"Yes."

"And you're asking them to travel into the middle of the war zone to do it."

Torlan nodded.

"That is correct."

Alex shook her head slightly.

"You realize most people would consider this plan impossible."

Torlan allowed a faint smile.

"Most people would not attempt it."

The two of them stood quietly for a moment longer.

Below them Havenfall slept peacefully in the valley.

The settlers had no idea that the next decision made aboard *The Long Path* might determine the future of their entire world.

Alex finally turned back toward the console.

"Well," she said.

"I suppose there's only one thing left to do."

Torlan nodded once.

"Yes."

Send the message.

The Messages Sent

The communications room was silent except for the low hum of the ship's systems.

Torlan stood at the transmission console while Alex remained beside the observation window, watching the dark valley of Havenfall below.

On the central display the message waited.

Two destinations were listed beneath it.

Valyra — Royal Command Network

Dravakar — Chancellor's Office

Samir Haddad sat at the adjacent communications station, monitoring the signal channels.

"Transmission arrays are ready," he said.

Torlan reviewed the message one final time.

The wording remained simple and precise.

It revealed just enough to demand attention—but not enough to provoke suspicion or fear.

Alex stepped closer to the console.

"This will reach them directly?"

Samir nodded.

"Priority diplomatic channels. Their command networks will flag it immediately."

Torlan rested his hand on the transmission control.

For a moment he paused.

Seven years of war.

Thousands of lives lost.

Entire fleets destroyed.

And now the possibility of peace rested on a single signal traveling through space.

Torlan activated the console.

"Transmit."

The communications system emitted a soft tone as the signal launched outward.

Two streams of encoded data raced away from Havenfall.

One traveling toward **Valyra**.

One toward **Dravakar**.

Samir watched the transmission progress indicators.

"Signal sent."

Torlan nodded.

"Confirmed."

The room fell quiet again.

Now there was nothing left to do but wait.

Minutes passed.

Then hours.

Night deepened over Havenfall.

Most of the colony lights dimmed as settlers returned to their homes.

Alex leaned against the console.

"You think they'll respond?"

Torlan studied the star map projected above the display.

"Yes."

Alex raised an eyebrow.

"That confident?"

Torlan answered calmly.

"Both leaders have been searching for a way to end the war."

The console suddenly emitted a soft alert tone.

Samir straightened in his chair.

"Incoming signal."

He checked the transmission source.

"Valyra."

A moment later another alert sounded.

Samir blinked.

"And Dravakar."

Alex stepped closer to the display.

The two incoming messages appeared almost simultaneously on the screen.

Torlan read them carefully.

Then he nodded once.

Alex looked at him.

"Well?"

Torlan answered quietly.

"Both leaders have accepted the invitation."

Alex stared at the display.

"They're coming here?"

"Yes."

Samir leaned back slightly.

"That means fleets will follow."

Torlan looked out the window toward the quiet valley below.

"Yes."

The fate of Havenfall—and perhaps the future of two civilizations—was now moving toward the small colony from opposite sides of the Kardrin Expanse.

The First Arrival

The Havenfall communications center had never been so busy.

Inside the small building near the landing field, several settlers gathered around the signal consoles while Samir Haddad monitored the long-range detection systems connected to the ridge antenna.

The new tower had already proven its value.

Signal data streamed steadily across the screens, showing ship movements across the surrounding region of space.

Samir leaned forward suddenly.

"Contact detected."

Alex, standing nearby, looked up immediately.

"Distance?"

Samir adjusted the scan filters.

"High orbit approach vector… coming from the Valyra sector."

The settlers in the room grew quiet.

Torlan stepped closer to the display.

"What is the identification signal?"

Samir expanded the transmission code.

"Diplomatic escort vessel."

He glanced back at Torlan.

"Valyra."

A low murmur moved through the room.

Mara Ellison folded her arms and watched the display carefully.

"How long until arrival?"

"Minutes," Samir replied.

Outside, word quickly spread across the colony.

Settlers stepped out of their homes and workshops, looking upward into the bright blue sky above Havenfall.

For a moment nothing appeared.

Then a small point of light formed high above the planet.

The object grew slowly larger as it descended into visible orbit.

The **Valyra vessel** was unlike anything the settlers had ever seen.

Its hull curved gracefully like a polished blade, reflecting sunlight in smooth silver arcs. Long, elegant structures extended along its sides, giving it a balanced and ceremonial appearance.

The ship was clearly powerful.

But it was also beautiful.

Alex watched from the communications doorway.

"That's not a warship," she said quietly.

Torlan studied the vessel carefully.

"No."

Samir confirmed the signal.

"It's broadcasting diplomatic credentials."

The Valyra ship settled into a stable orbit above Havenfall.

For several moments the colony remained silent as the settlers stared upward.

Mara finally spoke.

"After seven years of war…"

She shook her head slightly.

"…this valley just became the most important place in the Kardrin Expanse."

She looked toward Torlan.

Her voice was calm, but there was tension beneath it.

"Let's hope your plan works."

Above them the elegant Valyra vessel continued its silent orbit.

But everyone in the colony understood something important.

One side had arrived.

And the other would not be far behind.

The Second Arrival

The Valyra diplomatic vessel had been in orbit for only a few hours when the communications console sounded again.

Samir leaned forward instantly.

"New contact."

Torlan and Alex stepped closer to the display.

Samir adjusted the scan filters.

"Approach vector… southern sector."

Alex crossed her arms.

"That would be Dravakar."

Samir nodded.

"Signal signature matches Dravakar command codes."

The settlers in the communications center exchanged uneasy glances.

One war fleet in orbit was already unsettling.

Two fleets would be something entirely different.

"How far away?" Mara asked.

"Less than ten minutes," Samir said.

Outside the building, several settlers had remained gathered in the colony square, still watching the sky where the Valyra vessel glinted in the sunlight.

The second arrival appeared suddenly.

A bright flash high in the upper atmosphere.

Then the outline of another ship slowly emerged from orbital insertion.

The **Dravakar vessel** looked nothing like the graceful Valyra craft.

Its hull was thick and angular, reinforced with heavy plating and exposed structural supports. Engine housings and sensor towers protruded from its frame like armored machinery.

Where the Valyra ship looked ceremonial…

The Dravakar ship looked practical.

And dangerous.

Alex watched as the vessel settled into a separate orbit above the planet.

"Not exactly subtle," she said quietly.

Torlan studied the display.

"No."

Samir monitored the transmission signals.

"They're broadcasting negotiation credentials."

Mara folded her arms.

"So both sides came."

Samir glanced up at the orbital display.

The two ships now circled Havenfall on different orbital paths.

Each vessel clearly aware of the other's presence.

The tension between them was almost visible even across space.

Alex exhaled slowly.

"That's two fleets occupying the same sky."

Torlan nodded.

"Yes."

Below them the settlers continued watching the sky.

For the first time in Havenfall's history, two rival powers had arrived at the same world.

And both were waiting.

The war had not followed them here.

Yet.

But everyone understood that the next decisions made on Havenfall might determine whether the valley became a place of peace…

or the beginning of a new battle.

Concern Among the Settlers

That evening the Havenfall meeting hall filled quickly.

The settlers had gathered in the same room where Torlan had explained the discovery only a day earlier. Now the atmosphere felt very different.

Outside, two powerful vessels circled the planet.

Inside, the people of Havenfall waited for answers.

Mara Ellison stood near the center of the room while Torlan and Alex joined her beside the council table. Several dozen settlers filled the benches and standing space along the walls.

Through the tall windows, the evening sky had darkened. Every so often a faint point of light moved slowly across the stars as one of the orbiting ships passed overhead.

A farmer near the back of the room spoke first.

"So it's true."

He gestured toward the sky.

"Both fleets are here."

Mara nodded.

"Yes."

Another settler shook his head.

"We've spent years trying to stay out of their war."

A murmur of agreement moved through the room.

"And now the war has come here anyway."

Torlan listened quietly.

One of the younger settlers stood.

"What if they start fighting above the planet?"

The room fell silent.

Everyone looked toward Torlan.

He answered honestly.

"Then Havenfall will suffer."

No one spoke for several seconds.

The truth was difficult to hear—but no one in the room doubted it.

Mara watched the settlers carefully.

"These fleets came because of the message," she said.

"And because they're willing to listen."

One of the engineers leaned forward.

"You're certain they came to talk?"

Alex spoke before Torlan could answer.

"They came because they want to know what he discovered."

Torlan stepped forward slightly.

"This moment carries risk," he said.

"But it also carries opportunity."

He looked around the room at the people who had built Havenfall from empty wilderness.

"For seven years these civilizations have fought because they believed the other was responsible for a terrible crime."

The settlers listened carefully.

"That belief may soon change."

Another settler spoke quietly.

"And if it doesn't?"

Torlan did not avoid the question.

"Then Havenfall may become the battlefield you fear."

The room grew quiet again.

But Torlan continued calmly.

"Which is why we must succeed."

The words were not dramatic.

They were simply true.

The settlers looked at one another.

Many of them had faced storms, equipment failures, and years of uncertainty while building the colony.

Now they faced something larger.

But one thing had not changed.

They were still standing together.

Mara nodded slowly.

"Then we'll stand with you."

Several others nodded as well.

Outside the meeting hall, the two rival ships continued their silent orbit above Havenfall.

Waiting.

Meeting King Alaric

The following morning a shuttle descended gracefully from the **Valyra diplomatic vessel**.

It landed on Havenfall's small landing field with quiet precision, its polished hull reflecting the pale morning light across the valley.

Several settlers watched from a respectful distance as the shuttle ramp lowered.

Two uniformed Valyra officers stepped out first, their ceremonial armor gleaming softly. Their movements were calm and disciplined.

Behind them emerged **King Alaric of Valyra**.

He was tall and composed, with silver hair and a posture that reflected both authority and restraint. His uniform was formal but not extravagant—deep blue fabric marked with subtle royal insignia.

Torlan stepped forward to greet him.

Alex stood nearby.

King Alaric studied the small colony around him before speaking.

"So this is Havenfall."

His voice carried quiet strength.

"Yes," Torlan said.

The king's gaze moved across the valley for a moment before returning to Torlan.

"You are the one who sent the message."

"I am."

The king nodded slightly.

"You claim to know the truth behind the destruction of the royal convoy."

Torlan met his gaze calmly.

"I believe I understand what happened."

The Valyra officers exchanged quick glances.

For seven years the loss of the royal convoy had been considered an act of war.

King Alaric studied Torlan carefully.

"You realize the significance of such a claim."

"Yes."

The king continued.

"Many have attempted to explain the incident."

"None have produced convincing evidence."

Torlan nodded.

"That is true."

King Alaric's expression remained controlled.

"And yet you ask the ruler of Valyra to travel into a war zone to hear your explanation."

"Yes."

The king was silent for several seconds.

The wind moved gently across the landing field.

Finally he spoke.

"You must understand something about Valyra."

Torlan listened.

"Honor matters to my people."

The king's voice remained steady.

"The convoy that was destroyed carried members of my own family."

Torlan inclined his head respectfully.

"I am aware."

The king studied him again.

"If you are correct," he said, "you may have discovered something of great importance."

He paused.

"But if you are mistaken…"

Torlan answered calmly.

"Then the truth will reveal that as well."

The king allowed the faintest hint of a smile.

"That is a courageous answer."

He glanced toward the valley.

"You invited both sides to this world."

"Yes."

"And you intend to present your explanation to both leaders."

"Yes."

King Alaric nodded slowly.

"Very well."

He turned toward the shuttle briefly, then back toward Torlan.

"I will attend these negotiations."

His eyes sharpened slightly.

"But I expect proof."

Torlan nodded.

"You will have it."

Above them, the elegant Valyra vessel continued its silent orbit.

And now its king had come to hear the truth.

Meeting Chancellor Kade

Later that afternoon another shuttle descended toward Havenfall.

Unlike the elegant Valyra craft, the **Dravakar shuttle** arrived with a deep mechanical roar as its engines slowed for landing. Its hull was thick and armored, designed more for durability than appearance.

The ship settled firmly onto the landing field beside the earlier Valyra shuttle.

Dust rose briefly across the ground.

The ramp lowered with a heavy metallic sound.

Several Dravakar officers stepped out first, wearing dark, practical uniforms marked with command insignia. Their movements were efficient and direct.

Behind them emerged **Chancellor Darius Kade**.

He was broader in build than King Alaric and carried himself with the confidence of a man accustomed to command. His uniform was simple but precise, with very little ceremony.

Torlan stepped forward to greet him.

Kade looked around the small colony for a moment.

"So this is Havenfall."

His tone carried quiet curiosity.

"Yes," Torlan said.

Kade nodded once.

"The place where you claim the war might end."

"That is my hope."

Kade studied him carefully.

"You invited two enemies to the same location."

Torlan answered calmly.

"Yes."

The chancellor crossed his arms.

"That is either extremely brave… or extremely foolish."

Alex stood nearby, watching the exchange carefully.

Torlan replied without hesitation.

"The solution requires both of you."

Kade considered that for a moment.

Then he glanced briefly toward the sky where the Valyra ship remained in orbit.

"So the king accepted your invitation."

"Yes."

Kade gave a faint, humorless smile.

"That alone is interesting."

He turned back toward Torlan.

"You claim to understand the convoy incident that started this war."

Torlan nodded.

"I believe I do."

Kade's expression became more serious.

"Seven years of conflict began with that event."

"Yes."

"And many attempts have been made to explain it."

Torlan said nothing.

Kade stepped a little closer.

"If you are correct, you may have discovered something extremely valuable."

He paused.

"But if you are wrong…"

Torlan finished the thought calmly.

"Then nothing changes."

The chancellor studied him for several seconds.

Finally he nodded.

"You speak with unusual confidence."

Torlan did not react.

Kade glanced once more across the Havenfall valley.

"A quiet place to host the end of a war," he said.

Then he turned back toward Torlan.

"Very well."

"I will hear your proposal."

The Dravakar officers stepped aside as the chancellor followed Torlan toward the colony center.

Above them, two rival vessels continued circling the planet.

And now both leaders had arrived to hear the truth.

The Negotiation Location

Late that afternoon the two visiting leaders gathered briefly with Torlan and Alex inside the Havenfall operations building.

The room was simple—wooden tables, reinforced walls, and large windows looking out across the valley. It had served as the colony's council hall since Havenfall was first founded.

Now it would host something far larger.

King Alaric of Valyra stood near one side of the room with two members of his delegation.

Across the table stood Chancellor Kade of Dravakar, accompanied by several advisors.

The two leaders had not yet spoken directly to one another.

The tension between them was unmistakable.

Torlan stepped forward.

"Before we begin discussions, there is one matter to resolve."

Both leaders turned their attention toward him.

Torlan continued.

"The location of the negotiations."

King Alaric spoke first.

"I assume you intend to present your findings aboard your vessel."

Chancellor Kade shook his head immediately.

"That would place one side at a disadvantage."

The king replied calmly.

"And I assume you would prefer we meet aboard your warship."

Kade gave a faint smile.

"That would hardly encourage trust."

The room grew quiet.

Both leaders understood the problem.

Torlan spoke again.

"The negotiations must take place on neutral ground."

Both men looked at him.

Torlan gestured toward the windows overlooking the valley.

"Havenfall."

King Alaric considered the idea.

"The colony itself."

"Yes."

Kade looked toward the settlers' buildings outside.

"You intend for two enemies to sit down together in a frontier settlement."

"Yes."

Torlan's voice remained calm.

"Havenfall belongs to neither civilization."

He paused briefly.

"That is precisely why it must host this meeting."

Both leaders studied the room around them.

There were no military banners.

No political symbols.

Only the simple hall built by settlers trying to survive on a distant world.

Finally King Alaric nodded slowly.

"A neutral location is appropriate."

Chancellor Kade considered it a moment longer.

Then he gave a short nod.

"Agreed."

Torlan turned to Mara Ellison, who had been standing quietly near the back of the room.

"The colony council hall will serve well."

Mara looked slightly surprised—but she nodded.

"We'll prepare the room."

Torlan inclined his head.

"Thank you."

Within the hour, settlers began rearranging the hall.

A large table was placed in the center.

Chairs were arranged evenly along both sides.

Additional lighting was installed so that everyone in the room would be clearly visible.

By nightfall the preparations were complete.

Outside, Havenfall remained quiet beneath the stars.

Above the planet, two rival fleets continued their silent orbit.

Inside the colony hall, the negotiation table waited.

Alex stood beside Torlan near the doorway.

She looked at the empty chairs around the table.

"Tomorrow we try to end a war."

Torlan studied the room calmly.

"Tomorrow we begin."

Chapter 21 — Gathering Storm

The Meeting Hall

Morning light spread across the Havenfall valley as the settlers prepared the colony hall.

The building had once served as the settlement's supply warehouse before being converted into a meeting space. It was the largest structure Havenfall possessed, though by the standards of the two visiting civilizations it was still modest.

Inside, the room was simple.

A long wooden table stood in the center of the hall.

Frontier lanterns hung from support beams overhead, casting steady light across the room. The walls were reinforced panels and local stone, built more for durability than appearance.

Large windows looked out across the valley.

Beyond them, green fields stretched toward the distant ridge where the new antenna tower stood against the sky.

The setting could not have been more different from the massive warships orbiting the planet.

There were no ceremonial banners.

No military guards.

No symbols of power.

Only the quiet hall built by settlers trying to survive in a remote corner of space.

Torlan stood near the window for a moment, studying the valley below.

Farm vehicles moved slowly between irrigation lines. A few settlers worked near the water systems they had repaired days earlier.

Life continued.

That had been his reason for choosing this location.

When the leaders of Valyra and Dravakar entered this room, they would not see a battlefield.

They would see the people whose lives would be affected by whatever decisions were made here.

Alex stepped beside him.

"The room is ready," she said.

Torlan nodded.

Outside the hall, several settlers finished arranging the final details.

Chairs had been placed evenly along both sides of the table.

Two positions faced each other at the center.

One for **King Alaric of Valyra**.

One for **Chancellor Kade of Dravakar**.

Torlan looked once more across the valley.

Seven years of war.

Thousands of lives lost.

Entire fleets destroyed.

And now the leaders responsible for those decisions would soon sit together in a frontier hall built by farmers and engineers.

Alex followed his gaze.

"Do you think they'll listen?"

Torlan answered quietly.

"They came."

Alex nodded.

That alone was remarkable.

Above the planet, two rival fleets waited in orbit.

Below them, a simple colony hall waited for its most important meeting.

The gathering storm had begun.

Arrival of the Delegations

The Havenfall colony hall was silent as the first delegation approached.

Outside, the wind moved softly across the valley fields, and the distant hum of agricultural machinery could be heard faintly through the open windows.

Inside the hall, the long wooden table waited.

Torlan stood near the center of the room while Alex remained beside the wall display, watching the doorway.

Moments later the doors opened.

The **Valyra delegation** entered first.

King Alaric stepped inside with calm, measured movements. Two advisors followed closely behind him, their uniforms formal and precise, reflecting Valyra's long tradition of ceremony and discipline.

The king paused just inside the doorway.

His eyes moved across the simple room.

The wooden beams.

The lantern lighting.

The valley visible through the windows.

It was far removed from the polished halls of Valyra's royal command.

But he said nothing.

Torlan inclined his head respectfully.

"Your Majesty."

Alaric acknowledged him with a slight nod and took his seat along one side of the table.

A few minutes later the doors opened again.

The **Dravakar delegation** entered.

Chancellor Darius Kade walked in first, followed by several political advisors and two security officers who remained near the entrance.

Where the Valyra delegation carried the quiet formality of a royal court, the Dravakar representatives moved with direct efficiency.

Kade stopped when he saw King Alaric seated across the table.

For several seconds the two men simply looked at one another.

Seven years of war hung between them.

Neither spoke.

Alex could feel the tension immediately.

Even the settlers who had been helping prepare the hall quietly slipped out of the room, closing the doors behind them.

Now only the delegations remained.

Two civilizations.

One table.

Kade finally walked forward and took the seat opposite King Alaric.

The chairs settled with a soft scrape against the wooden floor.

No greeting was exchanged.

No ceremony followed.

Just silence.

Torlan watched both leaders carefully.

The moment was fragile.

Years of suspicion and anger could easily turn the meeting into another confrontation.

The room waited.

And so did the future of Havenfall.

The First Exchange

For several long moments the room remained completely silent.

The wooden table between the two leaders might as well have been a border line.

King Alaric of Valyra sat with straight posture, his hands resting calmly on the table. Across from him, Chancellor Kade leaned slightly forward, studying the room with a measured expression.

Torlan stood near the center of the table.

Alex watched from the side wall.

Neither leader seemed inclined to speak first.

Finally, King Alaric broke the silence.

His voice was steady but carried the weight of years.

"Your fleet has destroyed many Valyra ships."

The statement was calm.

But the accusation beneath it was unmistakable.

Chancellor Kade did not hesitate.

"Only after yours attacked our convoy."

The words landed heavily in the room.

One of the Valyra advisors stiffened slightly.

The Dravakar aides watched carefully.

King Alaric's expression remained controlled.

"The convoy that was destroyed carried members of the royal household."

Kade replied coldly.

"And the convoy your fleet destroyed carried Dravakar civilians."

The tension thickened immediately.

Seven years of war condensed into two sentences.

Neither leader raised his voice.

But the history between them was unmistakable.

King Alaric leaned forward slightly.

"You expect us to believe Dravakar forces were innocent in that attack?"

Kade met his gaze without hesitation.

"You expect us to believe Valyra ships were not responsible for the first strike?"

The air in the room grew heavier.

Torlan could feel the conversation drifting toward the same accusations that had fueled the war for years.

If it continued this way, the meeting would collapse before the truth could even be presented.

Alex noticed Torlan step forward slightly.

She recognized the moment immediately.

He was about to intervene.

Before the argument could continue any further, Torlan spoke.

Calmly.

"You are both correct."

Both leaders turned toward him at once.

The room became silent again.

But this time the silence held curiosity instead of anger.

Torlan continued.

"And both of you are wrong."

Torlan Intervenes

The statement hung in the air like a sudden change in gravity.

"You are both correct… and both of you are wrong."

For several seconds no one in the room moved.

King Alaric slowly turned his attention fully toward Torlan.

Across the table, Chancellor Kade's eyes narrowed slightly.

Neither man spoke.

Torlan stood calmly between them.

He had not raised his voice.

But the unexpected contradiction had forced both leaders to pause.

King Alaric finally broke the silence.

"You are suggesting that both of our governments misunderstand what happened."

Torlan inclined his head slightly.

"Yes."

Kade leaned forward in his chair.

"That would be a remarkable claim."

Torlan did not react to the tone.

"The destruction of the convoy was real," he said calmly.

"And the loss of life on both sides was tragic."

Both leaders watched him carefully.

Torlan continued.

"But the conclusion both sides reached afterward was incorrect."

King Alaric's voice remained measured.

"You believe neither side intended the attack."

"Yes."

Chancellor Kade folded his hands on the table.

"That would mean this war began with a mistake."

Torlan nodded once.

"That is correct."

The Dravakar advisors exchanged uneasy glances.

One of the Valyra officers shifted slightly in his seat.

The idea was almost unthinkable.

Seven years of war.

Entire fleets destroyed.

All because of a misunderstanding?

King Alaric studied Torlan closely.

"You understand the weight of such a statement."

"Yes."

Kade's voice was sharper now.

"Then you will provide evidence."

Torlan gestured toward the display console beside the table.

"I will."

Alex activated the console.

The room darkened slightly as a star map appeared above the center of the table.

Navigation paths formed glowing lines across the projection.

Torlan looked from one leader to the other.

"What happened seven years ago was not an attack."

He paused.

"It was an accident."

The room remained completely still.

For the first time since the meeting began, both leaders leaned forward to see the evidence.

The Evidence Introduced

The star map hovered above the center of the table.

Soft light from the projection illuminated the faces of the two delegations as the navigation routes slowly appeared.

Two lines traced across the map.

One represented the **Valyra royal convoy**.

The other marked the path of the **Dravakar transport fleet**.

Torlan stepped closer to the projection.

"These are the confirmed flight paths from the day of the incident."

He pointed to the first route.

"The Valyra convoy was traveling along its scheduled diplomatic corridor."

King Alaric nodded slightly.

"That is correct."

Torlan then indicated the second route.

"The Dravakar convoy followed a standard supply route."

Chancellor Kade studied the projection.

"Yes."

Torlan adjusted the map.

A third marker appeared between the two routes.

A blinking beacon signal.

"This navigation beacon served as a guidance reference for both convoys."

Alex expanded the data panel beside the map.

"Both fleets were receiving positional data from this beacon."

Torlan continued calmly.

"Shortly before the collision, the beacon began transmitting a faulty signal."

The star map shifted.

The projected flight paths subtly changed direction.

Both routes slowly curved toward one another.

King Alaric leaned closer.

"That alteration would place the two convoys on intersecting paths."

"Yes," Torlan said.

Chancellor Kade studied the data carefully.

"But neither convoy changed course intentionally."

Torlan nodded.

"The beacon signal made both navigational systems believe they were maintaining safe distance."

Alex highlighted the timestamp sequence.

"By the time visual confirmation occurred, the fleets were already within collision range."

Torlan pointed to the final section of the map.

The two glowing paths converged in a cloud of debris.

"This was the moment both sides believed they were under attack."

The projection shifted again.

Fragments of wreckage spread outward from the impact site.

Debris patterns drifted across the map.

Torlan highlighted the fragments.

"These debris fields match the trajectories expected from a collision."

He paused.

"Not from an ambush."

The room remained silent.

King Alaric studied the map slowly.

His expression had changed.

Chancellor Kade leaned forward, examining the navigation data with intense focus.

The explanation fit.

Too well.

For seven years both sides had assumed the other had fired first.

But the data told a different story.

The convoys had never intended to meet.

They had been guided together by a faulty beacon.

And by the time anyone realized what was happening…

It had been too late.

Rising Emotion

The star map slowly faded.

For several seconds no one in the room spoke.

King Alaric remained seated, his eyes still fixed on the space where the projection had been.

Seven years.

Seven years of war built upon the belief that his royal convoy had been deliberately attacked.

Chancellor Kade studied the navigation data again on the console display, his expression unreadable.

Finally, Alaric spoke.

"You are claiming… this war began because of a navigation error."

Torlan answered calmly.

"Yes."

The king leaned back slightly in his chair.

"That convoy carried members of my own family."

The room grew even quieter.

Everyone present understood the weight of that statement.

Kade spoke next, his voice lower than before.

"Our transport convoy carried thousands of industrial workers and supply crews."

He looked toward the map.

"They believed they were being ambushed."

Torlan nodded.

"Both sides believed the same thing."

Alex quietly added, "By the time the fleets realized what was happening, the damage had already begun."

Kade's gaze returned to Torlan.

"Then the first shots fired…"

"Were fired in confusion," Torlan finished.

Neither leader answered immediately.

The silence in the room changed.

It was no longer the sharp silence of accusation.

Now it carried something heavier.

Realization.

King Alaric spoke again, slower this time.

"If what you say is true… then every battle since that day…"

He did not finish the sentence.

Chancellor Kade completed the thought.

"…was fought for a mistake."

No one moved.

Torlan allowed the weight of that realization to settle.

He had learned long ago that people needed time to face the truth.

Especially when the truth carried the cost of countless lives.

At last, Alaric looked toward Torlan again.

"Even if this explanation is correct…"

His voice was steady, but firm.

"…the war cannot simply end."

Kade nodded in agreement.

"Too much has happened."

Too many losses.

Too many promises made to their people.

Torlan met their eyes calmly.

"That is why you are here."

He turned slightly and gestured toward the wide window at the far side of the hall.

Beyond the glass, the valley of Havenfall stretched into the fading evening light.

Green fields.

Amber plants.

Rivers winding through the valley floor.

A small colony struggling to survive.

Torlan spoke quietly.

"Because Havenfall offers something better than war."

Both leaders turned to look.

Neither of them yet knew what that meant.

Chapter 22 — Havenfall's Value

"Shared gain is stronger than victory."
Peace lasts longer when both sides benefit.
— *Wisdom of Cyrion*

Turning Toward the Valley

The meeting hall had grown quiet again.

Torlan stood near the wide window overlooking Havenfall Valley. Evening light stretched across the land, painting long shadows across the fields and riverbanks below.

He gestured toward the landscape outside.

"You have both spent years fighting over trade routes and territory."

Neither leader replied.

Torlan continued calmly.

"Your fleets have battled across half this sector of space."

He paused.

"But neither of you realized what lies here."

King Alaric slowly rose from his chair.

Across the table, Chancellor Kade stood as well.

Both men walked toward the window.

The valley opened before them.

Rolling fields spread across the valley floor. A river wound through the land like a silver ribbon. Clusters of amber-colored plants grew in patches near the water. Beyond them, the rocky ridge rose where the antenna tower now stood against the sky.

The Havenfall colony itself appeared small from this distance.

A handful of buildings.

A landing field.

Lights beginning to glow as evening approached.

Alaric studied the valley thoughtfully.

"This is the colony you risked your journey to supply."

"Yes," Torlan replied.

Kade folded his arms as he looked out across the land.

"A remote settlement on the edge of a war zone."

Torlan nodded once.

"Yes."

The chancellor glanced toward him.

"You believe this colony changes the course of our war."

Torlan did not answer immediately.

Instead, he looked toward the fields where the amber plants grew along the riverbanks.

"Yes."

Both leaders continued studying the valley.

For the first time since arriving, they were no longer looking at each other as enemies.

They were looking at Havenfall.

The Catalyst Plants

Torlan stepped back from the window and returned to the table.

Alex opened a small case and placed several sealed containers on the surface. Inside them were samples collected from the valley earlier that day.

The containers held pieces of the **amber-colored plants** that grew near Havenfall's riverbanks.

Torlan lifted one of the samples carefully.

"These plants grow naturally throughout the valley."

He set the container beside the console display.

"They contain a rare catalytic compound."

Alex activated the analysis screen.

A chemical structure appeared above the table.

Complex molecular chains rotated slowly in the projection.

Torlan turned toward Chancellor Kade.

"This compound accelerates high-temperature refining reactions."

Kade's expression sharpened.

Torlan continued calmly.

"It significantly improves industrial efficiency in heavy manufacturing systems."

The chancellor stepped closer to the projection.

He studied the structure carefully.

For several seconds he said nothing.

Then he spoke quietly.

"Our refineries have been searching for a catalyst like this for years."

Several members of the Dravakar delegation exchanged surprised glances.

Kade looked again at the sample container.

"You are certain this compound occurs naturally here?"

Torlan nodded.

"In large quantities."

Alex added, "We confirmed the concentration levels earlier aboard The Long Path."

The chemical projection shifted, displaying extraction data and density estimates.

Kade read the figures carefully.

The numbers were unmistakable.

The catalyst could dramatically improve Dravakar's industrial production.

After a moment, the chancellor looked back toward the valley outside.

"You are telling me that an entire supply of this catalyst…"

He paused.

"…is growing in the fields of this small colony."

Torlan answered simply.

"Yes."

The room fell quiet again.

For the first time since the negotiations began, something other than the war itself had captured the Dravakar leader's full attention.

The Shieldstone Mineral

The room remained quiet as Chancellor Kade continued studying the plant analysis.

Torlan allowed the moment to settle before speaking again.

"There is more."

Alex opened a second container from the case.

Inside were several **dark crystalline mineral fragments** taken from the ridge above Havenfall.

She placed the container beside the plant samples.

Torlan lifted one of the fragments carefully and set it beneath the console scanner.

The projection changed.

A crystalline lattice structure appeared above the table.

The mineral layers formed tightly packed geometric patterns, reflecting the scanner light in sharp angles.

Torlan turned toward King Alaric.

"This mineral formation occurs in the ridge rock surrounding the valley."

Alaric stepped closer.

He studied the lattice pattern carefully.

For a moment his expression remained calm.

Then it changed.

"You recognize it," Torlan said.

The king nodded slowly.

"Yes."

One of the Valyra advisors leaned forward to examine the projection.

"The crystal density…"

Alaric finished the thought.

"…matches shieldstone."

Torlan inclined his head.

"The same structural properties."

Alex adjusted the display.

Energy absorption readings appeared beside the mineral diagram.

"High resilience against directed energy fields," she explained.

"Excellent reinforcement material for planetary defense grids."

King Alaric picked up the mineral fragment and examined it in the light.

"This material would significantly strengthen Valyra's defensive shielding systems."

He looked toward the ridge visible through the window.

"You are telling me this mineral exists in the mountains surrounding this colony?"

"Yes," Torlan said.

"In substantial quantities."

The king returned the sample to the table.

For several seconds he said nothing.

Across the room, Chancellor Kade had turned away from the plant samples and was now studying the mineral projection as well.

Two resources.

Two different civilizations.

Both needed.

Both found in the same valley.

And both leaders were beginning to understand exactly what that meant.

The Balance

Torlan allowed the silence to linger for a moment.

Both leaders were still studying the samples on the table.

Two small objects.

Yet each one represented something their civilizations desperately needed.

Torlan spoke calmly.

"You now understand why Havenfall matters."

Chancellor Kade looked up first.

"Yes."

King Alaric remained thoughtful.

"The value of this valley is obvious."

Torlan nodded.

"And that value creates a problem."

Both leaders turned their attention toward him again.

Torlan continued.

"Neither of you can claim Havenfall."

Kade's expression hardened slightly.

"And why not?"

Torlan answered without hesitation.

"If Dravakar takes control of the colony, Valyra will see it as a strategic threat."

Alaric nodded once.

"That would be correct."

Torlan turned slightly toward the king.

"And if Valyra claims Havenfall, Dravakar will respond the same way."

Kade folded his arms.

"Also correct."

Torlan placed both hands lightly on the table.

"If either side attempts to control this valley…"

He paused.

"…the other will fight for it."

Neither leader argued.

They both understood the logic.

Torlan gestured toward the window again.

"The result would be predictable."

Alex finished the thought quietly.

"The colony would be destroyed."

The words settled heavily over the room.

Outside, the valley remained peaceful.

Fields moving gently in the wind.

Lights beginning to appear in the colony below.

Chancellor Kade looked out toward the settlement.

"So the resources would be lost."

"Yes," Torlan said.

King Alaric studied the valley again.

"And neither civilization would gain what it needs."

Torlan nodded.

"Exactly."

He let the moment breathe before continuing.

"But there is another possibility."

Both leaders looked toward him again.

"If Havenfall remains neutral…"

Torlan gestured toward the samples on the table.

"…both of you benefit."

For the first time since the meeting began, the conversation had moved away from accusation.

Now it was turning toward opportunity.

The Proposal

Torlan returned to the table and rested his hands lightly on its surface.

Both leaders watched him closely now.

The anger that had filled the room earlier had not vanished completely, but it had softened into something more cautious.

Curiosity.

Torlan spoke carefully.

"Havenfall does not belong to either of your civilizations."

He gestured toward the window again.

"It belongs to the settlers who built it."

Several members of both delegations glanced toward the valley outside.

The colony lights were now clearly visible in the growing darkness.

A small settlement.

Fragile.

Yet suddenly important.

Torlan continued.

"The resources here can benefit both of your worlds."

He paused.

"But only if the colony survives."

Chancellor Kade nodded slowly.

"That is obvious."

Torlan activated the console again.

A new projection appeared above the table.

Trade routes formed glowing lines connecting **Valyra**, **Dravakar**, and **Havenfall**.

"This colony could become a neutral trade world."

The projected routes pulsed softly.

Ships traveling peacefully between the two civilizations.

Cargo exchanges.

Commercial lanes replacing battle routes.

Torlan explained calmly.

"Both governments would recognize Havenfall as an independent neutral colony."

King Alaric studied the map.

"And the resources?"

"Harvested and traded," Torlan replied.

"The catalyst plants supplied to Dravakar."

"The shieldstone minerals supplied to Valyra."

Chancellor Kade leaned slightly closer to the projection.

"Under whose authority?"

Torlan answered simply.

"The settlers."

The room grew quiet again.

Torlan continued.

"In exchange, both of your governments agree to three things."

He raised a hand slightly.

"First — Havenfall remains independent."

"Second — both civilizations protect the colony from outside threats."

"Third — all trade occurs peacefully through Havenfall."

Alex added quietly, "No military occupation."

Torlan nodded.

"No military occupation."

The projection above the table shifted again.

Instead of war fleets, the routes now showed merchant vessels.

Supply ships.

Trade convoys.

The kind of movement that built civilizations instead of destroying them.

Torlan looked at both leaders.

"The settlers gain stability."

"Your civilizations gain the resources you need."

"And the war ends."

For several seconds neither leader spoke.

Both men studied the projection slowly.

A different future.

One none of their strategists had imagined.

But it solved a problem both sides had been unable to solve for years.

The Leaders Consider

The projection slowly dimmed.

For a long moment no one spoke.

King Alaric remained standing near the window, looking down toward the small cluster of colony lights scattered across the valley floor.

Chancellor Kade stood beside the table, studying the map where the trade routes had appeared.

The tension in the room had changed.

The anger that had filled the hall earlier had faded.

Now the silence felt thoughtful.

Measured.

Kade finally broke it.

"You are suggesting we turn this colony into a trading center."

Torlan nodded.

"Yes."

The chancellor folded his hands behind his back and walked slowly toward the window.

He stood beside King Alaric, both leaders now looking out across Havenfall.

A quiet settlement.

Fields stretching toward the river.

A handful of lights glowing in the deepening night.

King Alaric spoke without turning.

"You believe our people would accept this?"

Torlan answered calmly.

"If they see the alternative."

Kade glanced toward him.

"And what is that?"

Torlan replied simply.

"Endless war."

Neither leader argued.

Both men understood the cost of the conflict.

Years of fleets destroyed.

Resources exhausted.

Families lost on both sides.

For several seconds they continued studying the valley below.

Alex watched them carefully.

This was the first moment since the meeting began when neither leader appeared ready to argue.

They were thinking.

Alaric finally turned back toward the table.

"Your idea is clever."

Chancellor Kade nodded slightly.

"But clever ideas are not always practical."

Both men now faced Torlan directly.

Years of war still stood between them.

Pride.

Honor.

Politics.

Responsibility to their people.

Alaric spoke again.

"You have presented an interesting possibility."

Kade added carefully,

"But possibility is not proof."

Both leaders studied Torlan steadily.

"Convince us."

The room grew still again.

The real negotiations were about to begin.

Chapter 23 — The Cost of Ending War

Silence in the Hall

The meeting hall grew very quiet.

The discussion had ended, but the weight of it remained in the air.

Torlan stepped back from the table and allowed the silence to settle.

King Alaric stood near the window, the mineral fragment resting in his hand. The dark crystal caught the light from the room's lamps, reflecting faint patterns across the polished table.

Across the room, Chancellor Kade held the small container that carried the catalyst plant sample.

Neither leader spoke.

Both men understood what Torlan had revealed.

The resources were real.

The opportunity for peace was real.

But the war was also real.

Seven years of conflict had carved deep scars into both civilizations.

Entire fleets had been destroyed.

Cities had mourned their dead.

Families had buried sons and daughters who would never return.

Ending such a war was not a simple decision.

King Alaric turned the crystal slowly between his fingers.

"This mineral," he said quietly, almost to himself.

Torlan nodded.

"It exists throughout the ridge above Havenfall."

The king studied the stone again.

His voice was calm, but the weight behind it was unmistakable.

"Thousands of my people have died protecting our worlds."

Across the table, Chancellor Kade finally set the catalyst container down.

"Our losses have been no smaller."

No one argued.

The room carried the quiet understanding of shared tragedy.

Alex watched both leaders carefully.

They were no longer speaking as enemies.

Now they spoke as men who carried the responsibility of entire civilizations.

King Alaric finally placed the crystal fragment back on the table.

The small sound it made against the wood seemed louder than it should have been.

Chancellor Kade folded his arms slowly.

Both leaders looked toward Torlan again.

The evidence had convinced them of one thing.

Peace was possible.

But that did not mean it would be easy.

Alaric's Concern

King Alaric remained standing near the window.

The lights of Havenfall shimmered across the valley below, small and scattered against the darkening land.

For several seconds he said nothing.

Then he spoke.

"Thousands of my people have died in this war."

His voice was steady, but the weight behind the words filled the room.

No one interrupted.

The king continued looking out toward the valley.

"The convoy destroyed seven years ago carried members of my own family."

He paused briefly.

"Brothers. Cousins. Advisors who had served Valyra for decades."

The memory clearly remained close.

Alaric turned slowly back toward the table.

"If I return home and say the war began by accident…"

He let the sentence hang unfinished.

The meaning was obvious.

How could he explain such a truth to a grieving civilization?

Valyra's culture was built on honor.

On loyalty.

On the belief that sacrifices in war carried meaning.

To suggest that thousands had died because of a navigation failure…

The idea alone could shatter the trust of his people.

Alaric rested his hand lightly on the table.

"What will they think?"

The question was not directed only at Torlan.

It was directed at the reality he now faced.

A leader responsible for the memory of the dead.

Alex understood immediately.

For King Alaric, peace was not simply a strategic decision.

It was a question of dignity.

Of history.

Of how a civilization would remember its fallen.

Torlan studied the king quietly.

He understood the burden Alaric carried.

Ending a war required more courage than beginning one.

Kade's Concern

Chancellor Kade had remained silent while King Alaric spoke.

Now he stepped forward slightly, resting his hands on the back of a chair.

His expression was thoughtful, but firm.

"Our problem is different."

The room turned toward him.

Kade gestured toward the catalyst sample on the table.

"Dravakar's people believe Valyra attacked our convoy."

His voice carried the calm tone of a man used to speaking hard truths.

"They believe we were forced into this war."

One of his advisors shifted slightly but said nothing.

Kade continued.

"Our factories changed to wartime production."

"Our trade networks were redirected to support the fleets."

"Our people were told that survival required victory."

He paused.

Then looked directly at Torlan.

"If I suddenly return and declare peace…"

He shook his head once.

"…many will believe we have surrendered."

Across the room, King Alaric gave a small nod of understanding.

Though their cultures differed, the political reality was the same.

Neither leader could appear weak before their people.

Kade straightened slightly.

"Dravakar respects strength."

His voice remained steady.

"Our citizens expect their leaders to defend their interests."

He gestured toward the samples again.

"If I tell them we are ending the war because a neutral colony asked us to..."

The sentence faded unfinished.

The implication was clear.

Even if the evidence was convincing...

Even if the opportunity for peace was real...

The leaders still had to explain the decision to their people.

Alex glanced toward Torlan.

Both men had now revealed the same truth from different directions.

Ending the war would require more than logic.

It would require a way for both civilizations to accept peace without losing pride.

Without losing honor.

Without feeling defeated.

Torlan had been waiting for this moment.

Torlan's Answer

Torlan listened to both leaders without interrupting.

When the room grew quiet again, he stepped forward slightly.

"You do not need to tell your people the war was meaningless."

Both leaders looked toward him.

Torlan's voice remained calm and steady.

"Your people defended their worlds."

"That sacrifice will always matter."

King Alaric studied him carefully.

Chancellor Kade waited, arms still folded.

Torlan continued.

"What matters now is what comes next."

He turned and gestured toward the wide window overlooking the valley.

Outside, the lights of Havenfall shimmered quietly across the fields.

"This war revealed something neither of your civilizations expected."

Both leaders followed his gesture.

"The discovery of Havenfall."

He allowed the words to settle before continuing.

"For years your fleets searched this region for advantage."

"Control of trade routes."

"Strategic positions."

"But instead…"

Torlan pointed toward the valley floor.

"…you discovered something neither side had before."

King Alaric spoke slowly.

"A resource both civilizations need."

"Yes."

Chancellor Kade nodded once.

"And one neither of us can control alone."

Torlan met both leaders' eyes.

"Exactly."

He stepped closer to the table again.

"The war revealed Havenfall."

He paused.

"And Havenfall now offers both of you something the war never could."

Neither leader spoke.

Torlan finished quietly.

"A future worth protecting."

For the first time since the negotiations began, the idea of peace no longer sounded like surrender.

It sounded like opportunity.

A Path Forward

The room remained quiet as Torlan's words settled.

Both leaders were still looking toward the valley outside the window.

Finally Torlan spoke again.

"There is a way for both of you to explain this to your people."

Chancellor Kade turned back toward the table.

"I am listening."

King Alaric remained near the window but shifted slightly to hear him more clearly.

Torlan continued carefully.

"You do not present peace as an admission of failure."

He gestured toward the mineral and plant samples resting on the table.

"You present it as the result of discovery."

Alex nodded slightly as she began to understand the direction of the idea.

Torlan explained.

"Your fleets searched this region during the war."

"The conflict pushed both civilizations deeper into the Kardrin Expanse."

He paused.

"And in that process, Havenfall was discovered."

Chancellor Kade's expression sharpened.

"You would say the war revealed the opportunity."

"Yes."

King Alaric turned back toward the table.

Torlan continued.

"Both of your governments can announce the same truth."

He raised a hand slightly as he outlined the idea.

"The war revealed resources vital to both civilizations."

"Protecting those resources requires cooperation."

"Havenfall becomes a neutral world where both sides benefit."

Alex added quietly,

"A discovery worth ending the war for."

Torlan nodded.

"Exactly."

King Alaric studied the proposal thoughtfully.

"This allows our people to see the end of the war as a victory of wisdom."

Chancellor Kade considered the idea as well.

"And as a strategic decision."

Torlan met both leaders' eyes.

"Peace becomes the next step of strength."

For several seconds neither leader spoke.

They were no longer thinking about surrender.

They were thinking about leadership.

About the story they would carry back to their people.

A story that honored the past…

and allowed a different future.

The Leaders Reflect

The meeting hall fell quiet once more.

Outside the window, Havenfall's valley lay beneath a darkening sky. The last traces of sunset had faded, leaving the small lights of the colony glowing softly across the fields.

King Alaric stood silently near the window.

For a long moment he watched the settlement below.

A handful of buildings.

A few scattered lights.

Farm equipment parked beside the fields.

It was not a place that looked important.

Yet somehow this small colony had brought two civilizations to the edge of peace.

Across the room, Chancellor Kade picked up the sealed container holding the catalyst sample.

He studied the amber plant fragment inside.

"A small colony," he said quietly.

Torlan nodded.

"Yes."

Kade looked toward the window.

"And yet it may determine the future of two worlds."

King Alaric turned slowly back toward the room.

"There is wisdom in what you propose."

He glanced briefly toward Kade.

"But wisdom does not always overcome history."

The chancellor gave a slight nod.

"Seven years of war leaves deep scars."

No one disagreed.

Torlan did not rush to speak.

He understood that this moment belonged to the leaders.

They were not debating facts anymore.

They were weighing responsibility.

Alaric walked slowly back toward the table.

He placed his hand beside the mineral sample.

Kade set the catalyst container down beside it.

Two small objects.

Two different resources.

Together they represented a future neither civilization had expected.

For several seconds both leaders simply looked at the samples.

Finally Alaric spoke.

"Your plan may end the war."

Kade added cautiously,

"But agreements must be written."

Torlan inclined his head slightly.

"Then let us write them."

The decision had not yet been declared.

But for the first time since the war began, peace was no longer just an idea.

It was becoming a plan.

Chapter 24 — Writing the Accord

"Peace is built, not discovered."
Harmony between people requires patience, courage, and careful work.
— Wisdom of Cyrion

The First Draft

The large wooden table in the Havenfall colony hall was now covered with tablets, documents, and projected displays.

What had begun hours earlier as a tense confrontation had become something quieter—and far more important.

Work.

Torlan sat at one side of the table.

Across from him were King Alaric and Chancellor Kade.

Alex stood beside the console managing the document projections as the text of the agreement slowly formed line by line.

Several advisors from both delegations observed carefully, occasionally offering suggestions.

Near the back of the room, Mara Ellison and a few of the settlers watched silently.

They understood that the future of their colony was being written in this moment.

Torlan spoke calmly.

"The first issue must be Havenfall's independence."

A line of text appeared above the table as Alex recorded the statement.

HAVENFALL SHALL REMAIN AN INDEPENDENT AND NEUTRAL COLONY.

Torlan continued.

"Neither Valyra nor Dravakar may claim sovereignty over the planet."

King Alaric studied the text for a moment.

"That condition is acceptable."

Chancellor Kade nodded.

"If either of us attempted control, the other would respond."

Torlan inclined his head slightly.

"Which would destroy the very resources we seek to preserve."

The logic required little debate.

Alex updated the document again.

NO GOVERNMENT SHALL CLAIM TERRITORIAL CONTROL OF HAVENFALL.

King Alaric leaned back slightly in his chair.

"A neutral world."

Chancellor Kade considered the wording.

"A practical solution."

Torlan folded his hands lightly on the table.

"It is the only solution that allows Havenfall to survive."

Behind them, Mara Ellison watched the words appear on the display.

For years her people had struggled simply to keep the colony alive.

Now their independence was becoming the foundation of a peace agreement between two civilizations.

The first line of the accord had been written.

And with it, the shape of a new future had begun.

Trade Access

Once Havenfall's independence had been established in the draft, the next issue quickly followed.

Resources.

Alex adjusted the projection above the table. The document expanded, opening a new section.

Torlan spoke calmly.

"The next matter concerns access to Havenfall's resources."

He gestured toward the samples still resting on the table.

"The catalyst plants in the valley and the shieldstone minerals in the ridge."

Chancellor Kade leaned forward slightly.

"Dravakar will require a reliable supply of the catalyst."

King Alaric nodded.

"And Valyra must secure access to the mineral deposits."

Torlan looked from one leader to the other.

"Which is why neither resource should belong exclusively to either civilization."

Kade considered that.

"Shared access."

"Yes."

Alex began entering the wording as they spoke.

BOTH VALYRA AND DRAVAKAR SHALL HAVE PEACEFUL TRADE ACCESS TO HAVENFALL'S NATURAL RESOURCES.

King Alaric studied the text thoughtfully.

"Trade must be structured carefully."

He glanced toward Mara Ellison and the settlers watching from the back of the room.

"The colony must benefit as well."

Torlan nodded.

"That is essential."

Chancellor Kade tapped one finger thoughtfully on the table.

"Dravakar can establish long-term industrial purchasing contracts."

Alex added a line to the document.

King Alaric followed with another suggestion.

"Valyra will support stable trade exchange agreements for shieldstone extraction."

Torlan listened as the leaders continued shaping the details.

For the first time since the negotiations began, the tone of the conversation had changed completely.

Instead of arguing about fleets and battles…

They were discussing trade routes.

Supply agreements.

Economic cooperation.

Alex updated the draft again.

ALL RESOURCE HARVESTING AND TRADE SHALL BE CONDUCTED THROUGH HAVENFALL'S CIVIL AUTHORITY.

Torlan glanced toward Mara.

"The settlers will manage the colony's resources."

Mara Ellison gave a small, thoughtful nod.

Her people had struggled to survive on Havenfall for years.

Now the same land they had patiently worked might soon support peaceful trade between two worlds.

Chancellor Kade leaned back slightly.

"A neutral marketplace."

King Alaric allowed himself a faint smile.

"A better use of ships than war."

Torlan watched the agreement slowly take shape.

The idea of peace was becoming something solid.

Something practical.

Something both civilizations could build upon.

Protection of Havenfall

The agreement continued to grow line by line on the projection above the table.

Trade terms had been outlined.

Resource access had been defined.

Now Torlan turned to the issue he considered most important.

"Havenfall must also be protected."

Both leaders looked toward him.

Torlan spoke carefully.

"If this colony becomes valuable to both of your civilizations…"

He paused slightly.

"…it will also become vulnerable."

Chancellor Kade understood immediately.

"Other powers may attempt to seize the resources."

King Alaric nodded.

"Or disrupt the trade routes."

Torlan inclined his head.

"Yes."

Alex opened a new section in the draft document.

SECURITY AND PROTECTION PROVISIONS

Torlan continued.

"There must be a clear condition."

His voice remained calm but firm.

"No military forces from either Valyra or Dravakar may occupy Havenfall."

For a moment neither leader spoke.

The clause was important.

King Alaric considered it carefully.

"If either of us stationed troops here…"

Kade finished the thought.

"The other would see it as an attempt at control."

Torlan nodded.

"Which would lead us back to war."

Both leaders understood the logic immediately.

Alex entered the clause.

NO MILITARY OCCUPATION OF HAVENFALL SHALL BE PERMITTED BY EITHER GOVERNMENT.

Chancellor Kade folded his hands thoughtfully.

"Then how is the colony protected?"

Torlan answered.

"Through mutual guarantee."

He gestured toward the document.

"Both of your governments agree to defend Havenfall from any outside threat."

King Alaric leaned forward slightly.

"Meaning any attack on Havenfall…"

Chancellor Kade finished the sentence.

"…would be treated as an attack on both civilizations."

Torlan nodded once.

"Yes."

Alex added the wording to the accord.

VALYRA AND DRAVAKAR SHALL JOINTLY GUARANTEE THE SAFETY AND NEUTRALITY OF HAVENFALL.

Behind the negotiating table, Mara Ellison and the settlers exchanged quiet glances.

For years they had struggled alone on the frontier.

Now two of the most powerful civilizations in the region were committing to protect their small colony.

King Alaric looked toward the window again.

"A colony protected by two former enemies."

Kade allowed himself a small, thoughtful smile.

"That may be the safest place in this entire sector."

Torlan looked back at the agreement.

The framework of peace was nearly complete.

Ending the War

The agreement now covered Havenfall's independence, trade rights, and protection.

Only one matter remained.

The war itself.

Torlan allowed a brief pause before speaking again.

"One final section is required."

King Alaric and Chancellor Kade both understood what he meant.

Alex opened a new section in the projected document.

TERMINATION OF HOSTILITIES

For several seconds no one spoke.

Ending a war was not simply a matter of writing words.

The language had to carry meaning for entire civilizations.

King Alaric was the first to break the silence.

"The wording must preserve honor."

Chancellor Kade nodded.

"And clarity."

Torlan considered the problem carefully.

He then spoke slowly.

"The conflict between Valyra and Dravakar began through misunderstanding."

Both leaders accepted that now.

"But the war revealed something neither civilization expected."

He gestured toward the valley outside the window.

"The discovery of Havenfall."

Alex began entering the proposed language.

Torlan continued.

"The accord may state that the conflict revealed a new shared opportunity."

King Alaric studied the phrasing.

"That the war led to discovery."

Chancellor Kade added,

"And that the discovery now requires cooperation."

Torlan nodded.

"Yes."

Alex adjusted the wording as they refined the statement together.

The projection displayed the emerging clause:

THE CONFLICT BETWEEN VALYRA AND DRAVAKAR HAS REVEALED THE DISCOVERY OF HAVENFALL AND ITS SHARED VALUE.

IN RECOGNITION OF THIS DISCOVERY, BOTH GOVERNMENTS AGREE TO END HOSTILITIES AND ESTABLISH PEACEFUL COOPERATION.

The room remained quiet as the leaders read the text.

King Alaric finally spoke.

"This does not erase the sacrifices of the war."

"No," Torlan said.

"It gives them meaning."

Chancellor Kade leaned back slightly.

"Our people will understand that."

The war had not ended in defeat.

It had ended in discovery.

A discovery that created something stronger than victory.

Opportunity.

Torlan watched both leaders carefully.

The final barrier to peace had now been crossed.

The Signing

The final version of the agreement hovered above the table.

Every clause had been reviewed.

Every line carefully considered.

For several minutes no one spoke.

King Alaric read the document slowly from beginning to end.

Across the table, Chancellor Kade did the same.

Torlan and Alex waited quietly.

This moment belonged to the two leaders.

Outside the windows, the lights of Havenfall shimmered across the valley.

A small colony that had unknowingly become the center of a historic decision.

At last King Alaric placed the tablet down on the table.

"The terms are clear."

Chancellor Kade nodded once.

"And acceptable."

Alex placed two signature tablets on the table.

The room grew very still.

King Alaric stepped forward first.

He looked at the document once more before placing his hand against the signing surface.

His signature appeared across the final page of the accord.

A quiet breath passed through the room.

Seven years of war had just taken its first step toward ending.

Chancellor Kade stepped forward next.

He studied the document briefly.

Then he placed his hand on the tablet.

His signature appeared beneath Alaric's.

For a moment no one moved.

The war between **Valyra** and **Dravakar** was officially over.

Behind the negotiating table, the settlers of Havenfall watched in stunned silence.

Many of them had arrived on this world simply hoping to survive.

Now their colony had become the place where two civilizations chose peace.

King Alaric looked toward Torlan.

"You asked us to imagine a different future."

Chancellor Kade added quietly,

"And then you showed us how to build it."

Torlan inclined his head slightly.

"The future was already here."

He glanced toward the window and the valley beyond.

"We only needed to see it."

Chapter 25 — A New Beginning

The Fleets Depart

High above Havenfall, the sky had begun to change.

On the bridge of **The Long Path**, the main display showed the last movements of the war fleets.

Samir watched the sensor readouts carefully.

"For the first time in seven years," he said quietly, "Valyra and Dravakar ships are maneuvering in the same sector without targeting locks."

The display showed the elegant lines of the **Valyra escort vessels** drifting slowly away from the planet.

Their formation was orderly and precise, the ships turning gracefully toward open space.

King Alaric's fleet had begun its journey home.

Mateo leaned back slightly in his chair.

"That's a sight I never expected to see."

Torlan stood beside the main console, watching the sensor display with quiet attention.

Moments later Samir spoke again.

"The Dravakar vessels are adjusting course."

The heavier, industrial-shaped ships of **Chancellor Kade's fleet** began moving as well.

One by one, they turned away from Havenfall and accelerated into the darkness.

Two former enemies.

Leaving the same world peacefully.

Samir nodded once.

"Both fleets are clearing Havenfall orbit."

The stars on the display slowly returned to their normal patterns as the large ship signatures faded from the sensors.

Mateo exhaled quietly.

"Strange."

He glanced at Torlan.

"Seeing them leave without firing a shot."

Torlan watched the final signals disappear.

"That was always the better outcome."

The bridge grew quiet again.

Outside the viewing window, Havenfall rotated slowly below them.

Fields.

Rivers.

The small lights of the colony shining in the early evening.

For the first time in years, the sky above the planet held no warships.

Only stars.

The Colony Reacts

The news spread through Havenfall quickly.

By the time Torlan and the crew returned from **The Long Path**, settlers had already begun gathering in the open square near the landing field.

For years that same square had been a place of quiet worry.

Every passing ship might have brought danger.

Every signal from the stars might have carried bad news.

Tonight the feeling was different.

Hope filled the cool evening air.

Mara Ellison stood near the center of the gathering. Beside her were several members of the colony council.

The settlers formed a loose circle around them.

Farmers still in their work clothes.

Mechanics from the equipment sheds.

Families who had spent years building homes and fields in the valley.

Mara waited until the murmurs settled.

"The war fleets have left Havenfall."

A ripple moved through the crowd.

People exchanged surprised looks.

Some had hoped for peace.

Few had truly expected it.

Mara continued.

"The governments of **Valyra** and **Dravakar** have signed a formal accord."

She gestured toward the valley beyond the colony buildings.

"Havenfall will remain independent."

A few settlers nodded slowly as the words sank in.

"We are no longer just a frontier colony," Mara said.

Her voice carried calm strength.

"Havenfall will become a neutral trade world."

A low murmur spread across the gathering again.

Merchants instead of warships.

Trade routes instead of battle lines.

Mara raised a hand slightly.

"Both civilizations will send merchants and trade ships here."

"Scientists will study the valley plants."

"Engineers will survey the ridge minerals."

She looked across the settlers who had struggled so long to keep the colony alive.

"Our work here mattered."

The realization moved quietly through the crowd.

For years Havenfall had seemed forgotten.

A distant outpost barely surviving at the edge of known space.

Now two powerful civilizations had committed to protect it.

One of the older settlers spoke quietly.

"We were just trying to survive."

Mara smiled slightly.

"And you did."

She gestured toward the valley lights glowing in the darkness.

"And now the whole galaxy knows it."

The First Trade Plans

The following morning Havenfall felt different.

The valley had not changed.

The same river still wound through the fields. The same amber plants grew near the water. The ridge still rose above the settlement where the communications antenna now stood.

But the *purpose* of the colony had changed.

In the colony hall, representatives from both civilizations had begun discussing the first practical steps of the agreement.

Data tablets and survey charts covered the long table.

A Dravakar engineering team studied the chemical analysis of the catalyst plants.

One of their scientists spoke quietly to Kade's advisor.

"If the concentration levels remain stable, these fields could supply our refining systems for decades."

Nearby, two Valyra geologists examined mineral scans taken from the ridge.

The crystalline shieldstone structures appeared clearly in the data projections.

"This deposit is remarkable," one of them said.

"With careful extraction, it could reinforce our planetary defense grids for generations."

The discussions were careful but cooperative.

Instead of military briefings, the room now held conversations about trade routes, transport schedules, and long-term resource management.

Torlan stood near the window, observing quietly.

Alex joined him, folding her arms lightly.

"Quite a transformation," she said.

Torlan glanced toward the table where the teams worked together.

"Yes."

Only days earlier the same two civilizations had been enemies.

Now their representatives were planning trade agreements.

Alex smiled slightly.

"You turned a battlefield into a marketplace."

Torlan shook his head gently.

"The settlers did that."

Alex followed his gaze toward the valley outside.

Farmers were already moving equipment across the fields.

Work continued exactly as it had before.

Except now the entire valley carried a new meaning.

Havenfall was no longer just a distant frontier colony.

It had become a place where two worlds would meet.

A Moment of Reflection

Later that evening, Torlan climbed the familiar path toward the ridge above Havenfall.

The wind was steady but calm now, moving softly through the rocks and low brush that lined the slope.

At the summit, the communications antenna stood firmly anchored to the stone where they had installed it only days earlier.

Its signal beacon blinked steadily into the darkening sky.

Torlan walked to the edge of the ridge and looked down into the valley.

Below him, the lights of Havenfall glowed warmly across the fields.

Small homes.

Farm structures.

The landing area where The Long Path rested quietly.

Beyond the colony, the river reflected the last fading light of the evening sky.

The valley was peaceful.

Very different from the war-torn region of space surrounding it.

For several minutes Torlan simply stood there.

Then he heard footsteps behind him.

Alex appeared along the path and joined him near the antenna tower.

She followed his gaze toward the valley below.

"It looks different now."

Torlan nodded slightly.

"Yes."

The settlement had not changed physically.

But its future had.

Alex leaned lightly against one of the tower supports.

"Do you think Havenfall will succeed?"

Torlan studied the valley for another moment before answering.

"They already have."

Alex glanced toward him.

Torlan continued quietly.

"They built a colony where no one believed one could survive."

"They endured isolation."

"They endured the threat of war."

He looked again at the small lights across the fields.

"And they kept going."

The antenna tower hummed softly as it scanned the surrounding space.

Watching.

Protecting.

Alex smiled faintly.

"So the hardest part is already done."

Torlan nodded once.

"Yes."

For the first time since arriving in the Kardrin Expanse, the valley below felt safe.

Not because it had become stronger.

But because it had finally been seen.

Preparing to Leave

Back aboard **The Long Path**, the familiar rhythm of ship operations had returned.

Cargo doors stood open along the landing platform as the crew completed the final transfer of supplies.

Some containers that had once filled the cargo bay were now gone—delivered to the colony's clinic, farms, and equipment sheds.

The ship felt lighter.

The mission had been fulfilled.

Inside the bridge, Mateo sat reviewing the navigation charts.

The star map of the Kardrin Expanse glowed softly across the main display.

Samir adjusted a sensor panel nearby, running one final scan of the surrounding space.

"No hostile signals," he reported.

Owen Tark leaned against the engineering console.

"Strange hearing that."

Mateo smiled faintly.

"After the last few weeks, I'll take strange."

Torlan entered the bridge quietly.

He paused near the window, looking once more at the valley below.

From orbit the colony lights appeared like small constellations scattered across the dark land.

A place that had nearly been forgotten.

Now becoming something much larger.

Mateo turned slightly in his chair.

"Navigation systems are ready."

He tapped the chart display.

"So the question becomes…"

Mateo glanced toward Torlan.

"Where to next?"

Torlan studied the star map for a moment.

Countless stars stretched across the display.

Each one a system.

Each system a place where people lived.

Where problems existed.

Where someone might need help.

He answered calmly.

"There are always more places that need help."

Mateo nodded once and returned to the controls.

Samir began preparing the departure sequence.

Outside the viewing window, Havenfall continued its quiet work below.

A small colony at the edge of space.

Now the center of a new beginning.

Chapter 26 — The Long Path Continues

"A long path begins with a single step taken calmly."
Great journeys are made one wise decision at a time.
— *Wisdom of Cyrion*

Morning at Havenfall

Morning light spread slowly across Havenfall Valley.

The sun rose behind the eastern ridge, casting long golden rays across the fields and river below. Mist hovered lightly above the water before drifting away in the warming air.

The colony was already awake.

Farm equipment moved steadily across the fields. Settlers walked between buildings carrying tools and supply crates. The landing field buzzed with quiet activity as crews inspected cargo pads and storage areas.

Life on Havenfall had always required hard work.

But today the mood felt different.

Lighter.

Above the ridge, the tall communications antenna stood firm against the wind. Its signal beacon blinked steadily as it scanned the skies that had once carried the threat of war.

Now the sky was clear.

No fleets.

No weapons.

Only the calm blue arc of the morning horizon.

From the landing field, **The Long Path** rested quietly where it had touched down days earlier.

Nearby, settlers moved equipment that would soon be used to prepare new trade facilities.

For the first time in years, the colony was not merely surviving.

It was preparing for the future.

Farewell to the Settlers

The crew of **The Long Path** gathered near the landing ramp.

Mateo stood beside Owen Tark, reviewing the final departure checklist. Dr. Chen had already secured the medical bay aboard the ship, and Samir monitored communications from a portable console.

A small group of settlers approached across the field.

Mara Ellison walked at the front.

Several members of the colony council followed her, along with a handful of farmers and engineers who had worked closely with the crew over the past days.

They stopped a short distance from the ramp.

For a moment no one spoke.

Then Mara stepped forward.

"Havenfall will never forget what you did here."

Torlan regarded her calmly.

"You built this colony long before we arrived."

Mara shook her head slightly.

"You helped save it."

Torlan gestured toward the valley stretching beyond the landing field.

"You saved it."

He nodded toward the farms, the river, and the scattered homes.

"You only needed time."

Several settlers exchanged quiet smiles.

They had spent years working the land, repairing machinery, and protecting their fragile settlement.

Now their efforts had become the foundation of something far greater.

Alex's Reflection

Alex stood slightly apart from the others, watching the settlers as they spoke with the crew.

Families moved through the landing field carrying tools and supply crates.

Children ran along the edge of the clearing, laughing in the morning sunlight.

It was difficult to believe how much had changed in such a short time.

Only days earlier, Havenfall had seemed like a forgotten colony on the edge of a war zone.

Now it had become the center of a new beginning.

Alex folded her arms lightly and looked across the valley.

"I didn't expect this when I accepted the position."

Torlan stood beside her.

"Neither did I."

Alex smiled faintly.

"When I applied for the assistant role, I thought I'd be organizing reports and scheduling meetings."

Torlan raised an eyebrow slightly.

"You did those things as well."

She laughed softly.

"Yes."

Her gaze returned to the settlers.

"But I didn't expect to help end a war."

Torlan watched the activity across the valley.

"Sometimes the most important work is not the work we planned."

Alex nodded.

She had come looking for a job.

Instead she had found a purpose.

The Final Look

Before departure, Torlan climbed the ridge one final time.

The path felt familiar now.

Wind moved steadily across the rocks as he reached the summit.

The communications antenna stood where they had anchored it days earlier, its signal beacon pulsing softly into the bright sky.

Torlan stepped to the edge of the ridge and looked down.

From this height he could see nearly the entire valley.

Fields stretched along the riverbanks.

Farm structures dotted the landscape.

The colony buildings clustered around the landing field.

Small vehicles moved slowly between work areas.

The settlement had grown stronger.

Not because of the peace agreement.

But because the people of Havenfall had refused to give up.

Torlan stood quietly for a moment.

Then he remembered the words Dr. Ziv had spoken many years earlier.

"Leave the ground better than you found it."

Looking across the valley, Torlan knew the mission had succeeded.

Departure

Back aboard **The Long Path**, the crew moved through the familiar rhythm of launch preparation.

Mateo settled into the pilot's chair.

"Navigation systems ready."

Owen checked the engineering display.

"Drive systems stable."

Samir monitored the communications array.

"All external channels clear."

Dr. Chen secured the final medical cabinets.

Alex took her seat beside Torlan on the bridge.

The forward display opened to reveal the morning sky above Havenfall.

Mateo glanced toward Torlan.

"Where to next?"

Torlan studied the star field slowly forming on the navigation display.

Countless systems.

Countless worlds.

Each one holding its own challenges.

Its own stories.

He answered simply.

"Forward."

Mateo smiled slightly.

"Forward it is."

Into the Stars

The engines of **The Long Path** awakened with a soft vibration.

Outside the viewing window, the landing field began to shrink as the ship lifted gently into the sky.

The valley of Havenfall spread out beneath them.

Fields.

Rivers.

The ridge antenna standing strong against the wind.

The colony grew smaller as the ship climbed higher.

Clouds drifted across the view.

Soon the planet curved away beneath them.

Then the stars appeared.

Bright and endless.

Torlan watched them quietly.

The path ahead was long.

But it was the path he had chosen.

He spoke softly, almost to himself.

"The long path is just beginning."

The ship turned toward the stars and accelerated into the quiet darkness.

Appendix I — Havenfall

Havenfall began as a small frontier colony located within a quiet valley on an otherwise unremarkable world. For several years the settlement remained largely unknown to the surrounding star systems, its settlers focused primarily on survival and the slow work of building a stable community.

The valley itself proved unusually fertile. Streams descending from the surrounding ridges provided water for farming, and the wide floor of the valley allowed the settlers to establish fields, workshops, and modest housing structures.

For many years Havenfall appeared to hold little strategic importance. That changed when two significant discoveries were made.

The first was a group of amber-colored plants growing throughout portions of the valley. Scientific analysis revealed that these plants contained a rare chemical catalyst essential for several advanced industrial processes.

The second discovery came from the rocky ridges surrounding the valley. Beneath the exposed rock layers lay dense crystalline mineral formations ideally suited for use in high-energy shielding technologies.

These two natural resources—one valuable to Dravakar's industrial systems and the other essential to Valyra's defensive technologies—transformed Havenfall from an isolated colony into a place of great strategic importance.

Rather than becoming a battleground, Havenfall was ultimately established as a **neutral trade world**, protected by agreement between the two civilizations that had once been at war.

Today the valley continues to grow, its settlers building a community that stands as a reminder that cooperation can sometimes succeed where conflict cannot.

Appendix II — The Convoy Incident

The conflict between Valyra and Dravakar began with an event that later became known as the *Convoy Incident.* For many years both civilizations believed the other had deliberately initiated the attack that triggered the war.

Historical records now indicate that the encounter was the result of a navigation error rather than intentional aggression.

The Beacon Malfunction

Several years before the war began, an automated navigation beacon positioned along a major interstellar trade corridor began transmitting incorrect positional data. The malfunction went unnoticed for an extended period of time.

Because both Valyra and Dravakar relied on the beacon to assist with long-distance navigation, the error gradually altered the flight paths of vessels traveling through the region.

The Convoy Encounter

Two large convoys—one belonging to Valyra and the other to Dravakar—entered the affected region within hours of each other. Each convoy believed it was traveling along a safe and established route.

Instead, the navigation error guided both groups of ships toward the same location.

When the convoys encountered one another unexpectedly, confusion and defensive maneuvers quickly escalated into armed conflict.

The Outbreak of War

Both sides believed the other had intentionally staged an ambush. Communications between the convoys were brief and chaotic, and the initial exchange of fire destroyed several vessels.

News of the encounter spread rapidly to both home worlds. Political leaders on each planet interpreted the incident as a deliberate attack.

Within weeks the two civilizations entered a state of open war.

The Seven-Year Conflict

The war that followed lasted seven years and resulted in the loss of thousands of ships and countless lives on both sides.

Only much later did new evidence suggest that the original encounter may have been caused by a navigation system failure rather than deliberate aggression.

The discovery of Havenfall and the subsequent peace negotiations finally brought the conflict to an end.

Appendix III -- Wisdom of Cyrion

For generations the teachers of Cyrion passed down short sayings that guided their students in matters of judgment, patience, and leadership.
Torlan often remembered these teachings during difficult moments of his journey.

---

1. The quiet mind sees the farthest.
A calm mind notices patterns and truths that panic hides.

2. Observe first. Act second.
Understanding a problem is often more important than reacting quickly.

3. Strength grows slowly.
What lasts is usually built through patience rather than force.

4. Leave the ground better than you found it.
Every journey should improve the world in some small way.

5. Pride shouts. Wisdom listens.
Those who listen carefully often learn what others miss.

6. The storm does not change the mountain.
Difficult times reveal character but do not define it.

7. A small truth can stop a great war.
Understanding the real cause of conflict often ends it.

8. A steady hand guides the longest journey.
Consistency and patience accomplish more than sudden bursts of effort.

9. Anger clouds the map.
Clear thinking disappears when emotions take control.

10. The strongest bridge is built from trust.
Cooperation begins when people believe in one another.

11. The patient traveler arrives safely.
Haste often leads people into danger they could have avoided.

12. A wise leader speaks last.
The one who listens first understands the situation best.

13. Fear sees enemies everywhere.
Calm thinking reveals which dangers are real and which are imagined.

14. A single good decision can change many lives.
Small moments of wisdom often shape the future.

15. Every valley hides a purpose.
What appears ordinary may hold great value when carefully observed.

16. Peace is built, not discovered.
Harmony between people requires effort and courage.

17. The loudest voice is rarely the wisest.
Truth often speaks quietly.

18. A long path begins with a single step taken calmly.
Great journeys begin with steady decisions.

19. Shared gain is stronger than victory.
When both sides benefit, peace can last.

20. The future belongs to those who build it.
Hope grows wherever people choose to work together.

About the Author

Russell McFall is a lifelong storyteller who enjoys exploring the human side of science fiction. His stories focus on character, courage, and the quiet choices that shape a person's life.

Before becoming a full-time writer, Russell spent many years working in **software development**, where logic and problem-solving were part of everyday life. At the same time, he and his wife devoted many years to **children's ministry and homeschooling their family**, experiences that deeply influenced the themes found in his writing.

Many of Russell's stories first began as **bedtime adventures told to his children**. Those early stories gradually grew into larger worlds filled with explorers, young heroes, and distant planets where character matters as much as technology.

Russell enjoys writing **clean, thoughtful science fiction** that can be read and enjoyed by both younger readers and adults. His books often explore themes of perseverance, responsibility, friendship, and the quiet strength that grows through adversity.

He continues to write and develop new stories in his **Space Cadet series and other science-fiction adventures**, always with the goal of creating stories that inspire imagination while encouraging courage and integrity.

Russell lives in the United States and continues writing with the same sense of wonder that first inspired those early bedtime stories many years ago.

Also by Russell McFall

Ordained Path Books

Clean Science Fiction and Inspirational Writing for Thoughtful Readers

---

Contemporary Fiction and Short Stories

Stories of Community, Memory, and Hope

- **Squirrel Creek Estates — Where the Porch Lights Stay On**
- **The World That Chose**

The Space Cadet Richard Series

Where the Legacy Began

- **The Final Countdown**
- **The Dunes of Dinkytown**
- **The Mastermind's Maze**

The Space Cadet Legacy Series

Over 30+ novels of courage, friendship, and discovery — including

- **The First Gate**
- **Welcome Back, Player**
- **Flibber's Journey Home**
- **Stronger Together**
- **Phasegate Rising**
- **The Makers' Handshake**
- **Optimized**

(New missions continuing.)

Literary Humor and Reflections

Serious Nonsense — Sanity Sold Separately

Devotional and Reflection Books

- **Remembering God's Help — Stone by Stone**
- **Attributes of God**
- **This Is My Story, This Is My Song**
- **Lives of Faith**
- **Foundations of Faith**

Russell McFall writes clean fiction and thoughtful reflections designed to uplift the heart, sharpen the mind, and remind every reader that light still wins.

www.ingramcontent.com/pod-product-compliance
Lightning Source LLC
LaVergne TN
LVHW010631110826
845149LV00014B/2823

* 9 7 8 1 9 7 2 7 2 4 0 2 6 *